GW00383926

Puppy Love

A novel of
The Lycan Files

By
JP Cameron

Dedication

For Anna, Mark, Arina and Paul
Without you the Pack would be so much smaller
The Realms of the fae so much less crazy
And the sarcasm so less ... Real.

Thanks for feeding my imagination ...
By being yourselves.

Editorial

Copyright © 2018 JP Cameron
All rights reserved

ISBN: 9798691880025
Imprint: Independently published

Books in the Series:

Dog Days
Puppy Love
The Furry and the Furious
Barking Mad
Let Sleeping ~~Dogs~~ Gods Lie

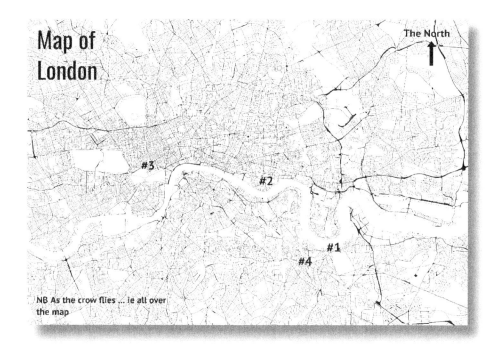

Map of
London

The North

#3

#2

#1

#4

NB As the crow flies ... ie all over
the map

Sites you might find of interest:

#1 University of Greenwich
The University of Greenwich is a British, United Kingdom based university.

It has three campuses in London and Kent, England. These are located at Greenwich, in the grounds of the Old Royal Naval College, and in Avery Hill and Medway. Previous names include Woolwich Polytechnic and Thames Polytechnic.

It was nominated the greenest university in the UK in 2012 as assessed by The People & Planet Green League.

The university has ranked well in terms of student satisfaction across all 20 listed universities in London – with it topping lists of 2010, 2011, 2012 and 2013 consecutively. It has not left the top five since its entry in 2010. The University of Greenwich has been ranked among the 200 institutions with the most global outlook and named one of the "most international" universities on the planet by Times Higher Education magazine.

#2 Wapping
Wapping is a district in London Docklands, England, in the London Borough of Tower Hamlets. It is situated between the north bank of the River Thames and the ancient thoroughfare simply called The Highway. Wapping's proximity to the river has given it a strong maritime character, which it retains through its riverside public houses and steps, such as the Prospect of Whitby and Wapping Stairs.

Many of the original buildings were demolished during the construction of the London Docks and Wapping was further seriously damaged during the Blitz. As the London Docklands declined after the Second World War, the area became run down, with the great warehouses left empty. The area's fortunes were transformed during the 1980s by the London Docklands Development Corporation when the warehouses started to be converted into luxury flats.

#3 Maddox Street, London
This extends from Regent Street to St George's, Hanover Square and was completed in 1720. Maddox Street was named after Sir Benjamin Maddox who owned the Millfield estate on which the street was built. The Mason's Arms, located at 38 Maddox Street, was built in 1721 and rebuilt in its current form in 1934.

Dickenson's Drawing Gallery, whose teachers included John Mogford and whose students included Emily Mary Osborn, was established at 18 Maddox Street in the early 19th century, the premises are now known as ArtSpace Galleries. Nearby, Maddox Gallery is based at 9 Maddox Street, one of several art galleries on this road. A Museum of Building Appliances, established in the street in 1866, no longer exists.

#4 Deptford Creek

Deptford Creek - 'Deep Ford' - was named after its tidal Creek. As the tide falls each day it exposes almost a kilometre of riverbed providing an opportunity for adventure and education that can't be found anywhere else in London.

Deptford Creek has a long history of fishing, shipbuilding and dockyards. Trades and industries from chemical works to tidal mills and slaughterhouses have all used its banks. London's first passenger railway crosses it and Bazelgette's famous sewage pumping station is alongside it.

The Creek's waters, muddy banks and flood defence walls are home to a wide variety of wildlife including shrimps, crabs, fish, birds and many species of wildflower.

Contents

Prologue

So, since I have your attention. Let's talk a little bit about the Real.

The first thing any mortal usually asks - if they ever somehow figure out they aren't actually the top of the food chain - is … "Is it Heaven and Hell?"

Well, after "Is Elvis still alive over there?"

Seriously, that's what you lot worry about. Not "Are monsters going to come and eat me and my family?" or "Am I going mad?", or my favourite "Does that mean Piers Morgan really *is* a troglodyte?"

Nope, nothing so sensible.

So, back to the inane question. My response these days … whilst I'm fixing the restraints and checking the damage to clean up … tends to be something like *"The Real is what you bring with you."* Usually with less mountain-top old mystic guru style and more swearing. Or at least a hefty dose of mocking laughter thrown in for good measure.

Fairy land. Middle Earth. Narnia. Earthsea. The Magic Roundabout … the names you mortals created for the Real are pretty much endless, almost as much as the descriptions you try to use to explain the place away. And to be fair, none really cover it all that well. In fact, you fall short like by bloody miles.

It's not your fault. The mortal imagination might *only* be bound by your own limitations … but those are still pretty crippling. Parents, teachers and every role model you're exposed to as you develop teach the next generation of children to believe in "reality", the reality that says monsters don't exist, that magic is only good for pulling rabbits out of hats and that the only way a man can change into a beast is in theatre, pantomime or state of the art special effects. The sort of reality which makes you pay your taxes on time and elect people into positions of power who at any other time couldn't find their arse with their elbow.

Is it surprising that mortal imagination gets crippled from such an early age?

As I've said, the Real is pretty much the sum total of everything that *could* be, as well as a lot that really shouldn't. The Ivory and the Shadow Courts work alongside the Furies to keep things in relative peace and harmony (and by that, I mean the sort of harmony you see between North and South Korea, requiring a mine field to separate them) and all bound by the Accords to keep their shit from spilling into the Mortal Realm. But that still means the place is as crazy as a box of frogs on Acid, auditioning for the latest Budweiser advert.

In Cantonese.

So, let's take a walk through the easier real estate.

You've got your *Eden* (or Lower Gan Eden in the Kabbalah, the garden of the Hesperides to the Greeks, Paradise to the Persians and so on), the immortal garden state with every species of flora and fauna that ever existed alongside some pretty freaky other shit never seen by mortal eyes. You've got your *Shadowlands*, where nothing is truly solid, instead an ever-changing mélange of dimensions untouched by the sun.

There's the *Wastes,* your rolling deserts filled with the spirits of the lost, the forsaken, cursed to trek the shifting sands until they reach gods know what judgement at the far end.

The Deeps, your bottomless ocean trenches where mighty Kraken drag unlucky sailors down to Davey Jones' locker whilst mermaids frolic in the freezing depths.

And let's not forget the rolling great *Verdance*, the sprawling forestlands filled with murderous trees, sharp knifed Druids and the many skeletons of those unwary enough to get lost under the innumerable boughs. Oh and Herne the fucking Horned and his Wyld court.

Basically, the Real has it all. I've thought about writing a tourists' guide to the place but figured it'd be a waste of my time, given how everything changes with disconcerting frequency.

Plus, we don't really encourage tourists. Except to feed the wildlife. Literally.

So, right now, I'm guessing you're asking ... if it's so amazing, why do us lycans kick around the Mortal Realm instead? Where I've made it abundantly clear you've thoroughly messed up the environment, and magic is about as strong as tissue paper?

For a couple of reasons, really.

For one, there's pretty much two states of being in the Real. You are either predator or prey. There's so much in-fighting within the Courts and the Wyld, between the non-factioned denizens and those immortals just too plain nasty not to let sleeping dogs lie, that you pretty much always need a benefactor or army backing you up. Just in case someone takes offense at your shadow brushing their foot or you looking at them in a funny way. Blood, ichor and all the other weird shit running inside denizens of the Real has been spilt over such lunatic excuses. And I know I've said us lycan are pretty bloody tough, but that sort of constant wear and tear only leads to an early grave.

With a shit load of pain along the way.

Secondly, one good thing about your Mortal Realm is - it's pretty predictable. You mortals tend to be fairly shallow, run of the mill sorts, driven by greed or lust or righteous indignation ... or just the desire to keep your head down and live a quiet life. The lunatics, the madmen, the troublemakers are mostly easy to spot amongst the herd. It helps that you keep promoting them to positions of power ... Prime Ministers, Presidents, Kings or Queens ... and then wonder why it all goes to shit in a handbasket. But this makes keeping the Accords a damn sight easier, when you can guess the motivations of the particular idiot trying to breach them.

Enough to reason with them or shut them down before they do too much damage.

On the other hand (claw or paw), the things you find in the Real, they aren't wired the same way. Immortal life breeds immortal emotions and grudges, to the point where denizens can kick off and start Armageddon just because they feel like scratching that particular itch. Or they remembered some slight done them by mortals centuries ago. Nursing a grudge is a favourite pastime of some of the crazier beings we come across in the Real. So, it's easier to let crazy deal with crazy, and let the Courts and the Furies manage the more big and nasty threats to the general order of things, and the survival of all our worlds.

Oh, and I almost forgot … ok, that was a lie. I just left the best for last. Finally, as I may have mentioned, there's Herne the ever-fucking Hunter. Lord of the Wyld Court. With him Real-side of the Veil, us lycan are more than happy to put up with the smell and noise you mortals fill your world with. It's irritating but far, far more preferable than enforced servitude in his Pack. Kinda like wearing noise-cancelling headphones to deal with noisy neighbours rather than blowing their house up to get a little peace.

So, yeah. The Real is a place of fantasy and magic, but it's also shit-scary and crazy beyond belief. If you mortals think it sounds inviting, I suggest you find some other way of amusing yourselves … like juggling chain-saws blindfolded or baiting great white sharks butt-naked in the ocean. 'Coz, trust me, there will be more of you to clean up after for your relatives to mourn over. Do us all a favour and think of them.

Don't go messing with the Real.

Chapter 1

There are many kinds of goblin-folk to be found throughout the Real. Hobs, bugganes and brags are known for simple mischief, shape changing themselves to fool mortals. More deadly are the Redcaps who dye their hats in the blood of their victims, or the Buabhan Sith, who appear as lonely maidens alongside roadsides but are really vampirish creatures seeking to slake their thirst. It is wise to steer clear of goblin-kin if you cherish a long and quiet life.

If you ever find yourself travelling through Mile End at two o'clock in the morning, you could be forgiven for thinking you'd stumbled onto some apocalyptic end-of-the-world horror movie.

Streets lit by neon lamp-posts flickering on and off with maddening infrequency. Scattered rubbish blowing across the road and collecting in spray-painted doorways. Shapeless forms staggering along the side-streets like zombies looking for their next feed, and everywhere you look the surfaces covered by jagged graffiti in blazing colours like tribal warrior motifs.

Me, I barely spared the neighbourhood more than a second glance as the taxi thundered through the night streets. Sightseeing was pretty much the last thing on my mind at that moment, seeing how the niece of a man I considered a solid friend had been kidnapped right from under my bloody nose. Taken against her will from under Pack protection. From under the Met Police's protection as well given she's also the sole witness to a spate of recent brutal murders in the City of London.

No, right now, what was running thorough my head was a lot simpler and cleaner.

Plain and simple ... *Rage.*

The desire to break bone. Rend flesh. Spill blood.

You *could* say I was a trifle annoyed.

The words ran through my head.

"Morgan, they took her!" Danny's voice was stilted and broken, emotion running high through his words despite a faint slur that told me he wasn't quite right either. "The bastards found me, and they've taken Felix! Oh god it's my fault, they've got Felix!"

The friend in question, Danny Price, lived on the corner of Maroon Street, in East London. Right by the canal and Mile End Park. At this time of the morning, the close was usually deserted and quiet, a haven from the buzz and chaos of London's ever wakeful madness.

But tonight, the madness had come knocking on their doorstep in full technicolour.

Flashing blue lights lit the end street, painting it in thunderous lightning even though the sky was clear overhead. On the normally empty road, uniformed policemen stood guard behind a flimsy wall of crime-scene tape, whilst the predictably nosey mortals lounged about on steps and pavement as they waited for the show to start. Police vans formed a blockade at the only entrance to the close, and men in black body armour and carrying serious guns lurked nearby. Across from the barrier, a car was parked up on the curb, windows dark but I caught the faint purr of an engine turning over and exhaust fumes wafting from the tailpipe. Probably a delivery order waiting to drop off tonight's kebab, or some unlucky Uber driver stuck waiting for his payment.

But what struck me straight of as the taxi pulled up in front of a man holding out his hand in the universal sign of *"Stop right now!"* was nothing these mortals could see or feel. A stink to the air, a reek that burned my nostrils and set my already fiery temper blazing like tossing petrol on a flame. Someone had used magic nearby, the scent leading like a stinking ribbon straight to Danny's home. Thankfully, there was no reek of death, but definitely violence had been done and some foul undercurrent made me want to spit the taste out of my mouth straight-ways.

All in all, *not* a normal night in the quiet close.

My unlucky cab driver pulled up just shy of the police cordon as instructed, and I signed the man over a fifty on the corporate account. Yeah, pricey for a short ride from the museum but given the company's strict code of silence, definitely worth it. Plus it always helps to tip the people picking me up at the dead of night in the middle of strange circumstances without asking any questions. Questions like "Is that blood all over you, Sir" or "Do you have someone in that exceptionally large roll-bag? I could have sworn I heard someone say something ..."

Getting out of the cab, I took a slow breath, forcing the urge not to spit at the rankness tainting the air. I was still wearing the remains of the night's gear, having divested myself of weapons and the more fanciful armour I'd worn to the fight with the Mistress and her pet shape-shifter. The heavy-duty cargo pants and t-shirt unfortunately were shredded in places, and liberally soaked in silvered blood, both from the shape-shifter and the fae bitch whose hand I'd had to cut off to stop her unleashing Armageddon this side of the Veil. Not *exactly* casual mortal gear to play down my intentions to the many watchful police officers, especially when approaching an active crime scene.

But shit happens, and nothing was going to stop me getting inside to see Danny.

Not even the unlucky policeman whose sole task it was to guard the crime tape barrier from anyone getting through.

"I'm sorry, Sir but you can't enter this area. This is an active crime sc…" The uniformed officer who had flagged us down started to say, stepping between me and Danny's house, holding onto the tape as if it was the border pole between warring countries.

Now I'd like to point out I *had had* a pretty bad day so far. I'd been in the mother of all fights with an immortal fae and one nasty sonabitch of a shifter. I'd been poisoned with the one thing that seriously messes us lycan up and, oh, lest I forget ... almost beheaded. I was bruised and battered from having bounced around the Natural History Museum, covered in what I will politely call *muck* from London's sewers and generally in the frame of mind you could describe as *belligerent*. And that's not to mention the lack of serious sleep I'd had recently, or the serious headfuck another ancient fae was playing with my head about details of my real parentage, and the spook-shit she had just dropped in my lap not an hour ago.

So my reactions at that moment *might* have been a trifle aggressive.

The policeman cut off as I grabbed hold of him, his uniform pulling tight as I yanked him through the yellow tape and, as he shouted for help, shoved him back. Hard. The man described an almost comic flailing arc as he powered through the air to land with a loud crash amongst a set of tin bins, scattering rubbish everywhere.

There was the unmistakeable click-clunk of weapons being cocked as the armed police gave me their fullest attention, whilst a half dozen officers ran toward me from where they had been working very hard on controlling the quiet and untroublesome crowds that hadn't gathered.

Maybe I could have handled that a little better.

"Stand down! Everyone stand bloody down!" A familiar voice barked out as I began to very slowly raise my hands and show just how weak and defenceless I could pretend to be. And there he was, ducking out of Danny's front door. Detective

Inspector Gregory Allen looking as rumpled and … well … just as normal as I remembered.

"For chrissake, Mr Black. He was just doing his bloody job!" The detective faced me, hands on hips, face creased into a hard frown. He smelt of stale coffee, frustration and more than a little anger, some of which he was throwing my way but mostly it was old and tempered from long years nursing it. Something from his past had left its brand on him. Burned deep, and that scar smelt of violence and pain.

And no, I'm not suddenly a psychic. All that stuff you can pick up by just listening to those senses Mother Nature gave you mortals … if you weren't so intent on dulling them with all the crap you fill your lives with.
Just saying.

"He might be doing his job, detective but my *friend* Danny called me." I growled back sharply, then shrugged slightly in pretend apology. "Look, I'm sorry. It's been one hell of a shitty day already and I just got the call …"
"Yeah. Got that. You know, with those fine-tuned detective senses I haven't got." Gregory rubbed a hand over his face, the rasp of stubble loud in the sudden quiet. "Any other night, I'd be happy to let you take the rap for assaulting a police officer or at least ask why you look like you got dragged through a paint ball slaughterhouse, but right now let's just get you inside before you do some serious damage to someone."

"Suits me fine." I growled as he waved me through the remains of the broken tape.

Ignoring the threatening looks thrown my way by the policemen and women, I followed the DI as he crossed the street, resisting the urge to grin at the man I'd thrown into the bins as he was helped to his feet. The carefully controlled look he threw back at me stood testament to his discipline, but I still made sure to mark his face for future reference … just in case. I find myself in and out of police stations a lot and falling down the stairs or slipping onto the boot of a policeman carrying a grudge is still a well-known "accident" that occurs behind closed doors. Or so I'd heard.

The steps up from the street to Danny's home were guarded by two more burly policemen, both who eyed me significantly as I followed the DI, ignoring the mocking salute I threw them.

My friend's front door was open, no obvious sign of forced entry showing so I guessed whoever had taken Felix must've gained entry some other way, out of sight from the street. That immediately told me the bastard had planned it. Probably staked out the house and chosen their moment instead of some spur of the moment thing. Hell, it didn't change anything much but at least the little grey cells were starting to work through the anger and tiredness. Details I could log and hopefully use later.

The stink of magic had gotten stronger as I entered, wafting down the main stairs and lurking like putrid fog round the ground floor. And that was another thing ... after a run in with something nasty from the Real a short while back, I'd helped Danny get his workplace and home subtly warded. Nothing too crazy, and nothing like the protection I'd paid for my block of flats. You know, those expensive and heavy-duty ones which had let two grimalkins and a Shadow Court fae come a'calling without invite. Those ones.

But ignoring my own personal problems with the sigils, Danny's place had the sort of protection that would have triggered if anyone had tried slinging magic around the place. Banished the bastards to Kingdom-come severely scorched, and left Danny and Felix untouched. Plus their neighbours none the wiser.

Instead, his place smelt *wrong*, the stink from whatever had happened reeking of violence and anger, and that underlying thread of lust.

DI Allen nodded me onward, through the door on the right of a single corridor, to the side from the staircase leading to the second and third floors. Another policeman waited just inside the open doorway, his scent of old spice, old sweat and rigid professionalism a credit to the man. More telling to me though, shreds of magic clung like sticky cobwebs to him and he also radiated the dull ache of a throbbing headache and gut-wrenching nausea.

I spoke without thinking.

"So I'm guessing you had men stationed in here. They were all knocked out somehow. Probably said afterwards they felt cold all of a sudden. Maybe smelt something rotten or the like. Next thing they know, they're waking up with the mother of all headaches and feeling shitty like they'd been drinking all night or eaten a bad curry. Am I close?"

The DI's expression was blank as he faced me, but I had those other supped up senses to tell me I'd scored a direct hit.

"Guesses like that, Mr Black, well they make the little voice inside me … the one I call *my suspicious bastard* … sit up and take note. I'm assuming you wouldn't like to share how you came to that astonishingly accurate guess?"

"Just a hunch, mister police officer." I lied through my teeth, knowing my own face could've won a poker tournament at that point. "You pick up a thing or two hunting lost kittens."

DI Allen grunted, totally not buying my answer but obviously guessing I wasn't giving anything there and then. He turned back to the man on the door, and I caught him ordering him to quietly take a break. Then the DI nodded me into the front room.

Danny was sat on his sofa, arms curled around his knees, head bowed with a weight of grief and pain I could smell coming off him like waves in a storm. A woman police officer was sat to one side, cradling a steaming mug, and keeping her eyes on the man. Her immediate job was to give him companionship and a sense of safety and offer up bottomless cups of tea since to the British there isn't anything that cannot be made a little better by a brew. It's incredible but it actually works … believe me, there's nothing mystical in tea leaves, but dunk them in almost but not quite boiling water, stir in milk and a heaped spoon of sugar, and hey presto you've got yourself the equivalent of a healing potion for all ills. Better than any fancy concoction brewed up by a hedge witch or phylactery bubbling away in some mad scientist's laboratory.

Just don't tell Elspeth that I ever said that. She'd skin me. With a blunt stick.

As soon as I stepped into the room, Danny jerked up, his face an open book – and it wasn't a pleasant read. The policewoman gave me a long, penetrating look, obviously aware of who I was but wholly disapproving. News like me travels fast. DI Allen gave her a nod, and with a quiet sigh she vacated her ward, giving me the chance to slide onto the sofa beside him.

"Oh thank Christ! Morgan, you came!" Danny gripped my arm with feverish intensity, strength surprising for one so slim and small. I reckoned he was doing overtime on sheer adrenaline, but the strength it gave him was totally lost in the ocean of grief he was feeling.

"Well, you called. I came. That's how it works, mate." I gripped his hands gently, trying to put some reassurance into the gesture. Everything I had already picked up as I walked into the house told me otherwise, but I still had to ask. "Look, Danny, are you sure Felix didn't just slip out? Go off on one of her usual wanders? She does do that, remember? You've called me before to go pick her up from just this sort of thing."

Danny shook his head vigorously, eyes narrowing as memories bit hard.

"No way. They fucking came and took her, right from under my nose. In my house. I've been so goddamn *stupid*." He swore, anger at himself dripping from every word. "I thought I'd been clever, that they wouldn't remember! How could I be so bloody stupid?"

They. They. They. Everything my friend was saying told me he knew who had taken Felix, that he also knew the reason why. But since the totally dependable DI hadn't shared that gem with me, I also knew Danny was keeping that fact from the police. Obviously, something he was not proud of. Something probably fairly illegal that could land him in even more shit.

"Look, mate." I grabbed his attention, cutting off his self-recrimination mid-flow. "I'm here to help, coz you called me. But to do that, you've got to tell me what's going on. Whose '*they*' and why'd they want Felix?"

Danny bowed his head for a moment before he eventually nodded, taking a breath and shooting a glance over to where DI Allen and the policewoman stood. Giving us space but staying near enough in case they were needed. Then my friend turned back to me, lowering his voice to an emotion-choked whisper.

"Morgan, it's just … I haven't been entirely honest with you, and I'm so sorry. It's just I've been hiding so long, keeping this thing quiet … it's not like I *wanted* to lie to you, I just didn't know how to …"

"For fucks sake, mate." I stopped him again, forcing a grin and knowing it probably looked a little toothy and wolf like but not caring. "So you didn't trust me enough to tell me the big bad secret. Fine, I can take you outside after we sort this shit out and kick your ass from here to bloody Big Ben, but for now, just tell me what this whole thing's about."

Danny grinned weakly, getting a grip of himself.

"It's ... the thing is ... Felix isn't my niece. She's my ..."

Fuck. I could tell what he was going to say in the next breath and beat him to the punchline.

"She's your daughter. What's so godawful about that?"

Danny froze for a second, obviously unsure why I wasn't completely fazed by the revelation. Hell, I hadn't known but the poor sap mothered the girl like she was his own anyhow, so it explained his behaviour. But that was no reason to put her in danger ... unless ...

"Because of who her mother is. Who her family are. The fuckers who stole her from me, the bastards I've been running from for over twenty years." Danny clenched his fists, then took another breath and looked at me with those anguished puppy dog eyes, his own guilt warring with the anger at what had been done to him.

"It's the mob, Morgan. The mob kidnapped Felix ... Because I stole her from them."

You know, I've got to admit. That I hadn't seen coming.

Chapter 2

"The mob? As in *organised crime* mob? Al Pacino, gangsters of New York. That kinda thing? *That* mob?" I asked dumbly, seeing Danny's eyes widen with alarm as I forgot to keep my voice down to a conspiratorial whisper.

Thankfully, both DI and WPC were caught answering some request from outside the house, talking into their hand and shoulder radios. Finding them otherwise occupied, I took a moment to consider what my friend had just revealed.

Now, London may not be the crime capital of the world or have so strong a criminal underworld to promote numerous action movies and CSI series based on location. But there is more than enough law-breaking to go around to support organized crime. And where you find that, the mob in some shape or form comes tritt-trotting along with size ten boots and knuckledusters. Gangs, mobs, family-run organizations, they all somehow exist alongside the rest of the city-dwellers and west-side citizens of London with only the grandest of their machinations making it into the mortal news.

But yes, the London mob exists. Us lycan know about the less-than-legal side of the city, but as a rule we don't generally go after many cases involving the mortal underworld. Primarily because vanilla criminals stay firmly on this side of the Veil and don't in any way jeopardise the Accords. Peddling narcotics, stealing millions in fine jewellery, blackmailing and extorting prominent members of the government … for us, the lawbreaking bastards could get away literally with murder if they did it in their own backyard and didn't mess with the fabric of causality. Or whatever. It was a phrase Jessica, our Alpha, had used once, and it sounded serious enough to use in these circumstances.

What fucked up this happy "don't poke us, we won't bite you" situation was the undeniable fact whoever kidnapped Felix had used *magic* to do so ... Some fairly nasty hexing to knock out the police and Danny, with some sort of masking spell to trick the protective sigils on the house and keep the crime hidden. Whatever else I was sure of, Felix would not have gone willingly, and she had a good pair of lungs on her. I'd been on the receiving end of her "vocal narratives" before, and I swear my ears had been ringing the next day. If my friend been taken, she'd have gone down screaming, and everyone in a mile radius would have heard.

I wasn't aware of any criminal organization consistently using magic in their wrongdoings, any open cases we were handling tied to this sort of thing. If only coz it was easier to rely on good ol' fashioned thuggery than learn to manipulate energies well enough not to blow their own balls off. Criminals, overall, just don't have the drive to be big time witches or warlocks. Elspeth had told me the most enterprising of law-breakers she ever came across using magic were the idiots making love charms and potions for foolish teenagers with too much money and not enough good sense to trust that the boy or girl in question just wasn't into them.

Our consultant witch had shared some stories over a bottle of wine, and the way she spoke about it, the peddlers of charms and trinkets to mess with emotions were akin to rapists in her book. Those she tracked down never made it to the Furies for Real justice, but I was sure they never ever brewed another love potion. Probably didn't have the right number of fingers to stir them or something.

Just to annoy her, one time, I'd changed her phone ringtone to Little Mix's "Black Magic". It seemed funny at the time, but Elspeth just jinxed me back in retaliation, and I spent the next twenty-four hours suffering from body odour akin to a grimalkin on a good day. As I'd mentioned, us lycan are fairly proof against direct harmful magic ... but simple odour issues somehow weren't considered a big enough threat to whoever designed us. Since then I'd learned to keep my horseplay in check, what with us employing a witch powerful enough to get round a lycan's natural resistance to most things magical.

She had been smug for a whole week, the cow.

So, back to the issue at hand. Someone or someone's had used strong magic to do over the police and Danny, then nab Felix. That didn't sound like any normal London criminal element, which made this certainly unique. And then there was the surprise fact Felix was Danny's daughter, and he'd admitted stealing her himself in the first place.

This whole thing was starting to stink the more I dug into it. But Danny was my friend, and Felix was too, so I did what any caring person would do. Shrug aside the doubts for the moment and get the full story.

"They're the Carteloni family." Danny admitted, shoulders slumping as he finally ripped the scab off the truth he'd been hiding. "Old school Italians from the Godfather days. Made it big in the US, and they set up shop here in London back in the 60s. They handled girls, drugs, guns, protection rackets, you know, the whole shebang. Kept smart with the police, made friends in government and stayed clean and out of the newspapers. Mr Carteloni Senior ... Anthony ... he was the head of the family back then. Knew when to toe the line, who to listen to. Kept the idiots wanting to be like the Krays in check, usually with the threat of leaving them floating in the Thames without their balls."

Feeling eyes on me, I glanced round and found DI Allen giving me a look that spoke volumes ... the *what was I being told*, and *how much was I going to admit to the police* sort of look. I just shrugged in reply, my priority here to find out what had happened and who was responsible. I'd be happy to let the Met Police tidy things up for Danny and Felix after I'd found the bastards responsible and beaten them to a bloody pulp.

Turning back, I let Danny take a swig of tea before motioning him to get talking.

"Ok, so we've got these Carteloni lot. For fucks sake, seriously, they sound like a pizza delivery store, not some bad-ass crime family. But ok, I can go with that. What I'm left wondering is where you and Felix fit in."

Danny cradled the mug in his hands, looking down into the brown liquid as he answered.

"What you've got to know is, I was just an idiot kid back in the day. I was brought up on stories about the Krays, all those East End crime families we all thought were like Robin Hood to the government. Just small-time heroes taking on the rich and powerful who didn't care about the little guy. My family were already on the take, and I ended up doing small jobs to help out, which turned into bigger jobs. Eventually I was approached by one of Anthony's cousins, and made *the* offer. Told me I had a trustworthy face, that people naturally liked me, made me perfect to be a frontman for some of the jobs they had going. I was fifteen, young, idiotic and full of myself, and pretty soon I was up to my arse in the business. Handling drug deliveries, collecting protection money, sitting in on deals as the 'nice guy'. Anthony noticed me, and I was brought into some of the family gatherings, made to feel a part of them."

"And that's where I met Ashley. Felix's mother."

"Anthony's youngest daughter."

"You're bloody kidding me." I shook my head, not able to help myself. This was sounding more and more like a poor B-movie script or daytime soap. The handsome teenager getting in too deep with the wrong crowd, meeting the beautiful young girl and falling madly in love. Slush pulp crap that normally ends up as a Hollywood blockbuster for idiot teens to drool over. And yeah, idiot ass lycans bored out of their mind at 3am with only channel-surfing left to alleviate the tedium of waiting out a few healing bones. Guilty as charged.

Danny must have read my expression as he dropped his gaze to his mug of tea, wincing and shrugging.

"I know, I *know*. It sounds so bloody stupid now. I was a naive idiot, but it all seemed too good to be true. Ashley was younger than me, a complete bloody princess back then. She treated me like shit to begin with, but I was simply happy to take whatever she threw me, and eventually I guess she decided to have a bit of fun. Mess around with the new kid, Daddy's favourite. It's not like I was ever going to say no when she ... well, you know."

"All too fucking well, mate." I sighed and shook my head. "And I'm guessing Felix was the result of that "*you knowing*"? Not a great fan of protection, you and her?"

Danny shook his head.

"The Cartelonis were good Catholic mobsters whatever else they believed in. Didn't believe in contraception. Sanctity of life and all that. Ashley went crazy when she found out she was pregnant though. Said she was going to get rid of the baby, our *baby*. It had done nothing wrong and she was just going to … So … so I went to Anthony and admitted everything. He almost had me tossed in the Thames but he wasn't going to let his own daughter get rid of his grandchild. Too traditional for that sort of shitty thing."

"Ash had to have Felix, and I was made one of the family. Brought into the fold, sworn by blood, and forced to marry to seal the deal. That was the final straw for her. Ashley always dreamed of marrying someone rich and famous, getting away from Daddy's control. Instead she was lumped with a jumped up nobody and a baby as well. She swore to me she'd make our lives a living hell. That we'd both regret what we'd done to her for the rest of our lives. And god did I believe her."

"So, what, you decided doing a runner with the grandchild of the bloody mob-family's head Don was the *sensible* option here? How the hell did that seem clever?" I wanted to gently bang my head on the nearest table, or for that matter, bang Danny's not so gently to see how much emptiness echoed inside, but I restrained myself with the simple knowledge this was old news, done and dusted. Felix was missing, that was what mattered.

"No, it didn't seem clever or smart or anything, but I really did believe Ashley. You didn't know her, mate. When she said she would destroy us, she wasn't joking." Danny took another swig of tea, the thoughts of his - I'm guessing – now ex-wife still making him shake with remembered emotion. None of them good. "So I acted the good family member, did whatever they asked me to do, but kept a track of everything. All the shipments I'd handled, the people I'd helped extort, the important 'names' I'd met in meetings. That sort of stuff. I'd also managed to put aside a fair amount of cash … you gotta remember this was in the days before e-banking and digital records so it was easy to stash. I worked out how much we'd need to disappear, then grabbed Felix during a family gathering. They were all busy getting drunk or high or whatever, it was almost too easy."

"I'd made copies of everything I had, and left Anthony a note with just enough details to show I was serious. Where I'd left copies that in the event of something happening, well, you know … ones to post to the few uncorrupt police of legal officials I knew, that sort of thing. I made a deal. Our freedom for our silence. Ashley didn't want me or Felix, and I wasn't good for the family. Anthony was smart, so it seemed like a win-win to me."

"For a smart kid, you sure made some stupid-ass assumptions." I told him bluntly. "Blackmail a crime boss with details of the family's dealings, and expect them to see the *sensible* solution? Like that was ever going to work."

Danny looked like he wanted to snap a reply, then his shoulders slumped, and he just nodded and continued the story.

"You're right. But it was all I could think of to save us both. So I ran. Made it to the US and spent the first five years moving round every few months like I expected to see the Cartelonis on our doorstep any moment. It was hell, but we were free. Five years went by, then another five, and nothing. I kept an eye on the news from London. I heard all the crackdowns on organised crime, saw some of the family in the news being put away and doing time. I settled on our new names ... made Danny and Felix Price up, paid for the fake identities and back stories. It was easier then with no proper computer records, and I let Felix grow up with a fake story about her being my niece by marriage, given into my care when her parents died. That way she never wanted to ask about me or any missing mother, or do anything like start investigating her roots."

"She was thirteen when I reckoned we were finally safe, that no one was following us. I wanted her to have a good education, to put down roots. But I missed the UK, missed London especially and I really wanted her to know the place like I did ... I hated being away. So, like some bloody naive idiot, I booked us tickets and brought her over. Bought a little place out of town for the both of us and enrolled her in school. She'd been in and out of places across the US, but I wanted her to make friends, grow up normally and not feel so all over the place as I did."

"I picked up the cafe after she had got her A-Levels and wanted to go to university in London, and bought the house here so we could be close. Up until I met you, there hadn't been any trouble, nothing to make me think there was any danger of our past coming back to bite us. My mistakes seemed to be dead and buried, Felix was doing well and settled, and I just forgot to worry."

"But I was so bloody wrong. And now they've taken her."

Danny curled back in on himself as the tears started to flow again, and I caught a barely muffled "tsk" from the WPC as she saw me reduce the man back to a crying wreck. Throwing her a shake of my head, I settled back on the sofa, thoughts quite honestly a little fucked up.

The mob. Danny Price, the cheerful easy-going cafe owner I'd saved from a Real incursion had been in with a mob-family. Had gotten their sweetheart hell-cat pregnant and then done a runner with their daughter. And now, nineteen plus years later, it looked like they'd decided to get even and kidnap said daughter in revenge.

Knowing there was no reason for him to lie to me now, that what he'd told me, he'd *believed* so much ... every lycan sense, every trick from the Real was telling me the story was true. But that old cynical and world-weary voice in my head wouldn't shut up. Things just didn't add up here, and not just because I expected ... any moment ... for someone to call "that's a wrap" and the scene to end, and all us actors shunted off set so they could change the scenery and powder my nose.

No, it all came back to the use of magic. Not guns, baseball bats or the usual mob tools. Magic. And that just didn't gel with the facts.

"Danny. Danny!" I reached over and laid a hand on my friend's thigh, gently pulling him out of his grief. The little guy looked up, red eyes raw and face soaked with tears.

"You said there was no warning. No signs. No one staking out the shop, hanging round the university that Felix spoke to you about? Nothing that made you think someone was following either of you?"

Danny shook his head, rubbing his hands together.

"I swear, nothing like that. I know I should have seen something but … no, nothing. No warning signs. I thought I was careful, keeping an eye out for anything not right but … god, I promise Morgan, I didn't see anything."

Warning signs. Something went click in my head and I was already up and halfway out of the house before the rest of my hindbrain caught up.

"Hey, Mr Black? Mr Black!" DI Gregory Allen hurried behind me, but I just shook a hand in his direction as I lengthened my stride and burst out the front door. Police officers on either side turned, and I again felt the decidedly nasty sensation of weapons pointed in my direction. Ignoring them like flea bites, I focused entirely on the one thing that had me tripping.

The car. Sat idling in the street across from the house. Blacked-out windows and no sound of music coming from inside. At 2am in the morning. Probably an Uber waiting for their fare to come out. Not suspicious at all.

I guess I should have tried a little subtlety, since I was only halfway between the house and my target when the engine coughed to full life and the car screeched off. I resisted the urge to give it a serious run for its money, as I reckoned the spectacle of seeing me leap over cars and keep pace with a vehicle doing thirty plus mph would need a little explaining. The number plate was purposefully disfigured, but I at least made the make and model. Four people inside from the faint flickering movement even through the dark glass, and they were definitely agitated as I picked up shouting over the engine throb. The car made the corner, screeching round and almost rising off two wheels, before vanishing into the greying morning.

"Shit!" I vocalised profoundly as I ground to a stop, even as I heard the police slowing behind me. I had to pull hard on the urge to crumple the nearest car into scrap metal as I turned on my heel.

DI Allen faced me, hands on hips, with a half dozen police officers backing him. I wasn't sure if they had come to help me, or hold me back ... either way, I just shot them a grim smile and started walking back towards the house. The DI fell in step beside me.

"Was that anything pertinent you should consider sharing?" He asked, but I just shook my head.

"Probably just some kids, smoking weed and wanting to look cool." I tried to make the lie sound genuine, but the DI just snorted and gave me a dirty look. "Ok, ok, it *might* have been persons of interest in this investigation, but I wasn't sure and wanted to ask them first. Polite like."

"So you just lost us our most solid lead because you wanted to chat to them first? Really?" The cold sarcasm from the DI stopped the anger roiling inside me for a moment, and I shook my head, knowing I was thinking with the beast, not the man.

"They were most likely just spotters. Probably hired just to see who turned up then report back to their contact. It wouldn't have led anywhere."

"You. Don't. Get. To. Make. That. Call." He grated, facing off against me, hand out and pressed to my chest. "Listen to me because I will say this only once. I get that Mr Price and the young woman are your friends. That you feel responsible for some reason for letting this happen. But this *is* *my* investigation and if you get in my way, or let any harm come to Felicity Price because you were too goddamn arrogant or proud to tell me something *pertinent,* I will haul your ass in for obstructing an active police investigation and lock you up and throw away the key. Do you understand me?"

The anger and old pain roiling off the man stopped me in my tracks better than his hand, like a bucket of cold water in the face. This was personal, definitely linked to something he'd suffered before. And here I was, tromping my size eleven boots all over his turf. Not the brightest move, Morgan.

I nodded and bit back any number of sarcastic comments that sprang to mind. The DI grunted, turning and angrily strode off to the nearest knot of police gathered round a large open backed van.

Oops. Pissing off my one ally on the side of law and order. Not the best first step, even by my standards.

"Verily done, Knight. I see that you are making friends with your usual grace and good charm."

The cold, dry whisper of an arctic breeze ruffled around me as the words bit through the air from behind me. My anger faded momentarily, swept away as ice rippled down my spine. I slowly stopped, turning on my heel, knowing exactly what I was going to find waiting me. Well, who, to be precise.

Standing in the open, clad in rags of ash and ruin, she leant on a crooked staff of black wood, scarred and bloodstained from numerous battlefields. A hood was pulled high over the newcomer's head so that darkness shrouded any features ... except for the blood-hued orbs that stared back at me with immortal mockery.

"My, what big eyes you have, grandmother." I mocked as a slim tattooed hand rose to pull the hood slowly back, revealing fox thin features of corpse white, covered in intricate runic script.

"All the better to watch you kneel and grovel before you die, pup."

The Morrigan. Mistress of War. Crow of Winter. My own personal Sidhe of Shade answered as the blood chilled in my veins.

Chapter 3

Trolls fall into three main categories … lesser, greater and elder. The lesser trolls, known to haunt bridges and have a pathological hate to goat-kin, are easily distinguished by their smaller stature, weasely features and long ears. Greater trolls can easily be mistaken for hairy ogres, sizing upwards of ten or twelve feet in height and have a perpetual hunger for mortal bones. The elder trolls thankfully are rare, having mostly died away when their mountain homes were discovered. These vast creatures ranged the prehistoric world and gave the dinosaurs a run for their money … the sight of an elder rising on the horizon, blocking the sun, was sure to strike fear and dread.

"You know, you showing up makes this morning truly complete." I snuck a look around, expecting at least one mortal to start screaming in fear or pointing their phone camera at the newcomer. Your instincts in the face of mortal death … to make high pitched noises or to take its picture. Hilarious that you've lasted this long as a species.

The Morrigan just smiled thinly. On her shoulders, two massive ravens eyed me with red rage and casual disdain … her bodyguards in their not so threatening form. I'd met them before and almost crossed claws with them. Not a dance I'm particularly keen on repeating, but I was damned if I was going to get eyeballed by bloody birds and lose.

Around us, life continued on as normal. The police threw me the occasional suspicious look, but in no way reacted to the absurdly obvious character who had appeared from nowhere and now stood in the middle of their crime scene. A glamour, I was guessing, and so subtle that I didn't get even a sense of it. Immortals had had a lot of time to practice their art.

"To what do I owe this grave honour?" I decided formality was the best way forward, since trying to match wits and sarcasm with an immortal was doomed from the start. I'd had the headache to prove it.

"Nicely recovered, Knight." She replied with a chill smile. That was the second time she had mentioned that word. Knight. Thrown at me like a slap in the face, but I know all she was doing was reminding me of my recent elevation. With a lot of personal gratification, I was also sure.

"It's ok, I've had a lot of practice from all the times I've had to apologise. So … ah, why are you here?"

The Morrigan remained silent for a long moment, then she took a gentile step to one side. Somehow, she had hidden the presence of a second person behind her … someone I immediately recognised and had a lot warmer feelings toward.

Elspeth MacElvy smiled broadly as she stepped away from the fae. Good Deed's witch-consultant, with her striking red hair and gypsy style clothing, was a vibrant figure compared to the immortal of the Shadow Court … but one I equally wasn't expecting to see at this hour at this place. She was supposed to be back at the Pack's office, headed there from the Natural History Museum debacle, assisting our Alpha hand over the traitorous Mistress to the Furies for punishment. Once done, I'd expected her to slope off home and do whatever it was she did to get over a night like the one we'd all had.

Drink cocoa. Knit some socks. Brew some potions or curse some idiot who got on her wrong side. Any or all of the above.

Not to show up at 2am in Mile End at the site of some seriously bad juju.

"Jessica thought you might like a hand with whatever happened here." The witch's expression grew grim as she looked past me, towards the crime scene. "We both agree this thing is a little too personal for you to handle solo, and if it has anything to do with your friend Felicity's testimony, Ms Walker feels the Pack owes a measure of responsibility for what passed here tonight."

"Huh. Reckon I can't argue that." I probably should have been pissed that my Alpha thought this too close to home to let me check things out on my own, at least at first before calling in help, but truthfully, after the Museum fight I was feeling rough as hell and none too sharp. Elspeth was a perfect choice for sniffing out the bad juju that had been thrown round here, and definitely would pick up on anything more subtle than a glowing sign painted on a wall detailing the perpetrator and where I could find them.

Just once, I'd like it to be that simple.

"And the Morrigan *just* happened to be in the vicinity to offer you your very own faerie taxi? How convenient." I remarked with more than a dollop of sarcasm and smiled a snarl as the pair of ravens gave very un-avian like squawks of anger. Want to piss off anyone from the Courts in one simple step? Call them a faerie ... then duck real fast, if you want to survive the experience.

For her part, the Mistress of War just gave one of her more chilling smiles, tapping those long fingers along her twisted oaken staff. Like the countdown to World War Three.

"Aye, but I'm not one to look a gift horse in the mouth, and it's a long cycle ride from the office to here." Elspeth gave the fae a nod of respect. "Her reasons for appearing at our workplace and asking after you are her own. For now."

The Morrigan had no reason to be hanging round either our offices or the site of an attempted breach of the Accords, but I had recent proof that this particular immortal didn't exactly play by the rules. Between her and her Queen, they had played a game with me that had had little to do with reason and almost cost me my head. So I guess I should just be thankful the fae been around to bring me exactly the right person when I needed her the most. Without me having to ask for help.

Yeah, right. Not suspicious at all.

"Fine, let's just leave it as fortunate timing. Or was there something specific I can do for you?" I addressed the Morrigan directly.

"We do have business, pup. Our Queen has words for you, but she requested I seek you out this early morn to guide her newly appointed Knight accordingly. Know you your suspicions are right. This be no mere mortal tale of indiscretion and revenge. Seek your answers at a place where knowledge is worshipped and yet enslaved, and over water where things be out of sight and forgotten. But do not tarry, the young one's life is indeed in peril. Until we next meet ... Knight."

The Morrigan nodded to me, then drew back as shadows curled and shrouded over her. A chill wind knifed through the close, rankness of rot and spoiled matter stinging the air as the Veil split and enveloped the fae, drawing her back from the mortal realm. Leaving a single black feather spiralling down to rest on the concrete.

And as a sign of the guardians' disdain for me, this was liberally stained with guano.

Leaving the mark to dissolve in the mortal air, I turned to Elspeth and decided to be upfront and frank with her.

"You ok for this? It's rough in there." I warned her. I know she was on a handsome retainer with the Pack and all, but that's the thing with working around lycans. We treat those close to us like kin, and as such, Elspeth was closer than any colleague and someone I respected. I had to at least try the big brother thing, despite knowing how well she could handle herself in most situations.

The witch nodded her thanks for asking but motioned me onward, the steel which lay under the surface all too apparent in that moment.

"I'm going to ignore the fact your companion appeared from nowhere, and just ask … is she going to be as much trouble as you?" DI Allen was waiting for us on the steps, having called off the policemen guarding the door, warding the portal all on his lonesome. Shabby, worn looking around the edges, I still saw the man behind the badge, the sort in medieval days who would have worn battered armour and carried a notched sword. And stood against dragons to guard innocent maidens. His righteous anger was held in check but burning bright inside for what had been done here, and I had been giving him nothing but grief since I'd shown up.

I should've felt bad, but I was just too bloody tired.

Elspeth stepped up and laid a hand on the other's arm, facing him directly and staring him straight in the face. She didn't smile, flaunt her breasts, or even work any sort of charm that I could tell … all it took was that direct contact. Skin on skin. Something passed between them, unspoken but all the more real for it. The Detective Inspector nodded once, shooting me one last look, then stepped aside to let Elspeth through.

Following her in, I once again felt the nausea bubbling up from the nearness of the foul magic used here. Elspeth stopped a few steps inside, steadying herself against the banister, bowing her head for a moment before drawing a long slow breath. Straightening, she looked around herself, and this time the ambient power of Nature glowed from her eyes. The breath of a summer's day whipped round the ground floor as she took a step forward, then another … away from the front room where Danny waited. Instead, she made her way slowly towards the stairs. To the first floor, where the bedrooms waited.

Seeing movement, I motioned for the WPC and police-officer guard to stand down as they moved to intercept. Danny joined them, peering from behind his warders with red-rimmed eyes. Seeing a complete stranger in his violated home, he shot me a questioning look, but on seeing me shake my head he managed to crack a smile through the sorrow and self-recriminations.

"Find her. Please." He mouthed, and I nodded, then turned to follow the witch upward.

The first floor was like any town house, with the main bedroom up front and a bathroom set to one side. Felix had taken the back room, since it overlooked the small park and canal. She'd said she wanted to have a little of nature to herself in the middle of London, something beyond the concrete and car fumes. For a party girl who lived for the bars and clubs of the big city, that little fact was all the more endearing ... and something I ruthlessly exploited in our habitual mick-take.

Elspeth moved purposefully up the stairs, almost in a trance as she walked deeper into the fog that the hex cast here had left behind. Invisible to the mortals, I could feel it rolling off my skin like oily spillage. Worse than the stink of a grimalkin, or the filth I'd had to wade through in the sewers beneath London. This stank of lust and violence, rank and petty. And madness, gibbering merrily along behind.

She stopped outside the open door to Felix's room, already adorned with bright crime scene tape. Breaks in the door's frame and panels showed someone or something had come through like a battering ram, the blows leaving ragged slices where claws had done their violent work. There were bloody marks on the splintered frame, possibly a handprint badly smudged. Small, feminine. Fear shivered like a spike amongst the filth in the air, and I closed my eyes as an image of Felix ... scared, alone, hurt ...

sprang to mind. The beast inside took hold of that and screamed its fury.

A little pointer for you … don't try drawing a calming breath when you are standing in a magical fug. It did my image no good, bending over and coughing like a reformed smoker after his first marathon. Elspeth turned and looked down at me, quirking one eyebrow.

"Need a hand there? A glass of cool fresh water maybe?" She asked, and I shook my head, holding up my hand.

"Make that a good bottle of red, and you've got a deal. For now, let's get this over with."

The witch nodded and turned back, pushing the tape aside and stepping into the room.

Any parent will tell you that the average state of a late-teenager to early twenty-something's room is terminal chaos, bordering on violent explosion. Felix was no exception, thinking that chairs and upright surfaces were equal to the task of keeping discarded clothes off the floor, if not better than the drawers and wardrobes near to hand. Posters of semi-nude and artistically rendered men in various strutting poses dotted the walls, mostly with lipstick kisses adoring their manly chests and cheeks. Postcards from a variety of places adorned one corkboard, with scribbled notes and letters, fetishes tagged to them with drawing pins as reminders of good times gone by.

But that was where all pretence at normality ended. The level of destruction in the room went beyond anything explained by girlie haphazardness. The bed was overturned and shattered, broken into three pieces. Given it was wrought iron, that alone spoke of unnatural fury. But holes had been punched in the bedroom walls, exposing wiring and insulation like the colourful insides of some long-forgotten pharaoh's tomb. The bedroom light, in a twisted frame of rose gold, had been ripped from its socket and crumpled underfoot … and two full length mirrors had been struck enough times to leave bloody webs of glass hanging from the frames. The window looking out onto the park had been ripped from its frame, with more bloody marks staining the brickwork.

All in all, the place looked like someone had tossed a grenade inside, or possibly an enraged bear that hadn't been fed for several weeks. But then again, you never really know ... "So, I'm just asking but ... I'm guessing this isn't the state you'd expect to find a *questionably* stable young woman's room in?" I hazarded as Elspeth stepped daintily into the wreckage.

"I can honestly say, having been a young lady of her age and of questionable mental stability, that this is *not* normal. In any fashion." The witch answered quietly as she reached the centre of the room. Her hands slowly rose, as emerald fire sparked along her fingers and wove out in a web through the air. "Now Morgan, shush. I need to concentrate."

I stepped into the room and settled into the nearest corner, letting my own senses tell me their own tale. I smelt fear and fury, mingled with the foul hex like ribbons entwined. Felix's scent came off almost every surface, a mingling of her mix of perfumes, perspiration, and hair spray. Oh, and just in case you think I'm one of those strange types who think women don't sweat ... they do. Every mortal does, it's a biological fact. Nothing to be ashamed of, it's just a waste process. But if we're talking volumes, then Felix is in the perspiration bracket, along with most of the successful models and, of course, the Queen. Models and Royalty seem to know how to do such bodily functions lightly and discretely. Something in their genes. I guess it's a talent not to dissolve into a puddle under the hot sun wearing all the ridiculous paraphernalia designers love to call fashion or court-frippery.

Anyhow, her scent was all over the room, as was to be expected. Mingled in with this though was someone else's. Male from the stronger scent, and reeking of a typical poor choice of antiperspirant. Lynx or something equally animalistic, which I guess is to makes the wearer think it's a good musk to wear. If anyone had smelt actual lynx musk, then they'd know just how mis-named that brand is.

The man's scent was riddled with madness and fury, also filthy desire, riddling the air. This level of intensity made me think serial psychopath, as there was little emotional stability to be found amongst it, little rational thought. Someone was acting purely on raw emotion, and that is never a good thing amongst you mortals. Wars have been started by such people, and some of the most despicable crimes committed by people saying "I just felt like I should *do* something". Usually with an axe or hammer.

The odd thing was the fear seemed to be as much the stranger's as Felix's ... laced through both their scents strongly. Anger and fear in equal parts, but no clue as to what the attacker had been afraid of. What had terrified Felix ... well, that took little guessing.

"Morgan, dear. I think I've got it." Elspeth broke my concentration, bringing me back round as I faced her. Emerald fire now wreathed her entire form and spun out in tendrils which knitted through the air and formed an intricate lattice work. All of which would take one hell of an explanation if any of the mortals below walked in on the two of us right now. For whatever reason DI Allen had kept the rest of the team downstairs, and I once again thanked the man silently for his experience where we lycan were concerned. He didn't know anything but guessed enough to keep his colleagues well clear.

"There are wards on this dwelling, which would have triggered if the attacker had simply attempted to gain entry with brute force." Elspeth spoke as she wove traces of green fire through the air. "They are of modest proficiency, but there are always flaws built into the working since no act of the craft can be completely perfect. Our Mother detests such attempts at perfection. These wards would only react to an entry that was not first invited ...”

The witch twisted her fingers, and the fire merged and soaked into the room, covering everything in a glittering layer. This then lifted and reformed, so that I found myself looking at a ghostly image of a young woman sat on her bed ... itself rebuilt from the three pieces it now lay in. The rest of the room had been healed of all traces of damage, and I guessed Elspeth was recreating the events from the imprint left here. More difficult to do than what she had done with Felix's memories, but the strength of the magic that had been loosed in the room probably made things easier.

I watched Felix rise and dance along to music only she could hear, stopping to write something in a journal. She seemed relaxed, at ease, and my gut twisted with a cold wrench as I knew things were only going to go very wrong right about ... now ...

Something happened outside the room, whatever it was loud enough to disturb the young woman. She set aside phantom earphones, left the journal on the bed and walked towards me and the door. I wanted to reach out, grab hold of her, stop her... so strong the pack sense for the daughter of my friend ... in fact my friend herself as well ... but my hands slid through her and her image barely rippled as she stepped through me.

Whatever the disturbance was, Felix didn't seem alarmed in any way, shrugging to herself after a moment. She walked back to pick up her headphones, but then cocked her head and looked at the window. Something had attracted her attention, and she walked quickly over and drew up the sash, sticking her head out into the night air. Whatever was out there, whatever she said, was lost as Elspeth and I watched but she seemed to be having some sort of conversation, shaking her head one moment but then finally nodding and making a beckoning motion. An offer to whomever it was to come in.

An invitation. Fuck, Felix had short circuited the wards herself without even knowing.

The next moment, the spectral image of the window and the surrounding frame was ripped outwards, and what I could only describe as a shifting cloud burst into the room. It landed on the bed, which flipped over. Felix staggered back, and I looked through the back of her head as the intruder rose up before her. There were no words, no sound, but I could almost imagine her screaming.

From the bedside, Felix reached out and grabbed up a baseball bat of all things, already swinging from the shoulder as her assailant came at her. The blurring storm ripped the room apart as it filled the space, but Felix seemed not to care, hitting at the thing and dodging to one side, then lashing out again. At least one strike must have hit home as the surging cloud stumbled and hammered into the door, and out of the writhing mass claws slashed and ripped at the frame.

"Whatever this thing was, it first set off some sort of distraction out front to draw the attention of the guards below, then convinced Felicity to grant it access to negate the wards. This confirms it knew they existed and planned the assault." Elspeth commented as she moved around to look at the thing. Twisting one hand, she slowed the image, freezing the boiling mass in place. "It must have charmed the room with silence otherwise by now someone would have come to help."

Unfortunately, even frozen in place, there wasn't much I could tell from the image it presented. Whatever this thing was, it was cloaked heavily enough that the recreation didn't reveal the attacker's identity. Just spikes, boiling masses of cloud and wrath. Claws showed somewhere inside, but for whatever reason this thing hadn't simply torn Felix apart. Instead it flinched as she struck at it, dodging around her.

Danny's daughter was screaming silently, but still no-one came to her rescue, as she lashed at it with her bat. Then the cloud darted forward, wrenching the weapon from her grasp and crumpling it to shards that exploded all around the pair. Her attacker surged up and lashed out to grab hold of Felix, but she dodged and kicked out, the scrappy fighter she was. And somehow she must have scored a direct hit as the cloud folded and convulsed.

"Good girl." I told her, but then winced as the intruder seemed finally to lose patience. A lump of the writhing cloud lashed out, and Felix's head snapped back as blood sprayed. She staggered back, hands to her lip and torn cheek, blood already running free. She hit the door, hand reaching out to grasp at anything, and silently screamed ... but the cloud wrapped around her, wrenching her around. Some sort of struggle went on inside the cloud for a moment before it stilled in form, spikes receding back as its own turmoil seemed to lessen.

"I'm guessing it knocked her unconscious. Hence it not needing to use any further force to subdue her." Elspeth sighed, rolling her hands. The image sped up, and I watched as some sort of crawling tendrils wormed out through the air from the cloud, surging with unnatural vigour as they sank down through the floor. "What we're seeing is whatever nightmare it used to knock out the police and your friend below. Nasty shit, vile and strong, to linger this long."

I focused back on the scene in front of us and watched as the attacker surged back round the room, doing even more damage. It seemed to freeze in front of one of the full-length mirrors, then lashed out, splintering it with violent strikes before gathering itself up onto the bed, shattering this into the three pieces, and dove out the ruins of the window.

"It left through the hole it had made getting into the house and took your friend's niece out the back." The witch told me, following the image to stick her head out of the gaping hole. "There's a drainpipe by the window, and the ruins of a shed directly below. The fence at the end of the garden has been broken, looks like it was forced outwards. I can only assume it used stealth initially to get to the house but once it had your friend's niece it just bulldozed its way out."

"Daughter." I corrected her as I moved to join her, looking out across the wreckage below. The gaping hole in the fence led out onto an area of green scrubland, stunted trees and wild bushes, and the canal leading back to the Thames.

"Really? Ok, his daughter." Elspeth reached out and gently gripped my head, turning me back to face her.

"What?" I squashed the urge to break free, knowing she knew what grabbing hold of a lycan's head normally resulted in ... Loss of fingers, at the very least.

"Morgan, the Morrigan was right in what she told you. This was no random hit. The taste of this thing, this is the same creature, the murderer Jacob has been tracking. Which Felicity witnessed." Elspeth told me flatly. "The essence of the thing, what it left behind before and now here is the same, but much, much stronger. Whatever this thing is, I would call it dangerously strong and definitely unstable. And now, it has your friend's daughter."

Shit, indeed, had just gotten Real.

Chapter 4

Hags are often mistaken for witches, a much-used mistake by the Inquisition to label mere wiccans as beings to fear. Black Annis lurk in the Shadow Courts, weaving their webs to trap mortals in their talons, whilst the Jennies haunt waterways and delight in drowning unruly children in the weeds.

There are days when I can shrug off pretty much most situations you throw at me. Mobsters? No problem. Murderous clouds breaking into houses and kidnapping young women? No sweat. Keeping my friend off the police radar for previous links to organised crime? Give me something hard, c'mon.

This day, I've got to admit, I was feeling off my game just a touch.

My immediate instinct was to throw myself out the gaping hole that once was a window, drop to the ground and follow whatever remaining scent there was. Track the bastard down all on my lonesome, and to hell with consequence.

Problem was, that would leave Danny with no clue as to what was really going on, and probably still blaming himself for the whole shit hitting the fan. It would leave the police chasing ghosts, with no solid leads, and most importantly it would leave me decidedly alone and exposed if I actually did manage to find whatever had Felix. As a pack, we're taught not to go lone wolf if there was any chance the target could be nastier than you. Sensible thinking, and it had saved the skin of most of my mates, and more to point me, more than once.

So, instead of following base-born instinct, I took a deep, slow breath then turned away from the gaping hole.

"Thanks Ellie." I nodded and let loose the frustrated sigh that had been locked inside since I'd started watching Felix's kidnapping. "You'd best head off, and I'll wrap things up with the police and Danny. Tell Jess I'm happy to work with you, Jacob, anyone she wants but I'm not walking away from this. Personal or not, I've got to see this through."

Elspeth gave me one of her knowing looks, wisely keeping quiet as to how she expected Jessica Walker to react to my ultimatum. Our Alpha allowed a certain level of pushback amongst the Pack, as long as none of us were put at risk foolishly. But that didn't mean I wasn't looking at a serious dressing down when this was all said and done if I pushed too hard. That I fully accepted if it meant I stayed on the case and found Danny's daughter.

I waited in the room as the witch let the reconstruction die, emerald fire fading into the furniture and floor, the magic drawn back into herself. Her eyes slowly returned to a nice friendly mortal brown, and her hair settled back into its non-witchy state ... so guys, just remember the next time you mock a lady for having a bad hair day, you might end up finding out she has the capacity to make yours oh so much worse. Just saying.

Finally, having gathered herself she stepped up and gave me a quick peck on the cheek and a hug, then left the room. I remained behind, eyes slowly roving over the wreckage of Felix's most private hideaway, thinking. Something nagged from the vision, a little detail ... and finally it clicked. Dropping to my knees, I hunted amongst the shards and shrapnel that once had been the bed, running my hands through the stiff carpet. Until I felt the small oblong shape I had been hunting for.

Her diary. She had been writing in it just before she had been attacked. Anything out of the ordinary, a gem that might point to whatever had happened here …. it was a slim chance, but I'd read enough crime novels to know diaries often contained that one vital clue mixed up with all the day to day garbage mortals think makes a day important enough to write about. Pushing it into a side pocket, I closed my eyes and took one last breath before pushing myself up.

"I'll find you." I told the room, not caring that there was no-one to hear me, then left.

I met the good and doggedly predictable DI Allen downstairs, as he waited patiently with arms folded and that closed expression which still spoke enough volumes to put Shakespeare to shame.

I'd given myself a few moments to get my head together and try to formalise a plan ... well, enough of something to pretend I knew what the next few hours might look like. And as much as the idea of having the combined might of the Metropolitan Police force backing me up for once sounded like a great way of covering my ass, having them underfoot if there was any danger of tangling with a magic-wielding perp only meant I was adding to the bastard's body count. They just weren't prepared for this sort of thing. So, with the best will in the world, I knew there really was only one course I could take.

Lie through my back teeth.

"So? Anything ... *odd* up there?" He asked me as I stepped down into the hallway. The WPC had moved Danny back to the sofa and re-joined him, offering up another mug of tea and shooting me a flat look as I glanced their way. For his part, my mate just gazed at me with hope and need like a raw open wound painting his handsome features. Not wanting to give anything away, I just nodded once and let the mortals around me make up their own mind as to what that meant.

Danny got the hint and slumped back onto the sofa, cradling the steaming mug.

Turning back to the DI, I motioned him forward and we left the house. By now, the locals had decided nothing more was going to happen that required their immediate time-wasting skills, and all but one had gone back indoors. This last lone soul stood at the edge of the police tape, talking quietly to the nearest policeman. The pen and open pad made me revise my opinion, realising he wasn't a local, just someone who needed to fit in wherever he might find himself. A reporter. Definitely someone I wanted to avoid, as Jessica had made it perfectly clear her thoughts on any lycan being stupid enough to appear in the mortal news. Thanks god ... gods, whatever ... I hadn't chased the lookout's car and forced it off the road ... suitable material for most of the papers that thrived in London. If I'd done it naked, with a bikini clad woman helping me along the way, that might guarantee me a top slot in the other ones.

So, keep a low profile whilst lying to the friendly police officer. Easy peasy.

"Look, Danny wasn't completely honest with you." I told the DI, as we stopped at the bottom of the steps to the front door. DI Allen simply snorted in response and motioned for me to continue. I guess the job had made him fairly used to people keeping things back or telling the odd lie here and there.

No way was I going to let the police know about Danny's past, the stupid decisions he'd made that meant he'd had to flee his home and country. Nor was I going to share what Elspeth had shown me, as that was well and truly out of their remit. Instead, there was still a way I could give the DI and his lot a stick to fetch without throwing them into direct harm's way.

So I spun a nice little story, where Danny had failed to let me and the police know that some fairly unimaginative individuals had been putting pressure on him at work, had been hanging round both the cafe and his home at all hours, and had approached him weeks ago demanding he start paying protection money to a certain Mr Carteloni. I didn't try to add too many details ... I was well enough versed in lying to know to keep thing simple. Nope, the police would be keen to ask their own questions, dig into the events themselves and spend a lot of time safe and unharmed doing background checks, character references and financial searches on this mysterious person or persons of interest. I knew for a fact that the protection racket was as rife throughout London now as it had been in the 50s, where every movie of that time seems to be about gangsters. Some types of criminals never go out of fashion, and some types of crimes are never left to gather too much dust on the shelf, when they make easy money.

No mention of magic. No linking this in any way to what Felix had witnessed. Nothing unusual for me or my lot to be involved in. Nope, just plain old fashion strong arming, kidnapping and home invasion to deal with.

Did I feel bad about spinning a load of bull to the DI? Well, to be honest, if it kept mortals from running headlong into violent and potentially lethal magic? Call me one hell of a cynical knight in battered armour, but I wasn't going to lose any sleep over this particular lie. Hell, I'd deceived my ex for well over a year about what I really was and she was probably as close to someone I might have had romantic tendencies toward as I'd found this side of the Veil.

Mr Romance, me.

Oh, and if you think I should feel bad about lying, just think back to the shining example of truth and paragon of virtue, Sir Lancelot ... and look what he got up to with King Arthur's wife, Guinevere. They played *hide the lance* shamelessly right under the King's nose. Though having now met Artur in the flesh, I couldn't say I blamed old Guinee for looking elsewhere for attention. That Ivory Court stooge had been so arrogant and self-obsessed it made my teeth ache.

DI Allen listened as I explained away an obvious attempt to strongarm Danny into paying the protection money owed by kidnapping his beloved niece ... his expression not shifting one bit. When I decided I'd spun enough to make a boatload of jumpers, he grunted and shook his head.

"Mr Black, that's a fairly thorough story you've got there. Ties all this up nicely for us to go and start making enquiries. I'm sure Mr Price will think twice before hiding any such relevant facts from the authorities, when it so obviously put his own flesh and blood in danger. And as his friend, I would hope you would make sure that is the case." The DI nodded to the open door. "I must insist that you leave this in the hands of the Metropolitan Police now, and don't decide to do anything ... *unadvised*. Mr Price will need a good friend soon enough, when we have finished establishing all the facts, and it would make things even more difficult for him if I've had to arrest you for meddling."

The DI managed to roll out his speech without a single blink or twitch, but there was enough heaviness ladled on certain words for me to guess I wasn't half as good a storyteller as I thought I was. But hell, if he swallowed only half the story, that would give them enough to steer them well clear of the direction I intended to take. So I just nodded and gave him a reassuring grin.

"Absolutely. Wouldn't want to get in your way. I've got stuff to be getting on with anyhow, so just give me a call when I can come over and see Danny again?"

The DI nodded and I started walking off. I'd had managed to almost get to the tape before I heard a gentle cough. Bugger. There's always something.

"Thing is, Mr Black." DI Allen walked up to stand beside me. I was perhaps a foot from the security tape, with a bunch of policemen and women close enough to seriously impede my freedom if they so chose. Bolting right now would be highly suspicious, no matter how I just wanted to be away and free from hindrances. Time to follow the lead out the back of the property, where that stink from the attacker surely led.

Just five more steps.

"There a problem?" I asked him, feigning innocence enough to make angels weep.

"Not a problem, not really. Your story ties up just fine." He nodded again, reaching into his jacket and removing a pad and pencil, tapping these against his leg. "Just fine. It's just that ... well ... you're saying Mr Price had been approached for protection money by men saying they represented a Mr Carteloni. Now I happen to know that name, and I very much doubt that particular family are still in the protection racket game. Far too low-key for them these days. Cyber fraud and drug running, maybe, but not simple strong-arm tactics."

"And this kidnapping of the niece to force Mr Price to give in to their demands? Whoever did this managed to keep off the CCTV in this neighbourhood and disable uniformed officers both outside and inside the residence with some sort of nerve gas or chemical agent which left absolutely no trace. And finally, they disabled the niece and took her out the residence without leaving a single fingerprint whilst still inflicting the sort of damage to her room that I would equate to a minor earthquake. No gunpowder residue, no sign of any weapon used except what forensics think might be the remains of a baseball bat thoroughly destroyed."

"So, as you can see, there are one or two things which don't quite gel with your account of things. Let alone why Mr Price wanted *you* here, in particular, and what you and your colleague were doing upstairs for so long?"

I shrugged, knowing every fact he was rolling off without even having made any notes screamed *liar*. None of it meant squat, nothing I'd said meant he could hold me here for any reason. So I met his eyes and let him make up his own mind.

"See, I don't like loose ends, and these are flapping around like knickers in a storm, as my granny used to say. Would you have anything to add? Any means of clarifying the situation for me?"

Playing dumb, I decided silence was the best option. My storytelling skills were obviously rusty, and I'd raised too many doubts when I simply wanted the police to be looking in an entirely different direction.

"I assumed you wouldn't. Fine then, I can only suggest you make yourself available if we have any follow up questions that I think you might be able to help with. I'm sure you won't find that too much of an inconvenience? Whilst you have things to take care, as you say?"

"Oh absolutely. I'll be glued to the phone, anytime you want a chat." I lied and stepped up to the tape, lifting it with one hand, my intention plain. "If that's all ...?"

"Just one last thing?" DI Allen asked, and I sighed, cursing my good fortune to have found the only DI in London with an active imagination and the instincts of a goddamn bloodhound.

"Yes?"

"Your colleague. Miss ...?"

I honestly wasn't expecting him to have even remembered her, given her brief appearance, so I guess my expression must have been comical. He grinned and shook his head.

"Just need a name, for the report. Since she was at the crime scene too. Miss ...?"

"MacElvy. Elspeth MacElvy. No idea if she has a middle name. You need her phone number?"

"No, that's fine. If you can ask her to drop me a call so I can confirm her details, at her convenience?"

I grunted and waved a hand in farewell, dropping the crime tape behind me. The policemen and women watched me leave, but DI Allen must have made one of those mystical gestures you see on TV crime series and no-one challenged me. For my part, I let them alone, deciding tossing one into the trash this morning was enough for me.

See, I can be mature. Go me.

Chapter 5

Now, if this had been a normal run of the mill case, my first instinct would've been to head home and close the door behind me all this shit. Spend some quality time gathering my thoughts, going over the facts of the case and sharing a plate of food with Bear whilst I downed some wine, and made a halfway decent plan of likely suspects and leads to follow up. Or shake down, depending on the quality of said lead.

But all I had going my thick skull was the simple fact someone had kidnapped Felix, left Danny thinking he was a truly shit human being, and my ever-helpful murderous fae contact had all but confirmed this was the same twisted bastard who had butchered at least six men. Takes one to know one, I guess.

Finally, the bastard had Felix, having somehow found out she was a material witness or something, and her life was not safe whatever way I looked at things.

Not exactly the kind of thoughts to let me kick back, chill and plan.

Plus the Blooding was a week away, and that had me all jangled up royally.

Oh yeah, I hadn't gotten round to explaining that one. So, what is the Blooding? If the name isn't a dead giveaway or anything.

The Blooding is how we lycans let off steam, get rid of all the stress and pent-up violence that stacks from being this side of the Veil, forced to lead a pretend life so that no mortal freaks out and pulls a *Howling* on us. Watch the movie – it does not end well for the furries. But the Blooding is also a way for the various Packs to handle difficult issues like leadership, challenges or territory infringements or just plain dislike amongst one another.

We can't exactly throw down in the street when one of us has a problem with another lycan, so the Blooding acts to contain and manage the mayhem if two of us get tetchy-like.

It harks back to those good old times when, I think I already mentioned, some lycan took it into their equally thick skulls that we were better than mere mortals and didn't need to hide our nature. After the blood had dried up and the bodies were cleared away, it was mutually agreed amongst the remaining survivors that we would never let our nature take control in such a way, never let the beast threaten the pack. Instead, if anyone started getting all primal, they were restrained and kept under wraps until the nearest Blooding was called, and then dealt with as seen fit by the Alphas.

Usually, any issue is decided all medieval-like, with trial by combat to decide the outcome, who was right or wrong. That may sound flawed in your nice humane society, in that it normally just means the biggest bully wins, but for lycans it somehow works. Each Pack chooses their Claw, who represents the Pack in disputes and arguments. The Alphas are removed from all but the most serious disagreements since the damage they can dish out tends to be on the WMD scale and leaves the sort of marks that even time doesn't heal. It's kind of hard to keep these events from the public eye when the building we are using is left as a smoking pile of rubble. Plus it's hell on the insurance premiums.

Anyhow, being honest with myself, my adrenaline was jumpy like an addict needing a fix, and patience was proving especially difficult to manage. No way was I going to be able to curl up at home to take my time reading Felix's diary or logically working through the facts. Instead, making sure I stayed well and truly clear of Danny's house and its newly acquired police house-guests, I spent the next half hour carefully picking up the kidnapper's trail across the wasteland London so delightful calls *parkland*. In the middle of a city, anyplace where nature actually manages to claw a foothold is a testament to Her stubbornness and tenacity, given the pollution and toxicity that mortals live their lives swimming in.

Keeping low, letting my good old-fashioned senses lead me on, I picked up the kidnapper's trail while ducking through the dying shadows and slipping between the twisted stunted trees. See, I just wanted to give the police, who I knew must be watching, the least possible reason to come follow me and start asking questions. Last thing I needed was the dependable DI Allen wondering why I'd said this was nothing that needed my attention, to then find me poking my nose right back in this shit. I'd already proven I was not that great a liar.

The trail was easy to pick up even a short distance from Danny's house, and arrowed onward without deviation, the dirt and grass crushed in what should have been footprints. Whatever concealing magic this bastard had was just as strong when he'd come this way, disguising the prints into random jagged crushed patterns embedded in the dirt, but this actually made it easier for me to pick them out. Nothing in the mortal realm left anything close to that sort of mark. The stink of his magic, his lust, his fear, everything about this man painted a bright path for me to follow, mingled with Felix's scent ... right up until I reached the edge of the scrub and stepped onto worn concrete.

I'd guessed the bastard was smart, but I'd wanted to see just how much ... and as I stood on the edge of the canal, the trail unravelling and fading on the shifting surface below me, I realised he must have reckoned on being chased by more than simple mortal police. Maybe police canine units, or maybe he'd expected someone with supped up senses would track his scent and used the one route guaranteed to hide it from magic or anything like me. He'd taken to the river, and let it wash away any trace of him or Felix.

To be honest, a part of me expected something like this, if only because I'd long ago learned the easy route never, ever happened for me. Still didn't stop me from letting loose a whole string of curses, a habit I'd picked up from hanging around this side of the Veil. Totally futile, never helps solve anything but I'll admit, it certainly makes me feel better every time.

So, strike solving this thing nice and easy. Welcome to the long and dirty, the way these things almost always pan out for me. I took a different route away from Danny's home and the watchful police, trying to keep my pace to a non-suspicious speed in case anyone spotted me. Then I took a moment to check my phone. I'd had a text from Jessica Walker, our pack's Alpha, informing me the Mistress had been taken by the Furies without incident, asking me to check in with her on the mob angle of Danny's case. Another fine example of the Oracle at work, given no way Elspeth had had time to update her.

Aside from catching up on my texts, I was also checking the time given I'd left my watch with the more badly bloodstained gear I'd stripped out of at the Museum. And no, I wasn't sneaking a peak at my Facebook or Twister or whatever you call it, or any of the other multitude of social sites mortals seem addicted to these days. Nothing is sacred, everything is online and available if you know where to look for it. The whole internet thing just confuses the hell out of me, so I try to steer clear of it as best I can, which is fairly simple given most of the Real residents also don't like technology, or it tends to blow up on them after a few moments use.

Just coming up five in the morning.

Three hours since I'd found out about Danny, Felix, and the shitstorm they were involved in. Less than half a day since I was tussling with a shape-shifter in the Natural History Museum, and bringing a homicidal demi-goddess from Arthurian times to justice before she created a body count to rival a small war. And lastly where I'd been gifted something of the Shadow Court, the ability to use magic in a very small but specific way. Something no lycan had ever done before. Kinda cool on one paw, and bloody terrifying on the other.

Anyhow, I was wearing most of the clothes from that struggle, which were stained with river muck and powdered concrete, let alone bloodstained and ragged, though these days I hear it's call fashion. Especially around the knees, gods know why. The police, DI Allen included, hadn't commented though I'm fairly sure someone had noted my general disarray. Not that I really gave a monkeys what they thought. But my next destination was a little more public, and I figured I'd need a change, a shower and most definitely a quick tussle with Bear to make up for leaving him behind last night.

See, *something* had stuck in my head, something Felix let slip a few days ago. And that 'something', a little worm of doubt, had fed on recent events and grown big and strong. So now I had a fully grown Jormungandr rearing its ugly head. You know, massive worm of Norse mythology that ends up killing Thor. Not that the Marvel movies will allow that to happen … he's just too damn handsome to be worm-fodder.

Felix had told me she was studying occultism at her university, and the teacher had given her some seriously strange vibes. Took his subject matter too seriously, I think she said. And now she had been kidnapped by someone using seriously bad juju … and the Morrigan had been unusually helpful this time around. What was it she said? *"Seek your answers at a place where knowledge is worshipped and yet enslaved, and over water where things be out of sight and forgotten."*

The bastard had fled along the canal, so that ticks off the water bit. But the place where knowledge is worshipped yet enslaved? Sounded awfully like a university to me, with their rooms of books upon books storing up stuff that never saw the light of day. And I reckon anyone on the teaching payroll probably had to worship their chosen field, since they sure weren't doing it for the money.

So, a quick and simple plan had formed in my head. Head home, shower and change clothes so that I don't cause a minor panic when I take a leaf out of my Alpha's book.

Look at me, bettering myself.

Heading to uni. Go lycan on campus!

I bagged another taxi ride on the corporate account, with the sure knowledge I was in for a talking to from Jess later about using my own two feet to get around. London traffic can be a total nightmare most times of the day given the road systems were built for horse and carts, but most of the maniacs seemed to be late risers at least, so this early I made it home in fairly decent time.

Signing off the fare, I slammed the cab door and headed to the side entrance built specifically for me after I inherited the apartment block from a wealthy and very grateful client. I'd decided early on I needed a way in for me alone, for when I returned home still in gear from a run in with something Real, or when I had visitors who weren't all that bothered about blending in with the mortals around them. The side path is carefully hidden away with bushes and short trees and leads to what most people think is a utility room with the generator for the building's power, and is out of the way enough to give me a chance to check my surroundings at all times, suspicious bastard that I am.

And true to how my day was turning out, I immediately spotted the car sitting idling across the street, tinted windows closed shut to give no clue of the occupants. For any mortal, that would be good enough to ignore, but I wasn't a mortal. I could sense the watchers in the vehicle, focused on the main entrance, waiting for my obviously well-known features to make an appearance.

So, someone already had watchers on my home. If I challenged them, no doubt they'd just hit the accelerator again and I'd either have to chase them down and reveal my abnormal abilities, or be left like a total mug in the street, knowing I'd tipped them that I'd blown their surveillance. Instead, I decided to just let them waste their time watching my run of the mill and very normal residents come and go. If I decided they posed any sort of threat, I could always arrange for a few of the Pack to come lend a paw.

My private lift is disguised behind a simple false wall in the non-quite utility room which needs unlocking with a six-digit passcode. Nothing high tech but dependable enough that I only worried about supernatural entities breaching the wards and stinking up my expansive home or leaving bloody apple trees growing in the centre of the floor. I really needed to get around to changing the code though, since with whatever lousy good sense I had had, I'd opted to use my ex's birthday as the key-code. Way to jinx things.

I let loose a relieved sigh as I shut the flat's door behind me. The bottom floor of my pent-house was all open plan where visiting Pack mates could crash out and lounge as only lycan can, and I took the stairs up past the second floor and its separate bedrooms and bathrooms, kitchen and chow-down spaces I'd set aside for my Pack mates. My personal fortress of solitude took up the third and final floor, which I shared with Bear and no-one else.

So it was with some surprise that as I bounded up the stairs, I heard a high-pitched childish giggle echo down to me.

Big shaggy troll-hound, check. Children, to my knowledge and still fairly reliable memory, nope.

I slowed my pace and crept up the last stairs, wishing I hadn't left all my tools behind with the Pack at the Natural History Museum after we'd finished the job. It was protocol ... Jessica would have had Elspeth de-jinx each and every item used in combat with anything from the Real, just in case they were contaminated with anything magical from beyond the Veil. It was a pain, but then seven hundred odd years ago something particularly nasty was carried through and ... well ... you know the story of the Black Death? Boils and sores and mortal bodies left, right and centre? And you lot blamed the rats. Since then, we'd gotten a whole lot better at containment, and a whole lot more paranoid.

So, no weapon to hand but then, I'm a big bad lycan with tools aplenty to dish out mayhem. Clenching my fist, I surged up the last few steps and threw myself into the open living area, senses straining for whatever was lurking in my home this time.

Bear sat on his massive furry backside, great big grin slapped on his trollhound chops, tail thumping hard on the wooden floor. Behind him, the gnarled apple tree filled the centre of the room, a gift from the Morrigan to remind me of the true nature of my world, my life. No lurking monsters, nothing waiting to attack me, but that giggle lingered in the air. I sniffed, drawing in the scents, searching for whatever was different. The apple tree was alive and filled the room with a zip of magic, a pulse of life echoing around the open space, but nothing screamed danger or imminent harm.

It felt odd that the tree growing inside my apartment at the top of the block *wasn't* the weirdest thing at that moment in time.

"So who's the surprise guest, oh mighty watch dog of mine?" I asked Bear, who chuffed and shook his massive head. He padded up and rubbed himself against me in welcome, then bounded quickly away, heading towards the cloakroom and no doubt to grab his harness and lead. All for show, of course, since if Bear wanted to go someplace, whoever was holding that lead would end up being dragged that way anyhow. I'd agreed with the trollhound that tug of wars were to be enjoyed away from the general public, so it was rare that I got my arse shanghaied around the Thames path.

Usually only when he saw a cat or squirrel. Then gods help me.

That niggling feeling that the two of us were not alone continued to bite, so I did a quick circuit of the flat but found no sign of anything untoward. Conscious of time ticking away like a B movie thriller with the prerequisite bomb at the end to deal with, I squashed my concerns and stripped, dumping the clothes in the bin for washing … or burning later before throwing myself into a steaming shower. Hot water soaked away the aches in my muscles, the bruises already fading away, the cuts healing. The joys of being a lycan, but don't think I simply shrug off injury. It still hurts like hell getting hit, still stings getting cut. I particularly like the way the recent movies have portrayed Wolverine, showing him feeling the pain of his wounds even though they heal. More realistic, even though he's just a comic book hero.

Anyhow, hot water also helped slough off any lingering enchantments or curses that the Mistress might've used on me, the sort of sneaky afterbite that bitch would particularly enjoy employing. The fact the immortal had given wolfsbane to her pet muscle to use told me what level of nastiness the Goddess of the Sewers been willing to employ.

Note to self, check in with Jessica on where we were on tracking down which utter bastard supplied her with that stuff. There were very few suppliers of anything that nasty to lycans … we'd made sure throughout the ages to come down particularly hard on any alchemists or chemists brewing up such nasties. Suspending them head down in their own cauldrons was always a favourite teaching method!

Clean, scrubbed and feeling refreshed, I grabbed a change of clothes that fitted the role I was going to be playing shortly. Of course, a guy looking to check out the university for his young daughter wouldn't need the knives and other handy tools I strapped on or secreted away about my person, but then I was going expecting trouble. Lockpicks, a handy sampling kit that I'm sure Sherlock Holmes would have been proud to own, that sort of thing. My instincts told me the university was the right place to pick up Felix's trail, and having the Morrigan point me in that direction made me doubly sure I wanted to go there prepared.

Walking back out, I found as expected Bear waiting, his lead and harness held loosely in his jaws, tail thumping a fairly decent beat on the floor. Ducking into the kitchen, I topped up the mutt's food and water bowls with fresh produce ... I had tried a store brand's food one time, something it promised was 100% real chicken ... and then spent the evening cleaning the mess up from where Bear had spread the processed food in disgust. So now I kept things simple, and always had real meat for the trollhound, if only to spare the furniture and ceilings.

Snapping Bear into his harness, I cast one last look around the flat, trying to work out if anything was hiding or watching through the Veil. But no tell-tale signs glared at me, no more mysterious giggles greeted me so I just shrugged and followed my mutt down the steps.

"Going mad, definitely." I told myself and put the matter aside. For now.

I was going to regret that lapse in judgement.

Chapter 6

Giants are mostly lost to the mortal realm, having no place to hide their over-sized nature or brutish features. They once made their homes in the deep forests and mountains where Man feared to tread, living simple lives with rarely any encounter with mortals except when accidently treading on one. It is unknown which King or Queen grew tired of their presence or coveted their lands, but the tale of Jack the Giant Killer misrepresented these mostly peaceful creatures and led to their hunting and massacre in great numbers.

Sneaking out of the flat's side entrance to avoid my newly acquired watchers, I took Bear down along the Thames to stretch out his legs and allow him to assault the neighbourhood trees as was his wont. Checking my replacement watch, I had about an hour left before the university opened and I got to practice my subterfuge rather than bulldozing my way to a lead. Time enough to walk the pooch, give him a break from the flat, and try to still the growling anger in my head that hated the inactivity, the soft approach.

Bear was sniffing at one particular tree as I stared out over the Thames, trying to think through what might happen, how I'd best prepare. If it turned out the professor had Felix, I'd probably have to beat her location out of him ... before or after he used his magic to turn into whatever the hell that thing was, the beast he'd used to commit murder. That would probably not go down well on the campus, especially with it being a historic building site and all. Our Alpha had views on her Pack doing public and unnecessary damage, especially to landmarks. I think it was a little bit of national pride, her being from this island originally no matter how long ago, and ignoring the whole Scots versus

English debacle. Anyhow, a fight on the campus site wouldn't help Felix, so I'd have to draw him away somehow. Maybe offer to buy him a beer. If it was him.

"Lost in thoughts, pup? I am not sure my Queen favoured a dreamer for her new knight." The sarcastic voice drifted down to me like snowflakes on a summer's day, chilling an otherwise bright morning. Bear stilled at the words, hackles rising like jagged spines as he stared up into the branches of the tree. I shushed him, not wanting to provoke any sort of rash situation. Not just yet, at least.

Sat ladylike with her legs crossed demurely, grey bandage robes settled around her like some ash-coloured southern belle, the Morrigan looked down at me with that same mocking smile. The one that told me just how young and silly she saw me as, and how foolish I'd been in her eyes. Yet here she was, paying me another visit.

"To what do I owe the pleasure of your company?" I choked the words out, knowing "*what the fuck*" wasn't entirely appropriate. Swearing around this particular immortal tended to raise her ire like the needle on a Geiger counter, and I wasn't ready to throw down with the Mistress of Battle. Least of all coz I'm fairly sure she'd wipe the floor with me, and I really didn't need the embarrassment.

"I see you are slowly learning your manners, pup." The Morrigan smiled ever more widely, like the shark as it drew near on its prey. With way more menace. She pushed herself off the lowest branch and jumped to the concrete with the grace of a cat, one of those prehistoric ones with excessively big fangs. Her two ravens hopped along the limbs of the tree, eyeballing me with those crimson orbs of madness, just daring me to try something, begging me to give them a reason to beat me down.

I carefully stepped back, pulling Bear with me, as he loosed a low, threatening growl. The sort that is a lit fuse and ends with a violent explosion. Ruffling his massive head, I let him feel the fact I wasn't threatened or in any danger, and he got the point. Good, smart mutt. Huffing a deep breath, he settled down onto the pavement in a lounging sprawl and probably gave serious thought to licking his balls just for the look of it. Ok, so less smart, more sarky bloody mutt.

The Morrigan stepped over to the side of the Thames path, looking out over the surging water. I joined her after a moment and stood staring out at the deep tides whirling and eddying with deceptive sluggishness. A Thames clipper clove its path in the distance, taking its cargo of early morning city workers to their desks, whilst seagulls cried raucously, sounding like they were mocking everything. Which they probably were, the arrogant bastards.

"As I mentioned at our first meeting this day." The Morrigan reached down to her hip and drew out a piece of ancient looking parchment, tied with a neat black bow and splintered bones keeping it shut. Madb, the original goth. They probably should worship her if she wouldn't just kill them all for their idiocy. "My Queen has sent word, and I her messenger am here to bring you them."

"So, you're like the Court Royal Mail service now? You've been made into a postman?" I quipped, imagining her as some sort of nightmare Postman Pat with one helluva scary black and white cat.

"Only if you imagine the sort that nails the letter to your forehead and eats the dog." She smiled right back at me, and I laid a hand down on Bear's head again to let him know not to act rashly. His growling huff in response hardly reassured me.

"Ok, ok, so she wants something. I'm a little busy right now, so if the Queen of Ice and Shadow doesn't mind waiting ..." I started but stopped as the morning light immediately darkened, like someone had tripped the dimmer switch. The sound of the

Morrigan's fingers on the stone of the river wall was a sharp crack as concrete splintered and flew out in a burst of shards. Worst of all, her eyes lit with immortal fury, sprung to fire so quickly that I had only a moment's warning.

"*Wait*? You ask the Queen of the Shadow Court ... you, her newly sworn Knight ... to *wait?!*" She snarled, but hell if I didn't stand my ground ... even if I also braced for violence.

"Yes, W.A.I.T. The word means to hold on, have some patience. Let me finish the shitstorm I'm currently stuck with before I get thrown headfirst into something else. Do I need to explain it any more?" I snarled right back, letting the growl of my lycan-self add bite to my words. But the Morrigan seemed hardly bothered, shaking her head and making her dreadlocks clatter. At least the fire dimmed a notch in her eyes, if only by a little.

"I know the meaning of your words, pup. I was old when they were uttered the first time. But none ask my Queen to wait, not when she requests you fulfil your appointed role. If one remembers, one would not have managed so well against the Lady of the Lake had not my Queen ... *our* Queen intervened." She told me bluntly, nudging the scroll so that it rolled across the stone to sit in front of me. "The matter which bears so heavily on your thoughts will not conflict with this task, so you should not concern yourself unduly."

"I'll be the judge of what will or won't conflict, and what I worry about duly or not." I replied sharply. "*Your* Queen might not understand this, but I owe Danny *and* Felix too much to go prancing off on some foolish errand right now. This whole Knight thing is a joke anyhow. I'm not a member of the Shadow Court, I'm a lycan bound to my Pack, and unless my Alpha gives her agreement, I'm not doing anything for Madb."

The Morrigan's laughter was a cold, bitter spike that caused my breath to plume, and set the seagulls screaming anew. The immortal fae nodded to the scroll, a touch of smugness creeping into her savage expression.

"Read on, my pup, and you will understand."

Biting back half a dozen sarky responses that so begged to be voiced, I took a breath to calm my temper and carefully picked up the scroll. As much as I knew it was some sort of missive, it was always wise to handle such things with care ... the sort of care you normally reserve for an unexploded bomb, or telling your date you forgot your wallet after the bill has been delivered. You know what I'm talking about.

Initial contact confirmed my suspicions, and I eyed the Morrigan sourly.

"When are you lot going to start using actual *paper* for letters, and stop skinning some poor bastard? It's cheaper, quicker and a whole fuckload less creepy. Just a suggestion."

"The one who gave up his skin for this message was one of those poor deluded fools who so assaulted you in Madb's domain not so long ago. She thought it ... *fitting* that he serves as a message bearer to you, after his intent to do you such ill."

Great, so this was the skin from one of the Knights the twisted fucker had tricked into attacking me, using them as cannon fodder so the bastard could grab a cheap shot at taking my head. Last time I'd seen the survivors, they had been encased in ice and on their way to becoming a tormented twisted patch of frozen trees in Madb's backyard. Nice to know that wasn't enough punishment for encroaching on the Queen of the Shadow Court's territory and causing trouble.

Snapping the black cord, I unrolled the skin and scanned the neat and spiky handwriting contained within. The message was short, and bluntly to the point.

For the attention of Morgan Black, newly appointed Knight to Madb and the Shadow Court. The Lady Madb Na Cruam Crough Si does bid her Knight Errant to attend the Beltane Day Tourney as her Champion and representative, to stand against those that may bring lawful or otherwise dispute against her. Champions of the Ivory and the Wyld will be appointed to stand with, or mayhap against you so best prepare yourself.

Underneath this was a more familiar script, seen all too frequently on penned notes left for me in the office. Normally reminding me to finish my case report or to remember to wash my mug more often.

We will speak about this later, but Madb has approached me and we have discussed the matter. According to Contract, you are going to the ball. So best put your party dress on, Cinderella. Jessica Walker.

You know all those swear words I said I'd picked up from working this side of the Veil this long? I got through every single one in almost one breath.

"You're kidding me. A tournament? And I'm Madb's Champion? What the hell gives?" I demanded, crumpling the skin in my hand without a thought. The Morrigan gave me that ice-cold mocking smile and simply shrugged.

"Our Queen's decisions are her own, and I would not dare suggest I might see the wisdom or foolishness in anything she requests." The fae tapped the broken stonework under her fingers, stirring stone dust with one talon. "I am bid tell you that I shall act as your Second at this event, as the Queen is aware you have not yet attended such a gathering. You should get your affairs in order and find this lost child of your dear friend, so that you have no distractions. I have already indicated that you are on the right path, so listen to your suspicions and they will lead you to her."

"That's it? Listen to my suspicions? Even Obi-Won gave better hints than that! For pity's sake, just keep popping over and giving me such bloody useless advice, why don't you?" I cursed. Loudly. "So I'm right about this being about the university? That it's not the mob or some other random kidnapping? For gods' sake, a straight answer could solve this right here and now!"

"And yet I am bound in what I can and cannot tell you." The Morrigan gestured, and the two ravens spiralled down to rest upon her shoulders, shuffling like homicidal old men as they glared at me. "Trust yourself, and you will reach the answer you seek. But tarry not long, for the child's life hangs by a thread. Delay overlong and you will rue your tardiness."

The fae gestured, and the wind whipped up again, this time wrapping around her so that it seemed like she was the centre of a mini tornado. I gritted my teeth and refused to step back, as the reek of the Veil sliced through the morning air, the portal through which the fae now stepped back to the Real.

She stopped, turning back to look over one shoulder, spearing me with one ice-rimmed eye.

"Know this. Troubles brew both within the Courts and from without, and this tourney shall be a treacherous event indeed. Some might see this as a chance to strike at our Queen, for reasons that are yet unclear. Prepare yourself for violence, Sir Pup, for I doubt not, blood will be spilled. You have been warned."

With that, the portal folded in upon itself, leaving the charnel stink of the Veil wafting out over the Thames like some toxic spill. I drew a long, deep breath and looked down at Bear where he waited.

"You know, mate. I am really, *really* beginning to dislike this cryptic shit."

Bear's huff of agreement made me chuckle, dispelling a measure of the anger and frustration I had bubbling over in spades.

So, not only did I have a missing young woman to find, but now a potentially deadly tournament to take part in. It was a good thing I wasn't the sort of person to like using a day planner or anything, as I'd have to keep scrubbing out any notes as the shit continually hit the fan.

At least the Morrigan had given me hope I wasn't just on a wild goose chase, heading to Felix's place of study. That in itself was probably the best thing I could take from the whole encounter, and as such, it would have to do.

That decided, I got Bear back to his feet and headed back to home, to drop off my furry companion, avoid my watchers and get on with finding Felix. Before I got to *rue my tardiness* and lose Danny his only daughter.

No pressure. Not at all.

Chapter 7

Dragons, much like many kin from the Real, fall into two rough categories. The lesser serpents, wyverns and such were known for their lack of vestigial limbs beyond those bearing wings and no trace of intelligence beyond that of beasts. The greater wyrms were known to adopt mortal form and live in secret amongst those seeking their hordes, their bodily parts. It is fact that what St George and his kin hunted were simple snakes compared to their greater kin, and should the brave knights have attempted their hunt of these instead, England would have had a very different tale told of the man's fate.

So here's a little bit of interesting tat.

The University of Greenwich has, in fact, three campuses rather than the usual one that most universities seem happy to get along with. One is its namesake in Greenwich town, one is lost somewhere in the land of pristine land rovers and very rich housewives ... Kent. But the one I knew Felix attended was in the grounds of the Old Royal Naval College, that gorgeous white-stone establishment which harks back to the old days of savage piracy and naval battles. The place had in fact been known as the Greenwich Palace, and was the birthplace of two Tudor Queens before falling into ruin after your little internal spat ... ah, I mean the English Civil War.

Wondering why I'm spouting so much thoroughly useless facts? That's the joy of the internet. As much as I detest it, if you need to do some background research on things thoroughly mortal, just log on and have a browse. The great Oracle Wikipedia is sure to know the answer. For me, it was just enough information about my destination to help with my background story of a father checking out universities for his hard-studying and academically gifted daughter. You know, lying through my back teeth. It comes more easily than I probably should be comfortable with.

Stashing the iPad Jessica had so thoughtfully given me a whilst back into my canvas man-bag, I signed off the third taxi receipt of the morning and mentally winced at the tally I was accruing with Jessica. Stepping out onto the street corner, I took a moment to draw in the morning air as the hubbub of Greenwich poured around me, a mixture of tourists, students and locals all out about their business. Amongst the crowd, I sensed the presence of Real denizens, mingling freely with the unaware mortals. Probably either to steal from or deceive them somehow or just ignore them, like a dog ignores the fleas it carries.

Greenwich Market sat at my back, hidden away within a nest of buildings with four entrances or exits to each point of the compass. A crossroads, almost. That in itself was a draw to any Real creatures, something that was almost folklore in many of the medieval stories and wives-tales, and a very good reason for mortals to steer well clear. But of course, in your true idiotic nature, it had instead become a well-known and popular place to visit for people from all over the world. It was a place where deals were struck, where money exchanged hands for goods or services, and the sort of barters done which were attributed to ol' Nick himself. Souls traded for riches, beauty and love bartered for the first-born child. The list is long, and there is nothing much a mortal won't be willing to pay for a promise of their dream-desire.

Usually, I'd have taken a stroll around the place, just to speak to the few informants I'd befriended over the years and check for any leads on new cases. But right now, I had bigger aquatic denizens to barbecue. I'd agreed to meet the university's principal at 9am sharp, and as a loving father, I wouldn't even consider being late for a chance to get my darling little girl into her first choice of learning establishment. See, how good am I?

Walking through the gates into the old Naval College, I found myself stopping suddenly, catching myself in surprise. A sudden dizzy spell was *not* something I was used to suffering, no matter the fact I'd been on the go pretty much nonstop since my crash-out from the poisoning and I hadn't eaten in over twelve hours. The day was brightening up around me, the ebb and flow of the mortal realm bustling around me just like any other day ... but something was well and truly off kilter.

There are tell-tale signs to look for, when something gives a lycan a touch of the heebie jeebies. Usually screaming mortals running in the opposite direction. Flames brightening the horizon and possibly inhuman roars echoing like some prehistoric soundtrack over scoring the chaos.

Subtle stuff like that.

What I faced instead was ... normality. The university was set around a main open square with grass and trees lining the gravel pathways, marble stone steps leading up to the large and grand looking doorways, and all backed by the rise of the hill that comprised Greenwich Park with its observatory. Tourists cut through from one side of the main Greenwich high street to the other side, usually to get to the Trafalgar Tavern, one of the more famous pubs in the area ... or for the more knowledgeable, the Yacht down a side alley for a quieter drink with less tourists. Students huddled in clusters on their way to class, dressed in what passed as fashionable but rich clothing since this place had a definite reputation to maintain. No baseball caps and half slung trousers round the students' arses, which I must say was a vast improvement in my book.

It being early, there were still some students lounging out on the grass, books strewn around them, Starbucks and Costa cups lying nearby along with an assortment of breakfast snacks.

Seagulls circled and screamed, having learned that this wasn't the seaside and students were less agreeable at having their expensive food stolen. Someone had planted the flowerbeds with what looked like poppies but with large red bell flowers attached, making the place look semi festive except for it being almost summer.

Normal. Nothing worrying at all.

But that feeling of something being off remained, and my good ol' lycan senses were stirred. Something was kicking me for attention, but either I was too tired or too wound tight to make sense of it at that moment. So, best I just crack on and hunt for more clues, and hopefully my brain would play catch up and supply the answers in good time.

Stopping a gaggle of young ladies … another interesting fact, that is an official term for a gathering of young women, if only because at the time it was considered they made as much noise as a load of geese in one place … as they walked and shared their lives on their bling-encrusted phones, I got directions to the central office with enough time to nab a coffee and Danish from the seller parked just by the gate. Not my chosen way of breaking fast, but the rumbling stomach was a distraction I didn't need whilst trying to blag some answers from a complete stranger.

So, knocking back bad coffee and a crumbling confectionary with way too much sugar, I entered the small side tunnel and walked into another square, surrounded now by brick and worked stone. Taking the steps up to the nearest door, I slipped into the marble-clad hall which housed the office and main administration block. Inside, out of the sun, that big ol' chill gave me another case of the goosebumps. Something was seriously hinky about the place but whatever the hell it was, I wasn't getting any closer to guessing its source. Either that or I was just plain tired.

An ancient receptionist took down my details and left me to sit in a small office, whilst she went hunting for the Principal. Like any good detective, I could have taken the time to leaf through the paperwork on her desk, maybe cracked the code on her archaic computer and found the information I needed with just a couple of clicks. Me being me, I knew computers like I knew astro-psychics. It's out there, and there are experts on the subject but I'm not one of them. Instead, I closed my eyes and tried to work out just what was bugging me about the place, the thing that had my metaphorical fur standing on end since I'd walked through the gates. With about the same level of luck. All I could think of was a clock ticking away, and Felix somewhere dark and horrible, alone and shit scared. That fed my anger and kept me awake till the creaking old lady came back to fetch me.

Professor Charles Thorne-Davis, alumni of the university and now Principal in charge of the campus, was exactly how I expected him to be. Fussy, wearing tweed and a smart bow tie and shirt combination and definitely suffering a comb-over meticulously kept in place with old fashioned lacquer. Wearing some sort of flowery cologne, and with the faint tick of a reformed smoker on the mend. In fact, I picked out the chemical sting of nicotine patches, enough to know he was overdoing them to keep the cravings in check.

We chatted for an hour in his cramped office amongst towering shelves of books and ornaments from times long past, as I patiently explained the details of my fictitious daughter as a nice little compilation of Felix, Elspeth and Jessica as the three women I knew well enough to use. Well, there was a fourth, but since I'd recently assaulted her in the basement of the Natural History Museum, I was trying to keep my definitely-ex out of my thoughts right now. I knocked back several more cups of mediocre coffee as I listened to the man drone on about the many different courses on offer at this prodigious establishment and the extracurricular activities all the students oh so thoroughly enjoyed, as well as the many benefits offered to students to help them integrate into society at the highest of levels. Politicians, business leaders, the movers and shakers of the mortal world. The sort of thing a loving father should and would care about for their daughter. To me, it was just so much noise. I even found myself staring at a large vase of those weird looking poppies someone had set on the man's desk, attention caught by the one spot of brightness amongst the shambles.

"You know, there was something I did want to talk about." I cut in as the Professor poured himself another cup of tea, fastidiously pouring another thimble-full of milk in and stirring the cup exactly twenty times before tapping the spoon twice and setting it aside. If his drinking habits were anything to go by, I bet he had his clothes lined out for the entire week and labelled for each day, and probably had his meals in plastic pots labelled in the fridge. And his wife dreamt of banging him over the head and running away with her Mexican dance instructor. Oh yes, worn gold ring on the correct finger all right.

"Ah, yes?" The professor smiled and motioned for me to continue, probably still seeing me as the extremely large paycheque I represented, thanks to my story of being an independently wealthy and very generous donor to every and all institutes my daughter attended. Hell, it worked in the books, it had been worth a try … and predictably, greed won out.

"My daughter has a friend, a marvellous young woman she met whilst *dancing* in the West End several weeks ago. It seems she attends this wonderful institute, and is enrolled in a rather interesting course. Occultism, I believe she said the subject she's studying? And my Emily has long had an interesting in such matters. Purely in the fictional nature of the thing, I hasten to add. Her mother, god rest her soul, filled her head with such fanciful tales when she was a child."

Professor Thorne-Davis coughed and shuffled the papers on his vintage velvet-lined desk, before nodding slowly.

"Yes, well, we have indeed begun a new study within our ... *ah experimental sciences* division. Professor Robert Knox is a newly acquired member of the faculty, and we are trialling this subject matter as one of many alternative programmes. You say your daughter knows someone taking the course?"

"Yes, Felicity Price, that's the young woman's name. They share a passion for partying and dancing, as well as interests in less, well, standard subject matters." I shrugged like a long-suffering father, who wishes his daughter were more in line with his own hopes for the future but loves her enough to let her have her dreams. "I was wondering if it would be possible to meet the good professor, and discuss what exactly his course covers? I've not entirely been comfortable with my Emily's choices in the past, and would like to know that my daughter is not going to be learning anything ... *distasteful*."

"Oh I totally understand, but I can reassure you that all of our faculty are vetted most thoroughly, and I have personally discussed the course materials with Professor Knox. There is nothing I would not want my own daughter to study, if of course I had one." The faculty head thought for a moment, then waved his hands in acceptance. "It is perfectly understandable having reservations though. I cannot see a problem with us stopping in on the class if it will help allay your concerns?"

He turned in his chair and clicked on a very old looking keyboard, causing the boxy screen to light up with the eldritch glow of a witch's cauldron. I waited patiently while he tapped away with the speed of an arthritic sloth using its offside hindleg, totally not imagining ripping the computer off the desk and hurling it through the window, holding down the professor and threatening to beat the answer out of him. Once again proving my superhuman power of patience.

"Ah, there we are. You are in luck, Mr Grey." Professor Thorne-Davis exclaimed, and leant back in his chair, looking all-together too smug given how long it had taken him to find the information. "Professor Knox has a class this morning, and I am sure he won't mind us dropping in unannounced."

If you are wondering, yes, I'd chosen Grey as a last name. Not anything to do with Fifty Shades Of, I promise you. It's more I'm used to having a colour as my last name, and thinking spur of the moment I just picked something close enough to my real one that I wouldn't forget and blow the cover. Nothing says a guy is lying through his teeth more than when he doesn't recognise his own name when it's used.

So, accompanied by the slick haired poppin-jay of a professor, we quit his room with its stacks of books, weathered wood and memorabilia from god knows what era of human history, and made our way back out into the fresh air. Another short walk, then up a set of stairs and through a door that would have graced an ogre's fortress. There was a sign saying something about a painted chapel, but I wasn't there to sight-see. Instead, we ducked through a small door, following a winding staircase down. The feel of descending underground weighed on my senses, a heaviness that pressed like a thunderstorm behind my eyes so that I had to shake my head to clear it. All too recent memories of the immortal bitches's lair and those dripping corridors sprang all too readily to mind.

"We let the musicians and the ... well, more popular course subjects use the halls and offices that you see as you come into the grounds." Thorne-Davis explained ahead of me, as we ducked through yet another door. If this kept up, I'd be thinking the Royal Naval College was actually some well-built rabbit warren, or troll-hole. It wouldn't surprise me, some of the crazy shit I'd seen this side of the Veil, but hey, there's always something new.

"Ah, here we are." The Principal stopped beside a curved wooden door, hung with the truly enlightening sign *13c.* He rapped against its wooden surface and then turned the handle. Me, I took a slow breath, letting my lycan senses fire up and filling my muscles with an excess of oxygen. Ready to fight or ... well fight to be honest. Time spent in the Principal's office had whittled my patience down to a mere thread, and the beast in me was hammering at its cage to be let out and to hell with the consequences.

Then the door swung inward, so I followed the mortal inside.

Chapter 8

I was expecting bubbling cauldrons, roaring fires and the rich accruements that any Harry Potter fan will know and love from their time in Severus Snape's care. That or the clank of chains, the moans of the lost and forsaken and the sniggering snarl of their demonic keepers.

Do I ever worry where my head goes at such times? Not really, since it's been proved spot on at guessing on far too many occasions.

What I wasn't expecting were half a dozen or so round-eyed and surprised mortals looking up at me from behind pitted and ancient looking desks, with A4 notepads and pens in hand, caught midway scribbling down patterns and text. Not a laptop or phone to be seen anywhere, not that I guessed there was much signal to be had down here, and the dim lighting from fluorescent tubes highlighting the entire scene in pale radiance. Despite the lack of direct sunlight, a full set of pots held more of the red flowers, those odd poppies which made the place look slightly less like a dungeon. And I mean, *slightly*.

Someone coughed, and my gaze was drawn up to the left, where a small set of steps led to a raised platform. On this had been set a large white board running almost the full length of the underground room. And standing at the board, black marker in hand and one eyebrow quirked, was who I presumed to be Professor Plum in the dungeon with the pen. If we'd been playing some very strange game of Cluedo.

Professor Robert Knox was a man of medium height, medium build ... well, medium most things except his features. Dressed in cheap-looking theatrical robes that would have graced any Halloween wizard, he was balding with a fringe of ginger hair worked high on either side of his face. Some sort of illness had scarred his skin, leaving pockmarks all over his cheeks, and his left eye was covered by a black disk instead of the clear glass of the other spectacles he wore. Not exactly the most appealing visage to find myself facing in this underground chamber, far away from the sun. But did I get the big bad vibe of a murderous villain from him?

Not even a twitch.

"Can I help you, Principal?" The professor asked with the faintish lilt of a Scots accent, something I was so used to hearing from Jessica that I almost missed it. "We were just in the middle of a particularly complex problem ..."

"Ah, my apologies, Robert. This is Mr Grey, who is thinking of sending his daughter to attend our humble university." Professor Thorne-Davis beckoned me in, and he closed the door behind him, shutting us from the world. The closest thing to a window I could see were plates of glass set in the ceiling, probably set at ground level for the rest of the college, which let in the early morning daylight in very muted colours. "She seems to be an acquaintance of one of your students ... a Miss Felicity Price?"

I caught the quiet hiss of indrawn breath at Felix's name, and had to force myself not to whip around and face whoever had reacted. Casually I just looked around the classroom, taking in the four goth girls sat together in enough black eyeliner and lace material to grace any Marilyn Manson revival. They were joined by two skinny young men wearing designer ragged t-shirts and slashed jeans too big for them, obviously either picked up at the nearest market or handed down from older brothers. And then there were the three huddled at the back of the room ... one girl and two guys, dressed fairly normally from what I remembered as current fashion, all with their heads down and obviously not wanting to draw *any* attention to themselves at all.

Nothing to see here, nothing for us to be interested in.

Yeah, right.

"Miss Price? Felicity?" Professor Knox shook his head, indicating the room. "I'm sorry but she appears to have missed class today. Otherwise I am sure she would be happy to discuss details of the course, and her experiences under my tuition. I'm sure any of the other students would be more than pleased if Mr Grey has any questions? Samantha? Adrian?"

Hearing their names, two of the three completely innocent youngsters looked up, flicking their eyes from the professor to us then back. The young woman tried to smile, obviously going for the second line of defence - hiding behind a fake grin. The young man just scowled and looked back down again, biting at his nails with an obvious nervous habit learned over many years if the state of his fingers was anything to go by. Mystery young man number 3 remained looking at the desk in front of him, pad empty of any kind of coursework.

"How about you, Gregory? Would you like to say anything?"

Guy number three jerked as if someone had hit him with a taser and looked up, and I caught the expression plastered all over his spotty youthful features. Guilt and shock written plain like someone had slapped the words all over his fat cheeks. But guilty about what? These three were SO not what I'd expected to be mixed up in the shitstorm around Felix, or linked to the bloodletting in the city. But they reeked of guilt like they'd bathed in the bloody stuff.

Then I got the lucky break, thanks to the mortal delight in dropping someone else in the shit at any chance.

"What about Gary? He's always answering your questions, when he bothers to show up for class?" One of the goths spoke up, dwelling maliciously on her words as only teenagers who think they are adults can do. "He's your *number one* student, isn't he, Professor Knox?"

Principle Thorne-Davis eyed his faculty member with one raised brow, who in turn looked at the young woman with a testy expression before nodding slowly.

"Ah, Gary Weatherby. Yes, he is normally such an attentive student. But sadly, I haven't seen him for the past couple of days either." The professor shook his head like a beloved grandfather who just found the cookie jar had been raided. "I can get someone to stop by his home and see if he is unwell, if you'd like, Principal?"

"No, no need to go to that bother. I'm sure he's just sleeping off one party too many, if he's anything like my Emily." I chipped in, as things battled to line up in my head. The three at the back, if anything, looked even more guilty at the mention of this Gary Weatherby, so I drew a line between them all. Still made no sense ... they stank of guilt but I wasn't getting any taint of foul magic or hexes from anyone here. Just the scent from those bloody red flowers. But something was definitely out of whack here.

"In fact, I don't think there's much point in bothering your students or disrupting your class any further." I tried my best mollifying tone, bigging up the apologetic father like I was going for an Emmy award. Pity the audience didn't appreciate my efforts. The only ones looking anything but bored or mildly annoyed at my intrusion were the three at the back of the classroom, but I already had them pegged for a follow up. "We should probably let you get back to your lesson. It was most helpful meeting you, Professor Knox."

"That would be much appreciated. And thank you, Mr, ah Grey was it?" He nodded to me then turned away. "Principal. Oh, and Samantha, Adrian, Gregory? Would you remain behind after class for a word please?"

With that, I was dismissed, and unless I missed my guess, wholly forgotten.

I towed the Principal back towards the door and out the classroom, letting it swing shut as I tuned out the incessant chatter the man was throwing in my direction. Listening for anything from behind that closed door … oh I don't know, someone shouting *"Oh god, he's onto us!"* or helpful like that.

All I got was the drone of Professor Knox diving into the Salem witch trials, from their viewpoint. So, strike that.

But those three …

They knew something, and I was damned if I was going to let them keep it to themselves.

That's us, lycans. Nosiest bastards on the planet, with a bite to boot.

Chapter 9

Black hounds are known to be portents of ill, even of death itself across the mortal realm. They are said to stalk their prey, leaving burning pawprints in earth and stone, hounding the unfortunate till they cannot run any further. None yet live who have witnessed how these creatures treat their prey, but it is a well-known fact that all they leave behind is a trace of sulphur, and a singular drop of blood.

So … no solid leads, just three suspicious young mortals probably stressed over smoking for the first time, or having group sex whilst spaced. And the beginning of the mother of a headache bouncing round my skull. Not the best foot forward, I had to admit to myself.

Getting out of the university proved a whole lot harder than getting onto the campus, given how eager Principal Thorne-Davis was to sign up my mythical daughter to next year's roll-call. I didn't want him getting suspicious of me, so I wasted a good hour filling out paperwork and putting down a deposit that I knew would never get taken. I didn't mind too much … in all honesty, having seen the campus, I really didn't think they would miss one little donation. Probably would have to save on washing the marble steps that umpteenth time during the day, and let the rain do it au natural. Oh the horror of it!

Finally, I managed to extract myself from the man's cluttered office, and made a break for fresh air and freedom. All I had were suspicions, not a shred of hard evidence, and that stinking headache brewing … probably from all the paperwork I'd filled out without biting anyone's head off. Showing this level of restraint definitely had my blood pressure pinging like a volcano ready to blow.

Leaving the grounds by its gates, I drew a shuddering breath as I felt *something* tatter and leach away from its grip on me. Whatever was going on in the place was localised, definitely within the boundaries of the campus but I still couldn't put my finger on it. Rather than stand there like an idiot, trying to work out whatever the hell it was that was playing merry hell with my senses, I decided to get out of the milling throngs of mortals who by now were filling up the pavements and sidewalks with aimless meanderings sure to set me growling.

Five minutes later, taking in great lungfuls of the soup you mortals call fresh air, I stood by the Thames, picking through what little I had by way of facts.

Something about those three teenagers had my canny "oh fuckery" senses tingling, but whether they were linked to the actual kidnapping of Felix or just because they were doing something illegal, probably drugs, I couldn't say. But I'd been told that my instincts about the university were right. By one of the fae High Court no less, so I guess I should consider her guidance carried a little weight.

Knuckling my forehead with one fist, I tried to think through the headache but bugger me, it was hard. The way it was building, I knew I was in for a bad night locked up in my flat so as not to give in to my instincts and chew someone's head off. Literally. But I wasn't going to get much work done either, and the clock wasn't just ticking, it was going all Defcon on me. The kidnapper had had Felix for more hours than I wanted to think about, and my phone had remained silent ... a sure sign no one had been in touch asking for a ransom. No way would Danny keep quiet if the bastard had been in contact.

When a mortal has a migraine, I've been reliably informed they head home, close the blinds and knock back enough medication to dope a thorough-bred horse. Piece of cake. In terms of us lycan, thanks to our wonderful inhuman metabolism, over the counter drugs have about as much effect on us as drinking tap water. As in nada. So it was handy we had a witch on payroll to help with niggling little issues like headaches, splinters and the odd case of poisoning.

Jessica liked to make sure her staff had the best healthcare plan. I had a niggly suspicion it was so she didn't feel guilty throwing us into the grinder again and again, but hell if I was going to say anything.

I was pretty sure my only three suspects would be sticking to the campus grounds for now, if only so they didn't look suspicious high-tailing it straight after my visit and questions. So that gave me a little breathing space. Just enough time to go find our resident witchy-nurse and have her bestow some of Mother Nature's cleansing balm on my aching brain. This time of day, Elspeth was probably at the office already, doing some hocus pocus research or making sure we'd remembered to water the plants.

Besides, I was overdue checking in with the boss, to update her and find out what she already knew. Technically I was AWOL since she hadn't yet officially signed off on me picking up Felix's abduction no matter the personal connection, and technically the link to the city murders put this squarely in Jacob's corner. That sort of territorial mix up with work only led to messy endings, usually at the client's expense, which is why *normally* we don't act so amateurish. But hey, it had been a long couple of days. Forgive me my slip.

Oh and to add misery to my already fairly fucked up morning, now my hand had started to ache like a complete bastard, throbbing with the sort of pain usually associated with having belted it with something heavy by mistake ... you know, when you're trying to put together Ikea furniture and they say hit it delicately. That sort of pain.

At that point, my personal griping was interrupted by the violent buzzing of my mobile. Hooking the new one out, I gave at least a heartbeat of thought to tossing it in the Thames ... before I stabbed the accept icon and barked.

"What?!"

"Morgan, you sound most out of sorts. Did ah catch you at an unfortunate moment?" My Alpha's Scots broag slid out of the microphone like whiskey over ice, totally calm and at ease despite my less than enthusiastic greeting. One thing about Jessica Walker, she isn't easily annoyed. Which is a good thing, given her ability to hand a person their liver if she eventually took offense.

"Uh, sorry Jess. Got the mother of all headaches." I grunted, knowing it was a poor excuse for rudeness but hey, I wasn't at my best right now.

"Ah understand. Ah will keep this brief. Ah know you met with Danny Price earlier today, and are following up on Felicity's disappearance. Do you have any leads from yer journey tae the university?"

Leads? Hell no. Confusing snippets that led me down the garden path and into the swamp full of 'gators more like, but I wasn't going to whinge to my boss about little details like that. Especially as she already knew I'd started investigation without me telling her the details. Nope, I just gritted my teeth against a renewed bout of pulsing agony, and gave her the low down. Danny's revelation about Felix's origins, their father-daughter surprise, the organised crime element and my follow up at Felix's class and the three suspicious students.

Jess was silent for a long moment. For my part, I bit my tongue and stopped myself from hurrying her response, knowing it was the beast in me all riled up, anger feeding it, pain causing it frustration. Annoying my Alpha just wasn't the clever option here.

Finally, her voice slid out the phone.

"Ah am meeting with Elspeth in a short while tae discuss her findings at the Price residence." I could almost see the expression she was wearing, thoughtful and wary. "Trust yer instincts, Morgan, too much of this seems awry and ah dinnae believe a simple matter of kidnapping based on yer friend's ... ah *unfortunate* life choices. Mr Price's links to this Carteloni family seem the obvious instigator of the abduction, but why now, and involving such *non-traditional* methods? Ah will see what ah can unearth about this interested party and its recent activities without alerting the mortal law. Fer now, ah am happy fer you tae pursue this matter and follow where it leads. But please keep both Jacob and mah-self updated. There is nae the need tae think yer alone in wanting this resolved speedily."

"Yeah, more likely it'll be the three of them are into some weird kinky shit or have a weed farm somewhere in town." I growled, taking a breath as a fresh spike of pain bounced inside my skull. This headache was proving to be a right royal bastard. "But any help'll be great."

"Dinnae worry yourself. The child was and remains under Pack protection, and it lies with mah-self to address the debt we now owe both Mr and Ms Price." Jessica answered lightly, but I could hear the thinly veiled thread of anger underlying her mood. Felix had been guaranteed Pack protection, but before our Alpha had been able to make good on her promise, someone had snatched her and challenged the Pack's authority and ability to protect their own. Even if that bastard had no clue who they were crossing, that someone was going to *hurt* when we found them.

Jessica made some further comment, but the headache chose that moment to go full Vesuvius on me, and pain flashed like wildfire through my head. I spasmed, dropping the phone and slamming a hand to my forehead in the vain hope there was an off-switch located there. Which only added to the pain, as the only hand I had free was the one also vying for "bastard oh how I hurt" right now.

Funny how that works; you see it happen all the time but never ask yourself why do it. You have a headache, and the first thing you do is hit your head to make it stop hurting. Sense, why durst thou forsake me?

What made things even more darkly funny was I chose that moment to faint. Blackness reached up to engulf me as I felt myself falling over, pain edging everything in lurid crimson. I may have cried out, or cursed, but the only thing I was absolutely sure about was a last thought as I hit the concrete and something went crunch.

"Fuck. Broke another phone. Jess's gonna kill me!"

Then, blackness.

It's cold. Cold and dark, something covering her eyes so she can't properly see around her. Just shadows and hints of objects looming out of the murk. The place smells of stinking mud, old water and mould, that clamminess which only comes from long disuse and neglect. Her head aches like an absolute bitch, and the cuts and bruises on her body all cried out for attention.

She coughs, painfully, and tries not to choke as the stink of the place invades her mouth.

"H...hello? Is anyone there?" Her voice echoes slightly, sounding so vulnerable, quavering with a fear she has no control over. "Hello? Can anyone hear me? Anyone, please?"

Silence mocks her, the faint sounds echoing back from far, far away. Stifling a sob, she slumps back against something cold and wet, slimy and slick. She doesn't care.

She's alone.

Waking from a faint is not something I'd list as a particularly pleasurable experience. Just in case you were wondering. Thankfully, it was made marginally better by the immediate view of a curving pair of breasts held in a clean white t-shirt, overlain with some intricate necklace made to look like silver leaves. A clean fresh perfume filled my nose as I drew in a stuttering breath, dispelling the dank stink I'd just had swamp my senses.

Roses and woodland after recent rain. Definitely an improvement.

"He's awake." Elspeth's voice noted dryly as she took a step back, a smile creasing her lips as she noted where my eyes had rested. "And in good enough health to be headed for a HR complaint, unless he looks me in the eyes pretty damn quickly."

I jerked my head up, wincing as stars burst on the inside of my head, and found the witch was not alone. Jessica stood to one side of our consultant, clad in a formal business suit of fine linen, looking as sharp and professional as ever. Jacob loomed slightly back from the pair, sat on the edge of a desk cradling a mug of something which steamed and smelled so good I started salivating. I caught sight of at least three other Pack members lounging nearby, and decided I didn't mind voicing my confusion.

"Anybody going to tell me what the hell just happened?"

"What's the last thing you remember, Morgan?" My Alpha asked me quietly, expression as poker-faced as ever.

I took a moment, head still rattled by the whatever-the-fuck I'd just had ... dream, vision, nightmare ... before answering.

"Was talking to you on the phone. I'd left the university. Took a breather before coming in to catch up with you all on what we talked about. Then ... nada."

"Ah'm wondering if anything untoward or unusual struck you at the time? Anything nae right?" Jessica pressed.

"Uh, yeah, the mother of all headaches. Felt like someone had taken an axe to my brain. Felt kinda weak and ill, oh and my hand started feeling like shit ... then I think I just sparked out." I admitted, seeing Jacob grin at the show of vulnerability. I'd be getting jokes about fainting spells and being delicate for the next month, I just knew, given the bastard's sense of humour.

"Elspeth? Would you mind?" My Alpha directed her attention to the witch, who was eyeing me with those bright jade eyes of hers. Even as she gave me a frank up-and-down once over, I realised I was slumped in a seat in the Pack's office – when I should have been out cold on the pavement in Greenwich all the way across London – but even more worrying was the fact I was sat in the middle of a wide, empty space. The desks nearby had been pushed away, and far worse for the office cleaners, someone had marked out a fairly large and complicated protective ward on the floor. With me slap bang in the middle of the bloody thing, whilst everyone else remained just outside the outer perimeter. Ivory candles had been set at the points of the star, and a very faint scent of crushed salt following along the curving lines of the circle.

Now, I'm no expert on the ins and outs of waking up from blacking out, but doing so to find I was in the middle of some fairly hefty magical mojo just didn't seem a reasonable reaction on my colleagues' behalf. Me being me, I decided things had gotten hinky enough for one day.

"Just what the fuck is going on here?" I asked in my most polite and well-mannered way. "I just fell over, blacked out. Is this someone's idea of a joke?"

Elspeth and Jessica exchanged significant looks, whilst Jacob remained focused on me, expression blank as stone. Finally, Elspeth shrugged, coming to a decision and stepped in close to me, placing herself within the circle. She took my head gently between her cool palms and tilted it back so she could look down at me thoughtfully.

"How's the headache? Still feel weak or nauseous? Do you have a bad taste in your mouth?" She asked, thumbing one eyelid and looking at me closely.

It was tempting to snap, pretend to bite her, but there was a seriousness to her expression which quelled my urge to poke the usual fun. Plus Jessica was watching me with a level of scrutiny I was not used to. Mild exasperation, most times of the waking day, yes. Not this.

"Nope, headache's all gone and I feel like I could stomach some food. If, you know, anyone's offering." I lied, still feeling the lingering rumbles of pain bouncing around my head, and my stomach was definitely offkey and making funny noises. But it wasn't as bad as it had been. "So I reckon I'm all good, What was it? Food poisoning? Some shit left over from that wolfsbane crap?"

"Simply put, dear Morgan, something tried to take a bite out of your spirit." The witch told me calmly, taking up my hand and checking my pulse. Which of course chose that moment to rocket. "Your chi. Your soul, for any better description."

"My what? You're fucking kidding me?" I choked out the words, hoping this was something Jacob that thought up and gotten these two to go along with. The kind of prank he loved pulling. Eating my soul? What the fuck?

"Oh stop being such a baby. It grows back, otherwise mortals would be walking round with great big holes in their spirit from all the bad karma they commit. And then where would we be? Knee deep in zombies, most likely." Elspeth scolded me like a primary school teacher instructing a particularly stupid child. "If you were thinking clearly, you *would* be asking what tried to take a bite out of yours."

"Uh, Ellie, that one's easy. Door number 1 ... the Mistress? You know, big scary immortal we just ass-kicked back to the Real for an eternity of pain and suffering?" I so could act the child, if she wanted to treat me that way. "Kinda obvious, surprised you missed that one."

"Obvious, and totally wrong." She answered with a sarcastic smile, reaching up to pat my cheek. "The once-Lady of the Lake didn't do this. It's too recent, only an hour or so old. I can taste its nature, and it's certainly not the queen of the sewer. No, this happened sometime this morning. And there's more."

I rolled my eyes at Elspeth, biting back on my frustration at being *handled* like I was a perp or lead being questioned.

"Ok, hit me. What else?"

The follow up slap was light, playful and totally unexpected but before I could react, Elspeth just shrugged.

"You asked for that." The witch then held up the hand she'd been checking, still gripped as she kept an eye on my pulse and ticked off points with my fingers. "If you stop thinking with your muscles for a moment, you'd understand. Firstly, someone used magic to try and take some of your lifeforce. Secondly, you are a lycan, and as such normally resistant to any such attempts to directly bewitch or glamour you or harm you with the craft. But thirdly, this time, instead of your innate nature dispelling the attack, you blacked out. Ergo, something is not right with this picture. And I know what."

You could have heard the grinding of my teeth at least a mile away, so loud did I clench against the urge to pick her up and shake her to get to the point.

"Ms MacElvy, ah believe Morgan is nae in the right mind this moment tae enjoy this little game of *i know, and you dinnae*. So as entertaining as this be, if ah might suggest brevity?" Jessica interjected, obviously seeing bloodshed looming on the horizon.

"Oh fine. Take away all my fun." The witch mock-pouted and then shrugged. "It's this."

I looked at what she was indicating, none the wiser.

"My hand? Yes, I've had it all my life. Comes in a matched pair. Somewhat useful for everyday things, like opening jars and swatting annoying witches, but to date not known for causing me to faint."

"Save your quips. Your hand, yes. The same one you've had all the years you were put on this planet to cause me grief. But what you haven't had all this time is … this." Elspeth tapped the one thing I had quite honestly forgotten about.

The white lines looked like scars, tracing out an intricate pattern much like a snowflake. The mark the Morrigan had bequeathed me with, in the bowels of the Natural History Museum, as a newly minted Knight of the Shadow Court. Allowing me to use magic, at least in a very specific way, which was definitely not something any lycan was supposed to do.

Even as I stared at the mark, several good curse words ready to be loosed, Elspeth plucked out a long needle from the masses of her hair and, with no warning, stabbed me in the meat of my hand, just down from the weird tattoo.

"Ouch!" I jerked my hand out of her grasp, glaring up at her. "What the fuck?"

"Just confirming my suspicions. Check the wound." She told me, slipping the needle away again in her tresses. Gods knew what else was hidden up there. "Feel anything odd?"

"You stabbed me. I'm bleeding. What more do you … ?" I started to growl, then stopped as I checked the small wound. Blood, tick. That's normal when someone stabs me and something I'd gotten used to in my line of work. What *wasn't* normal was the heaviness I felt round the wound, as well as a sudden itchiness in my skin. Like someone had rubbed chilli flakes into the small incision and was pressing down on it. Not painful, per se, but unpleasant, definitely.

Knowing there was nothing for it, I told her, seeing her nod as I confirmed whatever she was thinking.

"As I guessed. You're showing a very small but very real vulnerability to pure cold iron. Like any of the fae, who'se Court you would now appear to be a member of." The witch stepped out of the circle, offering me a hand up. I pointedly ignored the offer, pushing myself up and looking across at Jessica. She seemed to hesitate for a moment, but then motioned for me to join them out of the protective circle. Thank god for small mercies.

"This strikes me as somewhat odd, since the only way I would hazard you suffering such vulnerability is through blood. As in inherited. Not the sort of thing you normally get just by being given a new title, is what I'm saying." Elspeth continued as I stepped free from the circle. No alarm bells sounded, no fireworks or explosions went off. Hell, I had no idea what I was expecting but it was definitely a let-down when *nothing* happened.

Jacob pushed himself off the desk, eyeing with me with that cold, closed expression I knew he wore as a prelude to imminent violence. He wasn't angry, his scent was more *wary anticipation*, as if he couldn't decide if he was going to hit me or offer to make me a mug of coffee. Nothing I'd done in the past few hours could have pissed off my packmate enough to warrant us throwing down in the office in front of our Alpha, so his reaction notched the weirdometer up a few decibels. Fainting fits, protective circles and my packmates unsure of me. I was totally confused.

When completely out of one's depth, the wise thing to do is take things slowly, find out the facts and deal with them one at a time. Me, I'd never really been good at the wise option, unless you mean *wise-ass*, so found sarcasm works equally well if you heap it on thick enough.

"Ok, so I fainted. Still doesn't explain how I ended up sat in a circle of protection in the office and not in some A & E in Greenwich, And, whilst we dwell on that, *why*?"

"When ah called you, and you were most unsettled, ah already knew things were amiss." Jessica answered quietly. "When ah heard the sound of yer pain, and you ended the conversation so abruptly, ah sent Jacob tae yer last location from the GPS on yer broken phone. Which ah will be docking from yer wages, just so you know."

"Found you sprawled ass over tit on the floor. People thought you were some drunken idiot and had called the police." Jacob grinned, his wariness easing back not a notch despite the easy mockery we shared. "Didn't take much to convince them to let me take you 'home', to sleep it off. *Poor sod still dealing with the breaking up with his girlfriend ... can't handle his drink.* You know the drill."

"Bastard." I swore but without much energy behind it. My love life, or lack of one, wasn't something I particularly enjoyed re-hashing, especially as the last time I'd seen my ex, I'd had to stand by and let my colleague jinx her ... the magical equivalent of tazing her. It *had* been for her own safety ... it wasn't my fault we'd almost left her under the rubble of the Natural History Museum, if the Mistresses' plan had gone as the immortal wanted it to. Seriously, not my fault!

So, I'd fainted, Jess had called in the cavalry and I'd been hauled into the office to be checked out. Fine so far, details lining up nicely. That left ...

"So why the protective circle?" That was a new one.

"When Jacob brought you in, you weren't, well, yourself." Elspeth spoke up, nodding to my rune enscribed hand. "That little mark of the Shadow Court was lit up like a Christmas decoration, and you were yelling about being locked in the dark. You honestly sounded afraid, not yourself at all. Even your voice was not really your own. So I suggested to Jessica we take some small precautions. Just to be safe. I've seen The Exorcist, you know."

Somewhere dark, somewhere wet. I'd been afraid.

The dream came back to me like the dregs of a night spent out drinking, disjointed and unclear. But definitely very real. It was probably something I should mention to the resident expert on all things weird and wicked, let alone my Alpha, but until I had a handle on whatever it was, I decided to be mulish and keep tight-lipped. It was bad enough fainting from a headache for fuck's sake.

"Ok, so I was off my face, and acting a little weird. So you stuck me in a circle, tested me for possession and now that I haven't started spouting pea soup or twisting my head round, I'm all good?" I growled, making to head past Jacob. Right now I felt wrung out like a wet rag, but that's wasn't anything a bucket of hot thick coffee wouldn't help banish. And a pile of pastrami and pickle sandwiches. Gods I was hungry. "Coz time's ticking and Felix is still missing. I've got to get back out there ..."

It was Jessica who moved to stop me, not Jacob, which surprised me. The Pack enforcer simply remained watching, obviously under orders, whilst our Alpha stepped in front of me and placed one hand on my chest. No threat, no strength used, just simple bodily contact. I might as well have walked into a wall however, and I knew from experience that if I tried walking over Jessica Walker, I'd be the one travelling places, and all of them painful.

"Nae, Morgan, you dinnae." She spoke quietly, but her eyes carried the gravity of her concern. "Tis obvious you are nae yerself, that the fae mark has disquieted you in ways we dinnae understand. It is nae yer fault. Ah am equally tae blame for letting them mark one of mah own so. But until we know what is happening tae you, ah cannae let you continue with this case. Jacob and Lucy will pick up the trail for Miss Price, whilst ah entrust your safekeeping tae Elspeth."

Now as I have said, we all follow Jessica's lead, not with blind faith and unspoken allegiance, but in the clear knowledge that she does what is best for the Pack first and foremost. Under her and her late husband's leadership, we've all grown and profited, and faced down some truly godawful situations and walked away with little more than scratches. She invites us to speak our mind and challenge anything that we feel is contrary to our own viewpoints, but so far, that has happened so few times I could count on one hand.

So it was with some surprise that I found myself pushing back against that hand, and glaring back at her.

"The fuck you are, benching me." I growled, putting the bite into each word. At my tone, Jacob took one step forward, muscles clenching on his forearms in preparation for unleashing a world of hurt. Charles and Emma, waiting behind him, also pushed themselves up and moved from lounging to aggressively looming. Elspeth made to reach out to me, one hand already extended, to either stop me with words or witchcraft but I halted her with a furious glare. I could feel the familiar anger - raw and molten - surging inside but this time it was joined with something new, an edge I wasn't familiar with. A touch of hoar frost and bitter chill, cracking alongside the lava, entwined and strengthening each pulse of rage.

Danny Price was *my* friend, I had promised *him* to keep them safe, and now Felix had been taken. Locked up someplace foul, away from the laughter and life that filled her days. She was in the hands of a madman, possibly, a murderer, definitely, and my Alpha was going to force me to sit this out and let my packmates handle it?

No. Fucking. Way.

For her part, Jessica just stared back at me, her eyes steady, expression still and composed. But her scent ... best way I can describe it is ... think of the air before a summer storm, the promise of lightning and thunder in every breath. The threat that something is going up in flames shortly.

But at that moment in time, I couldn't have cared less.

The moment held, as I kept glaring at her and she returned that stare, whilst Jacob waited for any sign, any hint, to put me down. Whilst the rest of the pack and our consultant stood frozen. Waiting.

Of course, it was that moment that all hell chose to break loose.

Chapter 10

The grounds of Good Deeds, as I think I have mentioned before, were donated to us by a very grateful ambassador, after Jessica and David cleared up some very embarrassing and politically devastating evidence on its way to every national and international newspaper and website. Given the building's previous use, she had thought it prudent to have the placed swept for listening devices and other surveillance equipment, both mortal and otherwise. You seriously never know who is keeping tabs on who.

Our Alpha had also decided that, with our particular job of keeping the Veil patrolled and unwelcome guests removed back to the Real with a big "fuck you and thank you for visiting" message firmly taped to their asses, the establishment should be heavily warded against any incursions. Bound with lock and ward, the foundations rune enscribed and trigger-traps set to raise merry hell if anyone was foolish enough to try to bust through from the other side.

So it caught us all a little unprepared when every alarm began ringing, the water in the various 'features' dotted round the office blazed up into fonts of mystical fire and the stench of the Veil openly oozed into the nicely air-conditioned office space like a dead skunk trapped in the vent.

At the same time, my senses lit from an oh so familiar presence, one who was turning up with far too much regulatory for my peace of mind. The mark on my hard crackled with witch-fire, and I swung around, seeking the presence I knew had to be there.

"I trust I am not disturbing anything of import?" Her voice sang with winter's ice and enough sarcasm to sink a battleship, as

I loosed a very long and very suffering sigh. Focusing on those tones, I found the object of my continued exasperation sat neatly on the edge of a desk, grey strip shift settled round her and long staff leant near to hand against a flowerpot. The blue wytchfire from the water fountains lit her ash-grey skin and black runes with wickedness, whilst her eyes danced with immortal delight.

"Morrigan. Just what the hell are you doing here?" I grated, taking a step back and away from Jessica. The rest of the pack reacted instinctively to the Incursion, Jacob slipping up to ward our Alpha as he drew a disturbingly large cold-iron knife from beneath the desk he'd been near. Emma and Charles were nearest, and by their scent were a breath away from the Change, leaving Siobhan and Lucille to smoothly reach down beside them and pick up crossbows and cock them in an easy *I've prepared for this and I know I can shoot you between the eyeballs before you realise your mistake* manner. Cold iron sang in the air, and I found myself wincing at the sharp tang, my senses never before finding anything but comfort in the stuff.

The Morrigan smiled like frost on the windowpane, braids clacking as she looked around the room, taking in the various weapons pointed her way. The threat of imminent violence seemed to delight her ... not surprising really, given her incarnation as the Bitch of Battle. There was no sign of her crow guards this time but I had no doubt the bastards were lurking nearby, ready to hand out a beating with the cool casualness of natural born killers.

"Time passes, Knight, like the flow of blood from a mortal wound. My Queen bids you join us for the Beltane Tourncy and take your place as her Champion. Betrayal beckons, so put aside your childish games for now. I am sure whatever *fun* you had planned can wait."

Her mockery wound the mood up several notches, as Jacob loosed a deep throated growl that had nothing mortal about it. For her part, the Shadow Court fae cocked an eye at him in undisguised amusement but bit back her response as Jessica spoke up.

"Ah believe there is a matter tae address first, Lady Morrigan, before anyone goes anyplace." Our Alpha spoke firmly, slipping aside from Jacob's protection and facing the immortal. Despite her slim figure and not exactly towering height, she managed to face the Morrigan toe to toe, wrapped in the strength and surety that as an Alpha, she could throw down with the best of them. And leave smiling.

For her part, the fae just shook her head, making the bones and silver ornaments in her dreadlocks clatter and ring out sharply.

"I had thought we had an accord, lycan? When last we spoke, you acknowledged my Queen's claim on your pup as valid, and agreed to his standing as Knight-Errant in the tourney. We were *agreed*. Do not think to take back your words, for that way leads to ruin."

Jessica shrugged and laid one hand on my arm, this time as a measure of comfort rather than a threat.

"Morgan here has suffered from the title Madb so recently bestowed upon him. It is conflicting with his nature, and before yer ... *surprising* appearance, we were discussing the matter of his health and how best tae heal the ill done tae him. He is in nae condition, in mah humble opinion, tae stand for anyone right now."

"Oi! Hold on a sec ...!" I started, feeling like the five-year-old being talked about over his head. It wasn't that I wanted to go fight in some stupid tournament, hell, all I wanted to do was get back out there and follow up on the leads on Felix. But I had *some* pride ...

The Morrigan's eyes narrowed, and somehow she managed to pass the space between where she sat and me in the blink of an eye. Finding her facing me, I went to step away, but she was too quick, reaching up and laying one ice-cool hand on my forehead.

Whiteness exploded inside my head, and I loosed a surprised grunt as the chillness stabbed through me. The fury I'd felt moments before was washed away, guttering and dying under the relentless onslaught of her touch. On the plus side, the sickness and pounding headache wound down to a grumbling murmur, better than a full pack of nurafen and a night's sleep for a mortal.

"Tch, tis nothing to be afeared over." The Morrigan stepped away, drawing her robes about herself like some fussy grandmother. "The boons granted by my Queen are a weighty burden, and I expected some small reaction with the wolf's churlish nature. I have settled the account for now, and the knight here shall be good to stand at the tourney."

To be fair, I did feel a whole lot better. Whatever the immortal had done, it was like a cold shower, a morning's sleep and a hefty dose of caffeine to my battered body and mind. Shaking my head to clear the lingering cobwebs I faced my Alpha again, but this time with the unnatural anger banked right down. Jess must have sensed my change in mood, as she studied me silently for a moment before turning back to the waiting fae.

"Ah should mention this *could* be construed as a breach of the Accords, with yer intrusion on protected ground with nae invite granted." Jessica commented dryly, facing the Morrigan even as Elspeth moved to my side, one hand raised, her expression somewhere between vexed and concern. I felt the prickle of her craft running over me as she gave me a full diagnostic, her frown deepening as she obviously found I was fixed. For the moment.

The Morrigan gave one of her wintry smiles, and waved one dark-tipped hand in my direction.

"No intrusion, when I am so invited to come and go at my whim, as so granted by my dear Knight here." She smiled, the sharp points of her teeth glinting with oh so pure delight.

Jessica arched a slim eyebrow in my direction, as the events of the day wound back through my mind, as I scrabbled to understand just what I'd done this time. The Morrigan laughed, opening her mouth, but the voice that came forth was ... decidedly and depressingly ... mine.

"For pity's sake, just keep popping over and giving me such bloody useless advice, why don't you?"

"Oh for fucks sake, you are joking right? That was *not* meant as a free pass to keep coming over here and ruining my day. You can't blame me for that!" I growled, hearing Jessica's heavy sigh and Jacob's snort of laughter. "I'm serious. It's not like I meant that ..."

"Ah do despair, my dear Morgan, sometimes yer still the pup we found in the Real. The fae will take any offer and make of it what they will, this you well know." Jessica reproved me gently, then shrugged. The shrug is a gesture most mortals get wrong, thinking it something simple like a "fine" coming from the female of your species. A shrug, in reality, is loaded with meaning, especially in the animal kingdom. You see an Alpha in a pack shrug, it means everything from "I'm gearing up to tear your throat out" to "Go on then, I'll allow you to eat now."

Jessica's shrug held resigned determination, worry over my physical or mental state and annoyance at my stupid mistake but also at the Morrigan for her arrogant assumption. And some general annoyance, just to settle her mood.

See, told you. A whole boat-load of meaning.

"Ah can then only note mah concern over mah pack member's well-being, and also note ah dinnae think he is fully fit tae stand in this role of knight in yer tourney." Jess told the

Morrigan sharply, but the fae just shrugged herself. The meaning of that gesture was all too clear and way less diverse.

"I will verily pass your worries onto my Queen, Jessica Mary of the Walker clan." She responded oh so formally then turned back to face me, expression settling into frigid calm. "Now, Knight. Time passes and my patience with it. Come if you will or remain and make a mockery of your Alpha's word, and break the accord between our peoples. Return us to bloody dispute from this day forward, on your next word."

"Fuck me, you don't have to lay it on so thick." I growled, then looked at my Alpha. "Fine, let's get this over with."

"We will follow up on yer leads in your absence, dinnae you worry." She nodded at my unspoken request. "Ah will have those three youngsters followed, see what comes of it, and continue investigating this family Danny Price had such ill luck with in the past. Watch yerself, Morgan, and we will speak of our next steps on yer safe return."

I didn't miss the 'our next steps' bit, knowing I was due some harsh words at the very least for my open defiance of Jessica but at that moment I didn't really care. She wasn't cutting me from the case, that was all that mattered.

The Veil opened like some rotten flower, folding in on itself as the alarms began screaming like a backing chorus to the damned. Elspeth stepped away from the gaping hole rent in the air of the office, but Jessica and Jacob remained standing firm, as the rest of the Pack moved up to back them. It was a bold statement, a show of strength but also just in case anything decided to take advantage of the sudden bridge and take a peek into the mortal realm.

Boy would they be in for a surprise.

I gave the gang one final nod, turned and was about to follow the Morrigan into the mouth of hell when I stopped and turned back.

"Oh, and can someone go feed Bear? Before he eats my sofa?" I remembered, before taking a deep breath and heading into madness.

Chapter 11

Kobolds are an ilk of the Wyld Court, strange lizard-like creatures known for their tribal beliefs and intricate art that mortals have found in many a cave. Mistakenly believing this to be of early man and seeking to claim the sites for their own, mortals have drawn the wrath of these territorial tribes by their abuse of burial grounds and sacred temples to spirits. The bones of these fools are offered up to their minor Gods as tribute.

I stepped from rent as the Veil closed in and sealed off the wound between Realms, and drew in a long slow breath, bracing myself against the incredible mix of scents assaulting me.

The Way spat us out in a heavily forested glade, with ruins of grey stone rising all around like fingers reaching upwards to beseech the heavens. Decay clung to the place in long strands of brown-green fronds, thick webs that spun overhead and a matt of thick vegetation underfoot. From the sprawling jungle setting, I guessed we were somewhere in the Verdance, that vast reach of forestland and shrubbery filling a stretch of the Real.

More Badh-Catha guard stood around the stone-strewn glen, their tall spears ramrod straight and their bird helms swivelling in every direction whilst they clasped sword-hilts in mailed fists. Definitely tense, and ready for trouble.

Boy, what had I walked my size eleven feet into? Seeing the guards so alert, I did a quick once over myself, cataloguing that I had pretty much walked into the Real without the normal heavy armour and weapons I brought along, as well as the host of accessories I normally pack into my pockets to handle anything a couple of feet of cold iron couldn't resolve.

So, here I was. Basically unarmed for a lycan in the Real, about to go head-to-head in some sort of tournament of the Courts. Against Gods knew what sort of monsters. Not my best judgement call, to be brutally honest.

Going to be one of *those* sort of weeks, I guessed.

Thunder rolled with the boom of waves crashing against the rocks, and I turned my face upward, taking in a deep breath. The stink of the grave mingled with a sharp acidic tang, like lemons tossed in vinegar. It was a faint flavour, a wisp on the wind, but definitely there ... and something I knew and had hoped I wouldn't smell. The scent of fae fear.

Oh *that* was reassuring.

"Is someone going to tell me what the hell I've stepped in, and how much scraping I've got to do to clean it off?" I joked, but lost the grin as the Morrigan faced me. If you've heard the term *wintery* as a description of someone's expression, then this ancient fae was wearing something positively artic. Ice had formed a crazed pattern over her grey-black skin, like the touch of hoarfrost on the first day of winter. And her eyes ... her eyes blazed with bloody intent, so that I almost wanted to step back and ward off an incoming blow. You think I'm being over the top, you face down a pissed off immortal and then we can talk.

"Stay thy tongue, Knight, for you have not the wit to even act the fool this moment." She snapped, and I felt the muscles in my jaws clamp tight. Magic, the touch of the fae. And yeah, normally us big bad lycan are proof against such tricks but it seems the mark of the Shadow Court made me vulnerable to their tricks as well as iron poisoning. Boy, this whole Knight thing was turning out to be a right royal buzz-kill.

"The tourney be a time-honoured tradition where the Courts meet on neutral ground, for discourse and agreement upon weighty matters touching both our fair realm, the mortal realm and the third realm. Disagreements are settled by right of combat between the duly affected parties, much like I believe your, ah, *blooding* but on a much grandeur scale. But this Beltane, something has changed. One has come forward, challenging the right of rule of the Courts and demanding my Queen and her cousins step aside to let others determine the path of the Ivory and Shadow, and all those who serve."

The Morrigan spoke as if every word was a bite of winter, sharp and cold. It took me a moment to process what she was actually saying, and then the good ol' warning bells started to chime.

"Hence our Queen's call to arms upon you, Sir Pup. As Knight of Shadow, your duty is to stand as my Queen's chosen defender and protect her right to rule the Court." The Morrigan let her gaze travel up and down me in one long slow glance, weighing me up and obviously finding me wanting. What a surprise. "Some ill will hath afflicted my Lady Madb's scryers, the ice is unclear, fractured. This Beltane, blood shall be spilled, but there is a purpose to the dissembling being wrought here. We just know not what."

"Riiiiiiiight, so there's a couple of things I think I need a little more help with." I admitted, stepping over to a fallen lump of masonry that might have been the remains of a pillar or just a very well moulded rock. Whatever, I parked my arse on its cold surface as I looked across at the Morrigan. Thankfully my jaw seemed to be working just fine now, the simple lock-charm released now that she had spoken her piece. Nice of her to allow me to speak, and boy was I going to take advantage.

"Ask on, Knight. My Lady has appointed me your page this Beltane, and as such I am here to answer your queries as best I may before battle is fought and blood spilled."

Again, the immortal dwelt far too much on those last words, a vicious wickedness to her words as she spoke them.

Creepy, yeah some.

"Fine. So ... three realms? Mortal realm, the good ol' Real, but what the hell is this third one I've never heard about?" I'll be the first to admit I'm not the world's greatest scholar, but I had definitely spent enough time jumping between realms to have heard about there being another one out there somewhere.

"That which we do not speak of?" The Morrigan asked simply.

"Yeah, that one."

The fae was silent for a moment, then looked me in the eye.

"We do not speak of it. Next question?"

Any number of curses sprang to my lips, but I didn't need any charm to lock my jaw to keep them from escaping. An immortal playing silly buggers ... what a surprise.

"Ok, ignoring that elephant in the room .... You're telling me that you expect someone to challenge Madb for her right to rule the Shadow Court, and *I* get the fun job of defending her claim?"

"In a nutshell, if that nutshell was the size of your mortal realm's surface then ... yes, simply enough." The Morrigan shrugged. "Do not fear, you will not stand alone. My Lady and I may think you at least tolerably adequate for the role we have appointed you, but we are not delusional."

"You might want to work on your pep-talk. Just saying." I growled in reply, then gestured down at myself. "One thing you might've noticed, I'm a little underdressed for facing off against some all-powerful bad-asses, if I'm to assume you and Madb aren't simply jumping at, well, shadows and possibly going senile in your old age ..."

My tone must've finally crossed a line, since two of the nearest Crow fae appeared like magic beside me, swords unsheathed and crossing my throat like some torturer's scissors. I'd sensed them, and probably could've gotten out of their way if

I'd wanted to, but that wasn't really the point. Dodging the homicidal maniac foot soldier wasn't the game I was playing here. Instead, I kept my attention fixed fully on the Morrigan as she stood, sheathed in ice and ire.

Those blood red eyes held mine as they flared, like the pits of hell banked up to roast a soul ... then died down as the fae smiled and tapped her chin with one taloned finger.

"You are indeed a breath of fresh air in the Court, Sir Pup. I might *just* understand what my Lady saw when she made your appointment. There are those who consider too much of themselves under my Queen's rule, and your uncouthness should force them to reconsider their own self-worth. Or land you in *very* hot water ... either way, I foresee interesting times ahead."

"I honestly couldn't give a fuck what the Court thinks of my *uncouthness*." I snarled back. "All I care about is getting this idiocy over and done with so I can get back to my *real* job, and finding a missing woman, the daughter of a good friend. Before she's torn apart by something particularly nasty. So, no rush, you know."

And then my vision tunnelled and I fell in darkness ...

"... Hello? Is anyone there?"

I'm back in the cold and wet, the smell of decay and stinking mud stifling through whatever has been thrown on my face. My head is swimming, I can't seem to think straight.

Where am I?

A sound, something scraping against brick. A foot? A harsh breath, somewhere off in the darkness. There's someone here with me!

"Hello?! Can you help me please?"

Hands grip me, so suddenly I cry out in alarm, but they steady me, pushing me back against the wet brickwork. Whoever it is, they are right in front of me. I can feel them looking at me but they don't say a word. Just stare at me, so hard I can feel them.

"Why won't you answer me?! Help! Help!" I start to struggle, to lash out .... Fight to get free ... but a hand clamps over my mouth, muffling me. Now they speak, fast and low, gibberish to my ears, but my head starts to swim and the blackness rushes in again.

"Help me ... please?"

I found myself back in the dismal clearing, down on my knees, hands braced before me and clenched hard on the bare stone. The dregs of the vision slunk away as I shook my head, the confusion and fear so vivid even though they weren't my own.

A curved cup hovered into view, steaming slightly, and I looked up to see the Morrigan staring back at me. Her eyes were cold and bottomless, a blood-stained void that had no soul behind, just the ancient echoes of ages long past. Yet there was something there, a faint spark ... even a little compassion? Surely not.

Grabbing the drinking horn I gulped down the hot wine, feeling its warmth leach through me, banishing the chill and the fear. It did nothing to still the anger I felt bubbling through me, realising like a stroke of lightning who it was in the dark. Who was so scared.

Felix.

Somehow I was sensing her thoughts, somehow stuck with her in whatever shit-hole she had been dumped. It wasn't possible, just as how unlikely it was for a lycan to do anything you'd call *magic*. And yet there it was. Filling my head with shit and generally pissing me off.

"The child is yet safe, as your connection shows." The Morrigan told me matter of factly, opening up a whole new raft of questions, like how the hell she knew what I was seeing, what it all meant and why hadn't she said something sooner. But I bit back on the demands for anything from the fae, knowing I was more likely to get answers from the stone underfoot than her. And it would probably hurt less in the long run.

Instead, I pushed myself up after setting the now empty horn cup aside and shook my head to clear the fog.

"You have asked questions, and I have answered. Now, Sir Pup, you had best garb yourself for battle, for the time fast approaches whence your attention shall be needed." The Morrigan smiled coldly, then used her long staff to point behind me.

Turning, I was wholly unsurprised to find a pile of garments and equipment sitting on the cleared stone where a moment before, it had been empty. Neatly folded, I recognised my kit immediately and breathed a small sigh of relief. I'd fought enough fights in the stuff to trust it, know what it could and couldn't do. I'd had some small suspicion the Morrigan was going to magic me up some sort of armour and weapons to use in the tournament, and I would've spent half the time worrying the bloody stuff would vanish at the wrong moment or turn into something specifically embarrassing to me for their entertainment ... fae have that sort of sick sense of humour. Don't ask me, it's got to be something to do with living so long. Turns their brains to mush.

Anyhow, I didn't waste any time pulling on my Real armour, checking each weapon in its sheath as I settled the kit on and rolled my shoulders, feeling a whole lot better now that I had my toys to play with. Yeah, I know that I've said before that none of it is as good as me properly "wolfing out", but it never hurts to have several edges ... especially ones made of pure cold iron that don't ring Herne's front doorbell straight off when I used them.

I drew a slow calming breath and tried to order my thoughts. Felix was out of reach, and the rest of the Pack would be off doing stuff to track down leads and hopefully get me what I needed once this idiocy was done with to put the hurt on the bastard responsible. So grouching around and wasting time only made things worse for her, and the kid didn't deserve that.

Time to man up, Morgan and go hit someone until they stopped being a problem.

I held up my hands in mock surrender, shrugging as I accepted my fate.

"I get the point. Enough questions. How about we get on with the hurting?"

"You seem suddenly blessed with wisdom. Let us hope it is not anything ... permanent." The Morrigan smiled nastily, but held up one of her hands in mockery of my gesture. "But stay a moment. We are joined ..."

Cold iron ripped from its sheath as I tensed, senses lit like wildfire, anger and fear warring like two great titans inside. That scent ... it *couldn't* be ... but my nose never lies.

Cold shivers washed down my spine as I threw a look of betrayal and "WTF?" at the Morrigan. Knowing who approached. Who ...

What.

Herne.

Chapter 12

The immortal Lord of the Hunt entered the clearing to the ragged howling of wolves, the baying of hounds scenting blood, and the cries of the hunted doomed to die beneath claw and fang.

I kid you not, the bastard has his own *soundtrack*.

I don't think I can express, in words you'll understand, what it felt like when Herne the Hunter stepped into the ruins where we waited. I'll try, though, coz I'm good like that.

Imagine a summer's day, hot sun on your face, gentle breeze flowing across the meadow where you stand. Birds singing in the trees, maybe the gentle sound of running water close by. Everything at peace, calm. Then ... BAM! Thunderclouds roll overhead, darkening the sky as lightning hammers through the air to scorch your senses and leave burning hot trails across the backs of your eyeballs. The ground shakes like it is under assault from a hundred thousand frenzied drummers, and your ears are filled with the explosions of a million fireworks all set off to go in one massive burst.

See ... I tried. Totally wrong in every way, but that's an inkling as to how it felt as his foot fell on the stone.

Around me, the Crow Guard smoothly shifted from guard to ward, swords and spears not *exactly* pointing towards the newcomer but definitely held ready in case things kicked off. For her part, the Morrigan remained still and composed, wrapped in her leather and rags, a cold smile lit on those thin lips as her eyes pulsed with bloody hue. Me, I was rooted ... no chance to run or hide, no way out of this fucked up meeting. I was trapped in the Real, wrong footed and still staggering from that last vision I'd shared with Felix.

Herne stopped after that first footfall, a legendary figure towering over us, eight ... ten feet tall. Clad about in skins and claws, his armour a mismatch of briar and horn, Herne leant on a massive spear carved with intricate patterns, what skin showing blazing bright azure with detailed wode swirl. His face was hidden within a hood of stitched skin, but his eyes blazed like feral suns out of the shadows, and his breath curled in the air with the heat of the hunt, of the kill. Horns that would have graced the eldest stag from prehistoric times curled overheard, vicious tines glinting with the shine of fresh blood. There was a stench about him, pure animalistic ... primal and real in the dead air, straight from the dusty plains of the savannah.

Surprisingly, he'd come without a pack, when normally his Hunt was ever close to hand. Given he ruled the Wyld Court, this comprised some of the maddest of the fae ... redcap goblins, hobs in their skulls and bones, thorn sprites bearing bows of twisted poison-ivy ... a host of scary as fuck nastiness. As well as whatever poor fuckers he'd captured to be his Hounds ... lycans more often than not. Part of me wondered where the merry little band had gotten to, but that was a very small part whilst mostly all I felt was the fear. The gut-wrenching terror that any of my kin feels in the bastard's presence. The pull, the desire to bend knee and serve beyond any will of my own.

Bastard.

The moment drew out, thunder threatening to break in the air all round, and then the Hunter spoke one word, the rasp of his voice the dying shriek of a hundred prey.

Kneel.

The command hammered at me like a physical blow, so that my bones screamed and ached to bend, my back knotting like a bowstring ready to loose. The word rebounded round the inner reaches of my skull like some crazed rubber ball bounced by a lunatic child ... but I gritted my teeth and snarled my defiance.

"No. Fucking. Way!" I spat the words, every muscle burning in the fight to resist the immortal's will.

Ice-cold fire burned on my hand, and I dragged my eyes away from the motionless figure standing before me, to see the sigil on my skin - the brand marking me as connected with the Court of Shadows - alive and afire with power. Flames danced around its curving lines, and I tried to focus on the pulsing might stored there, leashed to me for just such occasions. I couldn't help a snarl of laughter ripping from my chest as I imagined the blue flames blazing around my first, lashing out to slam into Herne and throw him off those fur-lined boots of his. Dumping him on his hoary ass. God I'd love to see that!

True to my recent experience, nothing like that happened, no matter me focusing so hard on that outcome. No Harry Potter moment, no hero getting to toss a fireball into the bad guy's face just when he needs to. The blue fire burned on my skin in time with the pulse of my hammering heartbeat, but despite the waves of power slamming at me from every side, at least I kept my feet and stayed standing in front of the horned fucker.

It could have been a heartbeat, it could have been an hour later but finally Herne turned from me and I sagged as I felt the grip of his focus loosen and die. The big bastard still filled the clearing with raw power and might, but now it was dampened down as if he'd thrown on a cloak and covered up. The Lord of the Wyld Court faced the Morrigan, who had remained silent whilst we contested, and rasped out one simple statement.

He'll do.

With that, the Hunter turned on one booted foot and strode back out of the clearing, the pounding beat of the Hunt fading with him until silence settled once more around us. I honestly don't know what I was feeling right then ... relief the bastard was gone, anger that the Morrigan had obviously been expecting him and more than a little righteous fury at such an offhand appraisal by the utter bastard. *He'll do?* What the fuck did he mean by that? But as I spun to face my lethal fairy page, she shook her head and then addressed empty air.

"Your Lord is in agreement then? We stand together this Beltane?"

For a moment I honestly thought the Morrigan had finally given into senility and was, not to put too fine a point on it, nuts. Then my lycan senses caught up on current events, ringing the bell in my head that something was not as it seemed. Focusing, I eyed the space the Shadow fae was addressing, and saw a faint disturbance in the air around *something*. It shimmered like a bad special effect in an 80s Star Trek movie, then resolved itself as a mocking voice drawled.

"Yes, yes, it's all so boring but as my Lord so commands. This day, Wyld stands with Ivory and Shadow. For as long as things remain ... *entertaining* ..."

The disturbance faded away and I eyed the newcomer warily.

In looks it seemed something like a small sized lion on steroids but without the mane. Instead, it bore a single Mohawk style ruff arching back from its brow and running to the centre of its knotted shoulders. Its fur was a constantly changing ripple of colours, blending in with the surroundings so that at any moment, parts of it seemed not real or missing. Its eyes were vivid pits of molten honey, glowing with an inner fire that was purely demonic. The cat beast lazily opened its jaws in a massive yawn, showing a disturbing number of fangs more suited for a great white shark's mouth than anything feline. Its claws were unsheathed and equally fearsome, with extra spurs of white bone jutting from each of its fore limbs. A stub of a tail twitched at its arse end, bristled and tipped with what looked like more spikes ... not the nice little kitty tail you'd enjoy twining around your ankles.

First impressions, the thing had *dumb predator* written all over it, but as always in the Real, nothing is entirely as it seems. Far too much intelligence glittered in those shining eyes, as the creature stretched and shifted into a seated position facing us both like a befanged and furry Yoda.

In mid-freaking air.

"Morgan, it be a pleasure to introduce the Bayun-Cat, of the Wyld Court." The Morrigan tipped a short bow to the beast, and it rolled its massive head in response. I wracked my brains for what was familiar about this thing, since in all my travels I definitely hadn't come across it ... hell, I could just image how Bear would be acting up right now if he was with me, seeing something furry to chase ...

"A pleasure, I'm sure." I greeted the Bayun-Cat, nodding a bow that was slightly more than half assed. Until I worked out where this thing sat in terms of being able to hand me my ass, I wasn't beyond showing a little respect.

"The Bayun-Cat will serve as Herne's champion in the coming tourney." The Morrigan added, as the Wyld-cat casually extended its claws and licked them, showing the boredom of any feline which wasn't getting what it wanted there and then. "The Ivory have already chosen a champion from their list of noble knights, and shall meet us on the field of battle. So best we are away before they grow wearied and decide to start matters without us."

"All so tiresome. I don't suppose anyone feels the need for a lie down right this moment?" Bayun-Cat looked around the gathered Shadow Crow knights, eyes glowing brightly, mouth stretched wide ... very wide in fact.

"Cheshire Cat. Damn it, I'd know that grin anywhere!" I realised with a mental kick, but the Bayun-Cat shot me a withering stare in answer.

"You have one warning, puppy, and one alone. Ask not where the Mad Hatter is, or if it is time for tea unless you desire to experience a most singular amount of pain that I promise will last you your brief lifetime. You have been warned."

With that, the Bayun-Cat rose up, its yellow eyes flashing madly. The shifting colours on its hide flowed together in a sudden burst of energy, and with one last hiss, it vanished from sight. One last muttered *"Cheshire Cat! Indeed!"* hung in the air with a fading imprint of its fevered orbs, and then it was gone, vanished from sight and my senses.

"I suggest you not bring that matter up with the Wyld champion again, if you wish to be able to return to the mortal realm to seek your missing woman-child with all limbs attached." The Morrigan told me with a sharp smile but I just shrugged. It wasn't the first time I'd put my size eleven foot in my mouth and it damn well wouldn't be the last. And how was I supposed to know the inspiration for a much-loved character from a children's cartoon was in fact a psychotic Wyld beast? These facts should be included in the credits.

Instead, I just gestured toward the nearest break in the ruins.

"Aren't we supposed to be going someplace? Times' a ticking and I'm sure your mysterious challenger can't wait to get his nose bloodied by yours truly." I finally decided it was safe enough to slip my short sword back into its sheath, having kept it in one fist all the time Herne and his little kitty had been present. They'd both ignored the rather obvious insult, for which I was thankful, but I decided I'd chanced my luck enough to be waving a deadly substance around the Real. People might get the wrong idea. Plus it was making my skin itch, damn this stupid weakness.

The Morrigan simply nodded and turned on one heel, walking off in the complete opposite direction to where I had indicated. The Badh-Catha honour guard fell into step around her, some taking to the air in their crow forms to whirl and dive on the air currents, crying out in harsh voices.

"Come then, Sir Pup, and let us meet our doom together. Or you can walk off that way, and I'll send your bones back to your pack leader bound up in a nice little bow." The Morrigan called out over her shoulder in her most infuriatingly calm voice, and I ground my teeth, fighting the urge to go slap that smile right off her face.

My thoughts must have been a little obvious, as she looked over her shoulder and grinned even more widely, as I hurried to catch up my guide in the Real.

The thing with the Real is ... no matter how many times you travel here, you never really know what you'll find, even if you have a good idea of what to expect. The place has an annoying habit of somehow knowing your expectations, then taking a perverse enjoyment in proving you thoroughly wrong.

Or it could just be that I'm really bad at this sort of thing. That's entirely possible too.

I'd been told this was the Beltane Tournament, a place where the Courts meet to discuss the sort of matters that make the United Nations delegations seem a jovial chat amongst friends. So I'd mistakenly thought the surroundings would reflect the gravity of the situation. Something grand, opulent, another too-obvious way of the Courts to show off in the Real to the rest of the Immortals. Kinda like the big-ass buildings they keep raising on the London skyline, a whole load of phallic "fuck you's" to make visitors feel humble and small.

I'd, as always, forgotten that Immortals have all the subtlety and style of a ten-year-old with a box of crayons.

We made our way through lush, dank forest of dripping decay, purple leaves reaching down from withered trunks to drape the canopy floor in a moist, rich carpet. Haunting inhuman cries filled the air as *things* skittered out of sight amongst the heavy foliage, but I felt eyes on us from above as well as around us. There was no sense of impending threat, nothing triggering to tell me we were walking into a trap or the like, but I still gripped the hilt of my trustworthy sword ... just in case. It's a man thing ... we like to grip something to give us some sense of safety. Or, yeah, something along those lines.

Finally, the trees parted, our hidden followers growing silent as we stepped into the open. I stopped, finding the Morrigan waiting for me, leaning on her gnarled wooden staff, one arm outstretched like some creepy signpost.

"Behold, Knight. The Beltane Tourney."

Ahead, the land sloped down in a gentle curve to what looked to be a crossroads of immense proportions. Following the pathways stretching out on either side, I could see roads leading back into sprawling forestland, up to foothills poking from the greenery and, far across from me, jagged mountain reaches spiking up to the sky. Crossroads are symbolic for the fae, and in the Real they tend to be either places of safety, where inns are pitched and travellers seeking haven can rest in peace, *or* places where great idiocies are committed ... pacts with witches, demons and suchlike ... as they draw those kith and kin you mortals slap together under the term "supernatural" like flies to a corpse. Nothing super about most of them, by the way, unless it's their super abilities to mess with mortals and cause us hardworking lycans extra headache. Me, having a moan? Well, maybe a little one.

Anyhow, back to the Tourney.

Rising from the centre of the four roads, taking up what our neighbours from across the pond might describe as a whole "block", a huge wooden structure filled the Real air. Flags and pennants adorned the curving walls, along with massive bones and what looked like a goodly number of broken weapons and armour. Probably the leavings from past disputes, on display to remind immortals of past jollies or something tasteless like that. There were turrets fitted atop ever tower, and massive gates jutted from the stained wooden walls, allowing the flow of all manner of creatures in and out.

All in all, the thing looked a lot like a medieval version of the Coliseum in Rome, if it had been designed by some mad barbarian in love with gothic style done in scarred wood. There were hints of olde England castles to the structure, and even a nod to the Disney Castle if you looked hard enough. Not ones to miss a trick, the fae, nor feel overly bad at stealing another's design.

It's not like Walt Disney was going to lodge a lawsuit for copyright.

Surrounding the edifice, a sea of brightly coloured tents and structures sat along curving paths made for passage around the main event. Some of these were tall and thin, swaying high above the populace, whilst others squatted like fat, brilliantly coloured fungi, spreading far and wide on every side. Poles sprang like spears above each tent, bedecked with flags and intricate script in a multitude of tongues. This being the Real, no immortal missed a chance to make a killing ... in a manner of speaking ... to sell on a wealth of junk and useless tat. There would be magical artefacts galore available for the taking, captured fae kin and other strange creatures from beyond the Courts, all available at bargain prices for their release, indentured servitude or for other more nefarious uses. Services to be provided, bodyguards to be hired, assassins contracted to resolve all manner of dispute.

Basically, think of any of the larger Asian markets you see in the travel programmes where it looks like pretty much everything is for sale ... then add in the fact, this being the Real, that *anything* is for sale. From our vantage point, I could see the flow of traffic around the huge sprawling marketplace. As ever, there was a truly startling variety of immortals out and about, obviously attracted by the Tourney and its standing amnesty throughout Beltane. I easily spotted Ivory and Shadow Court contingents by their ornate armour and long lances dancing with bright flames or swirling darkness, the ladies tall and thin and bedecked in flowing gowns of spun moonlight and dawn. Massive ogres knuckled their way through the crowds, bearing bundles and sacks of goods for whomever had contracted their services, whilst heavily clad dwarrow stumped through the gathering, ever-present clouds of sparks and soot filling the air above them as they carried portable forges on their backs or on wheeled carts. Fur and bone-clad goblins and kobolds, obviously of the Wyld Court, shrieked and cat-called through the crowds, bone spears waving dangerously in the air around them. Scintillating sprites and feathered serpents spun in lazy trails above the tents, harpies gathering on rickety struts to rain insults down on the passers-by below whilst thrusting out their naked chests for all to ogle.

All in all, it was a chaotic menagerie of both law and disorder, and the only thing that seemed missing from such a meeting of the Real were the screams or groans of those whose experiences were being terminally cut short. The Pact seemed to be holding true, as I could not taste any scent of blood and death in the air ... lots of pent-up aggression and the desire to commit murder, maybe, but no actual fulfilment of such wishes. It was almost too good to be true. Which, given the Real and the reason I was here, of course it was.

Our little company wended its way down towards the nearest edge of the great marketplace, and I quickly noted each road had been set with its own guard post and minor gates to allow or deny entry if the guards so wished. Given whoever drew the unlucky straw for watch-duty over the Tourney would face all manner of immortal fury if any breach of the Pact was allowed, I was unsurprised to see the soldiers manning the gate were of no Court, of no kith and kin themselves. Just like me and mine, they were outside the intrigue and politics of the Shadow and Ivory, even the Wyld.

Towering statues of gilded bronze and steel, the soldiers were all Golem. Powerful spirits bound into the substance of the intricately crafted figurines. Something akin to the creature Terrigylle had used to keep watch on his front door back in the mortal Realm, these were the super-hero and over-powered cousins of that simplistic gargoyle. Enchanted to be uncharmable and immune to any and all poisons, the golem soldiers had the rules of the Tourney enscribed into their very bodies so that they obeyed and enforced each and every restriction to the letter. Judge, jury and executioner, they were what must have been envisaged by the makers of Robo-Cop without the fleshy and vulnerable mortal bits. Given that the types of creatures attempting to break a rule here would be scary-powerful at the very least, it probably helped that each golem had a miniature sun contained in its chest that could be used in a variety of ways to turn offenders into smoking piles of ash.

Small details like that make all the difference.

The nearest golem stepped forward as we reached the guard post, raising one muscle-wrought arm and placing its palm out in an utterly unneeded gesture of denial.

"Halt. Visitors to the Beltane Tournament must surrender their birth names and intentions before they may enter the grounds." The golem grated as fire blazed up around that hand in an inferno to make Iron Man throw in the towel out of jealousy. "Deceit will not be permitted."

"The Lady Morrigan Na CrobDerg and her guards seek entry to the Beltane Tourney, escorting Morgan Black of the

Walker Pack, to serve the Lady Madb Na Cruam Crough Si as
Knight and Herald. Our intentions are simply to serve the Queen
of Shadows, and seek to thwart any that would do her harm.
Does that suffice, guardian?"

The flames roared around the golem's hand for a moment,
then dimmed and died as it lowered its arm.

"I detect no deceit in your words, Lady. Pass and fulfil
your service but remain within the rules of the Tournament at all
times." It grated, as its fellow golem reached down and pulled the
gates apart, unblocking the roadway. I nodded to the metal statue
as I passed, one law-keeper to another, but its cold face bore no
expression nor did it respond in kind.

The Morrigan beckoned me on, and we made our way into
the throng. I was used to the chaos that came with such immortal
gatherings, and prepared myself for the 'joy' that any mortal
knows if they travel on the London Underground at rush hour
but I hadn't factored the effect having the Mistress of Battle as
my personal guide would have.

Her warriors worked the crowds like professional Secret
Service personnel, their spears and swords turned so as not to
cause injury but to ward off anyone getting too close ... but that
wasn't a problem when the Morrigan herself seemed to need only
stare in anyone's direction and they melted back and away. I saw
massive ogres towering overhead cringe and bow and back off
like naughty children under that withering gaze, saw armoured
knights backpedal and duck out of the way as they caught sight of
our entourage heading in their direction. All in all, I was
beginning to feel a little useless as we approached the main gates
and the outer wall towering high overhead.

The gates to the massive wooden fortress stood wide open,
manned with more gold and bronze guardians. We went through
the ritual questioning once again, it seeming not enough that we'd
been cleared for entry by the last lot of impervious and

unbribable guardians, with the Morrigan swearing we were not up to anything devious or plotting to breach the rules of the club. Given how devious, sneaky and downright untrustworthy goes hand in hand with most fae, I did wonder at the seeming trust these golem put in simple spoken words. Me, I would have required a lie-detector test for each and every one of the sneaky bastards, not that it would do much good. Fae lie as easily as draw breath.

The golem once again let us through but this time helpfully provided directions to where the Shadow Court was in residence. Wisely, it seemed the two Courts were being well apart ... this being neutral ground notwithstanding, this apparently was not enough for the organisers to trust everyone would play fair. Or be able to resist the urge to stick a knife somewhere unpleasant. Whomever the planners were, they were obviously less gullible than their gate guards.

Once through the massive wall, I found the fortress was built around one huge open arena, sand floored and studded with massive wooden stakes to deter anyone inside from reaching the tiers set above. Rings of seating ran around the entire enclosure, rising up high to give unparalleled views over the arena floor, with some boxes and throne-like structures sat apart from the more basic bench offering. Obviously the VIP immortals got some measure of luxury for their viewing pleasure.

Sections had been penned off, access to each restricted behind striped rope and bunting. Huge draping flags denoted which House or Company or simply which immortal was in residence, with by far the richest and grandest sections being held for Ivory and Shadow, almost opposite each other across from the sandy arena floor. There were other, smaller enclaves that I quickly eyeballed as we passed, the most obvious being for the Wyld. Matted furs hung from hunting spears whilst bones were strung like festive baubles between the poles, from just about anything that could or had ever been Hunted. I wasn't surprised to recognise more than a few mortal bones hung amongst the gory decorations ... there was a long and bloody history of the Hunt chasing down ne'er-do-wells before the Accords prohibited Herne from having his fun in the realm unless authorised by the Courts. Mortals had a lot less issue with over-crowding in prisons back in the day, just saying.

Dutifully following the Morrigan, we wended our way away from the main thoroughfare already filled with immortals of every shape and size. Heading up several flights of stairs, we passed by a band of inquisitive satyrs who were obviously touting for bets but shied away as soon as they recognised the Shadow fae, and barged through the few earlycomers meandering aimlessly on their way to their seats.

As we approached their section, my senses lit up with the now familiar sense of the Court of Shadow, ice-cold fire sparking from the rune grafted to my skin and shooting though my body like a blast of artic frost. Looking up, I found the surroundings rather unsubtlety altered to be a home from home for the Shadow fae. Long shards of ice decorated spears of twisted ruin, banners of rippling grey and black rippling in an unseen breeze. Knights in hues of bruise-blue and bone-ash leant on curved halberds decorated with far too many spiky edges, eyes of bloody hue blazing from within crafted helmets of grinning skulls.

The Morrigan did not bother stopping, her Crows simply lifting the roped-bone barrier and darting inside as the dark fae guards banged their weapons on metallic bracers, creating a doleful boom that in no way cheered me for being on their team. I caught more than one distrustful glance as I followed their Herald of Shadow, but using all my tact and diplomacy, I simply grinned and made a few bows to the more butch-looking guards. It wasn't like I was here to make friends, and if they weren't tough enough to be promoted to Knighthood in their own Court, I was happy to rub their pointy noses in it a little.

Madb had bedecked her quarters for the Tourney in true fae fashion ... heavy on the gruesome and brooding. Canopies woven of twisted shadows hung overhead that billowed and shifted of their own accord, held aloft by long spars of twisted ice. Her Court milled around an area cleared of seating, almost large enough to call a ballroom if anyone had been of a mind to dance. I took in the spectacle of Shadow fae in all their finery mixing with dark skinned dwarrow kitted out in enough metal and leather to keep the smallest spot of sunlight from their sensitive skin.

Interesting fact. Unlike trolls and their gnome cousins, dwarrow don't turn to stone if touched by sunlight. For some wholly illogical reason, they metamorphosis into, of all things ... toads. Big, warty, long tongued toads. The sort you see mortal television presenters handling with mock disgust on Nature programmes, the ones with far too much intelligence in their bulbous eyes. So if ever you come across a stranded toad that looks particularly pissed off, I'd suggest giving it a wide birth just on the off chance it's a dwarrow in a foul mood at being caught out in the sun. If you think frogs peeing on your hand is bad, you *really* don't want to know what one of those buggers will do if you catch their attention.

So besides grouchy dwarrow and wisp-wrapped fae, there was the usual assortment of goblin-kin, gnomes, trolls and the odd lurking ogre. I spotted witch-kin, the black-skinned Annis and green haired Jennies who haunt the waterways to lure unsuspecting mortals to their deaths, and their goat legged cousins, the glaistigs. Nasty ones, those, preying on mortal men with glamour who only saw beautiful women up for a dance and frolic ... until reality bites, as well as the glaistigs as they fed off the mortal's blood whilst in the throes of passion. I'd had a few cases in some of the more dinghy nightclubs and hotels in London a few years back, made all the more easy for the predators given the drugged-up state of their prey. To this day I'm not sure what was more troubling to the victims, that their dance partner was sucking on their blood or the sight of those hairy hooved goat legs wrapped around them.

Anyhow, amongst the assortment of nightmares, I caught sight of a few regular looking folk, wrapped in long coats, obviously bearing weapons and keeping to themselves. Bounty hunters wearing warded leathers and probably toting enough tools to take on a small country. Lycans and hunters sometimes partner on Accord-breaker cases, using the simple logic that more hands make light the work, and the simple truth that having a bunch of crazed mercs chasing one's ass often made the runner panic and walk right into a patient lycan's waiting fist. I gave the nearest a nod, and received a tip of a broad-brimmed hat in response. A gesture between equals, at least from their viewpoint.

Madb herself was a thunderous presence overlaying all of the immortals in her Court, lurking amongst the deepest shade atop a throne crafted of ... yes, again with the decorative style and taste of a brick ... yellowed bones. I'd last seen something similar acting as a seat for the once Lady of the Lake, and hadn't been all that impressed then. The fact that Madb's one was even creepier, with the skulls actually animated and moaning softly in concert, only made me twitch that little bit more.

Clad in rags and twisted cloth, no hint of royalty about her, the little girl with the long black hair slowly raised her head at our approach. Dreadlocks of violet, ice-blue and murky green adorned her pale head, entwined with small bones and silver trinkets, and she had added intricate tattoos of black ink that made her cheekbones even more stark, her eyes even more sunken amidst the writhing black veins under her skin. The blue of her lips was the perfect shade of a hundred drowned souls, and her skin was the marble white of the recently dead, glowing almost with un-life.

But it was her eyes that once again stopped me dead in my tracks, those blazing orbs of ebony fire lit with all the intensity of Hell itself. That time I'd met her in the forest of ice, when a bunch of mostly-mortal knights were tricked into mounting a crusade to cleanse the darkness of the place ... oh and dispose of me in the bargain so I didn't go on and frustrate a crazed immortal's plan of revenge ... I'd seen the little girl let loose the merest shred of anger on the poor bastards, and those eyes of flame had run with such power and unholy might, it had left me wanting to keep as far as possible from the Queen of the Shadow Court.

And yet, here I was. A newly knighted member of her Court and summoned to defend her honour. Life truly has a shit sense of humour at times, I keep being reminded.

Madb cocked her head at our approach and a thin smile split those oxygen-starved lips. She clapped her hands once and once only, but the sound cut through the babble of conversation like a red-hot knife through butter. En-masse, every member of the Court and those others attending turned, and I found myself the subject of the *entire* gathering's undivided attention as the Morrigan led us forward, stopping at the foot of the Queen's throne.

"I welcome my herald's return to our Court, and rejoice in her companion, our newly joined Knight of Shadows. I greet you, Morgan Black, on this day of discord and strife. I trust you are well rested for the coming challenge?" Madb asked, one ebony clad finger scratching a thin line on the bone of someone's skull. It moaned in response.

"Can't complain." I answered glibly, but bit back any further sarcasm at the quiet but still easily-heard sigh from my companion. A simple shake of her head spoke volumes, but hell,

I wasn't here to have fun and make merry. I'd been shoehorned into fighting a battle against who knows what, right when I should be finding Felix and beating the living shit outta whomever had kidnapped her. Be disappointed in me all you like, I wanted to growl, but decided that baiting the immortal Queen any further probably wasn't in my best interest.

"Indeed." Madb proved her royalty by simply ignoring my glibness as if it had never existed, and instead looked across at the Morrigan. "Is our champion suitably prepared for the coming trial?"

"If he should bend his efforts to surviving the challenge, instead of wasting them on useless cleverness, I have no doubt he will prove worthy my Queen." The Morrigan answered dryly. "If wit were a weapon, I'd be suggesting unarmed combat be his strength. Thankfully, I doubt much he will have to talk his opponent to death."

Further discussion and observations on my obvious shortcomings were cut short as the clear sound of a horn cut through the air. Again it blasted, a doleful wail that echoed with odd timbres, making me grit my teeth against the vibrations.

"Ah, your arrival is most timely, champion. Our challenger is soon to join us. Best we not let them tarry too long, to make whatever mad claim of disgruntlement they have towards us." Madb pushed herself off her throne and stepped down the long-bone stairs to join us. Incongruously, she then lifted one waif thin arm and linked it with my own, looking up at me with a chilling smile.

"Lead on, champion. Let none delay us this fateful meet."

Feeling wholly off-balance, with the Queen of the Shadow Court curled into my arm like a child being taken for a walk, I looked across at the Morrigan. Who simply smiled coldly and stepped ahead, crunching her staff down with every step so that the thuds resounded like a drumbeat.

Behind, the Court filed in behind us in total silence as I and Madb walked slowly out and towards whatever waited in the arena below.

Chapter 13

Wizards as seen in Harry Potter or Lord of the Rings or any such popular mortal fantasy don't actually exist. A male witch is a warlock, and there is no requirement for long beards, wands, or any of the paraphernalia commonly thought to be needful for this profession. Instead, most warlocks tend towards the run of the mill, next door neighbour types with above average incomes to afford the private sanctum and steady supply of candles, ink and scribing tools to summon powerful entities and make deals with them.

The seating around the arena had filled up in the short time I'd spent with the Shadow Court, filling the air with the roar and thrum of hundreds if not thousands of spectators pumped for the big event. For all that this was a direct challenge to the Courts' rule, and something I guessed didn't happen often, the locals were definitely making a celebration of it ... with raucous laughter filling the air, hoots and howls mingling with more recognisable cries of enjoyment. Minor cantrips sent sparkling rockets into the air like fireworks to burst in showers of green and gold, chasing small sprites who yelled abuse back at those hurling the spelled explosives.

I caught sight of those satyrs from before working their way through the crowds, ticket stubs held in fists and small pencils gripped between their teeth as they scribbled down what I could only guess were bets for the coming match, giving Gods knew what odds.

The Morrigan led the Shadow Court contingent down a wide concourse, Real denizens bowing on all sides as I and Madb passed by, arm in arm. Fae soldiers in black enamelled armour waited ahead, long spears crossed to block the path, but these lifted as the herald strode towards them. The Shadow Court "box" was our destination, another ghastly affair bedecked with skulls and ice, shadow-strewn and lit by torches of blue and green flame. Looking out across the arena, I immediately saw the Ivory Court sat squarely opposite, red flames curling up into the air like writhing serpents whilst the guards shone in armour of silver and gold. Oberon and Titania were already seated on twin thrones, lounging out with their usual self-assured smugness.

We stopped just beyond the line of fae guards, and Madb slipped her skinny arm free, facing me.

"Now, champion, take thee down to the sands, and await our challenger. Prepare for ... *anything*." The Queen of Shadow told me bluntly, eyes dancing with ebony fire as she twisted formality with her words. "As no doubt my herald hath warned you, we are blind to the threat facing us this day, and for that to be so, bespeaks someone of Power assuredly be involved."

"Power as in *Court* power? You think someone in your own backyard is making a play here?" I asked, hating the fact I was going into this so blind. "And isn't someone going to explain the rules to me? Just so, oh I don't know, I don't go breaking them by accident?"

Madb deigned not to reply, instead turning her back on me and stalking off towards her own throne-like seat. Instead, the Morrigan stepped into view, braids clanking as she gave me a light but firm tap on the cheek to draw my attention. Obviously the Queen had said her piece and talking to the poor stupid lycan had worn her out so much, she needed to go rest her backside and recover.

"You know already my Queen distrusts her cousins, that we had placed a watcher in their Court to seek answers to her ... *concerns*." The Morrigan told me softly as she steered me toward a long flight of stairs. They were of the sort to instantly make me watchful of my step, knowing the last thing I wanted was to bounce down them and land in front of all the gathered fae on my ass.

"Yeah, and he ended up dead in the sewers, made to look he'd died in a fight with a lycan. I remember that, oddly enough. Still doesn't make sense." I whispered back, thinking of a dead weasely lycan and the disguised Shadow Knight, known to the Ivory Court as Sir Jasper Ne Cu Boireann or the Crying Knight.

"Before his untimely demise, our source reported trouble in the Ivory, murmurs of discontent and whispered betrayals. His presence with the wolf who transported the portal key to the mortal realm for the Lady is troublesome, for he would not have involved himself in its hunt without the say-so of my Queen." The Morrigan admitted in a hushed voice. She needn't have bothered … the noise from the crowds all around had ramped up a notch so that the air thundered, but there was always the chance someone would try to eavesdrop using non-traditional methods. In the Real, the meaning of "the walls have ears" is entirely different and ever creepier.

"But that matter is for another time. For now, you have asked the rules of the tourney. Sir Pup, they are simple. The challenger shall utter their lists of complaints before the Courts, to be witnessed by all gathered here. My Queen, our cousins of Ivory and Lord Herne may offer any restitution if they do desire but unless these are accepted, then the challenger passes the baton to their champions, and thee and thine companions shall decide by might of combat the victor this day. The tourney is to first blood, not death … my Queen does not desire to spend her newly made Knight needlessly."

"Ok, so just to confirm? The idiot with the issue gets to air their beef, the Courts try to bribe them to shut up and fuck off … which am guessing usually fails, call it a hunch. Then me and whatever fools also volunteered for this farce get to hit the other guys until they bleed, and we all go home happy. That about right?"

The Morrigan shot me that wintry look I was coming to expect whenever I tried even a little wit and shook her dark braids so that the charms clashed softly together.

"A child's explanation of what passes here, but I would be foolish to expect anything more. Someone wishes the nature of this challenger to remain hidden from the Courts, and has worked complicated magics to befuddle and confuse our seers. That alone should warn you this be no simple brawl. Expect trickery and treachery, and you will not be disappointed. Now, hurry to the sands before any think Shadow are afeared to stand against the challenge."

Thus dismissed, my guide turned on her heel and headed for her Queen's side.

I growled out a quiet curse and did a last check of my armament. Along with the various cold iron weapons that were good for all manner of beasties this side of the Veil, I had vials and samples of helpful herbs and substances known to affect a wide variety of nasties in truly awful ways. Anything to give a poor lycan the upper hand when dealing with whatever mug we were chasing. Much of the kit had been cobbled together through trial and error after encounters hunting down Accord breakers, and were the result of blood spilled and the desire *not* to repeat that again. At least if it was our blood.

Feeling anything but reassured, I started down the long flight of stairs leading to the arena floor.

On all sides, goblins and hobs leaned over the rail and cat-called down to me, some obviously cheering me on whilst others definitely less than complimentary. I sidestepped a spilled tankard of foul-smelling alcohol poured by one truly ugly mother of a hob, and made a mental note to look the bastard up later.

Flowers rained down on me, wreathes hitting the wooden stairs in multi-coloured streams like venomous snakes, and horns blared in a cacophony of wailing tunes that filled the air above me like a bunch of kids given the sort of musical instruments hidden in Christmas crackers, and no-one to tell them to keep quiet.

I reached the end of the stairs having run the gauntlet of half-drunk Real spectators, only slightly beer-stained and flower bedecked. I nudged a spray of black something-or other from my shoulder, and stepped onto the sand, feeling it crunch under my foot with a satisfying solidity. Nothing like good dirt beneath one's feet to help in a fight.

The huge arena stood empty around me except for one lone figure, who waited at the centre exact. Clad in bright plate armour of shining gold and vivid crimson, the knight stood comfortably and patiently at ease, despite the chaos echoing around above us. One mailed hand held an ornate, vicious looking lance with the pennant of Ivory snapping in the breeze, whilst the other rested casually on the hilt of a massive sword sheathed at its waist. The helmet, a crafted dragon with a raised crest and gaping jaws, slowly turned to face my way as I approached and I caught the glitter of embers blazing to life as the knight looked me over casually.

"So, I'm guessing you're the lucky champion for Obie and Tits, huh?" I broke the icy with my usual grace, grinning as I nodded up to the Ivory Court enclosure. "What did you do to deserve this shit-stick of a job?"

For a long moment the Ivory champion remained silent, then the hand on its sword hilt lifted and pressed something alongside the helmet's side. Metal shimmered and folded back, revealing a woman eyeing me with wry amusement. Locks of ginger-fire framed her angular fox-features, and her jade eyes danced with fire and acid mirth.

Bollocks, and didn't I just know this particular warrioress, from my last little jaunt into the Real.

"You ask what I did to deserve this *honour*?" She answered back to me, and nodded in my direction. "I let my idiot-brother be framed for the loss of one of the most powerful artefacts our Court keeps watch over, and I let a smart assed wolf-boy cause chaos before my Lord and Lady when he came asking questions."

Manisha Na Pendragon Cie, Artur Pendragon's sister. Guard captain who had greeted the Morrigan and I when we went seeking answers about the loss of Excalibur. And a fae who I knew wanted to discuss some of my less than smart comments over crossed swords when we found the time. The Ivory captain had magically bugged me to track her errant brother and almost caused an Accord incident when she blew up a fair chunk of one of our safe houses in her efforts to claim him.

"*You're* the Ivory champion?" I asked the obvious and totally stupid question, but Manisha just grinned mockingly and bowed.

"In the flesh, knight of Shadow. I'm gratified to see our cousin's choice is as *suspect* as ever, and their grasp on matters of seeming grave import is that of an enfeebled geriatric. The fact they chose you to represent them in this matter speaks volumes."

"You know, a guy could take that sort of thing personally. Anyone would think you didn't like me." I quipped back as I slid my shortsword free and tested its edge against one meaty thumb. Reassuringly sharp, but less reassuring was the numbness from the small cut. "Got any idea what the fuck we're likely to face?"

Manisha shrugged, adjusting her helmet so that it slid smoothly back over her features.

"I've yet to meet our Wyld companion, and have been told little more than a challenger comes forward to contest my Lord and Lady's right to rule the Court." The Ivory Knight sighed.

"The whole debacle reeks of madness, but now I know you are involved, that at least meets my lowest expectation."

"Gee thanks." I'd hoped for something, anything to give me a clue as to what we faced, but that of course was asking for too much. "Oh, I've met our friendly neighbourhood Wyld beastie and ... well, let's just say ..."

"Indeed, Pup. Let's just say *exactly* what?" Empty air spoke up with dripping tones of sarcasm, as glittering motes swirled around the pair of us. Manisha instantly went en-guard, spear lowering and pointing at the shifting light show, whilst I just grounded my sword and leant on it. I'd felt ... *something*, a tickling of my senses that wasn't alarm or danger but something blurring between the two. Either I was getting better at picking up on the clever bastard, or he hadn't been trying too hard to conceal himself.

The Bayun Cat shimmered into existence; twisting round like it had no bones, grinning that evil smile right back at me. Far too many fangs for a Disney appearance, this Cheshire Cat would have devoured Alice for a light snack.

"Let's just say ... he's at least a little psychotic, and having only met him once, I seriously doubt he's altogether sane." I finished, smiling back at the Wyld champion. Hell if I was going to back down.

"Ah, belligerent honesty. I do so prefer it to bald faced lies." The Bayun yawned, showing off more of those vicious teeth. "Tastes all the sweeter going down."

Manisha ground her spear into the sand and gave a grunt of dissatisfaction. Resigned acceptance, more like ... the usual sound heard from the female of the species across the ages when two males square off.

"Boys, boys. Let your discourse be set aside for now. I believe our quarry approaches."

The gates opposite us slowly ground open with a creaking groan straight out of any halfway good horror movie with big budget special effects. Silence rippled around the arena, the yattering chatter and drunken cries from the audience stilled as the two massive doors slowed and stopped.

For a long moment, the silence hung heavy in the air, as I let a growl fill my throat and brought my sword up. Ready to lay down the hurt. Manisha stepped up beside me, setting her long spear alongside my weapon, and gave me a short nod.

Finally, a slow thud echoed from the darkness, and forms shimmered slowly into view. Two abreast, massive and all too familiar. The golem strode out into the arena, massive swords resting over their shoulders and marching in time with each other. Two, four, eight of the metal statues ranged out, keeping pace with the one who shuffled along in the middle of their number. This one stood out like a sore thumb, tiny compared to its guards, wrapped in rags and lurching along with broken steps. Long hair the colour of ash fell loose from within a patched and threadbare hood, hiding any features as the figure hunched over. Its breathing rasped loud and slow in the air of the Real.

The golem slowed their solemn gait until they ground to a halt, ranging out four on each side, leaving their prisoner standing alone in a circle on the sand. Swaying slightly on its own two feet, the figure waited as silence settled all around, heavy with expectation. For my part, I just kept my sword ready and let my eyes range around the arena. Surely this wasn't it ... one opponent who looked small enough that Elspeth could've taken them down with one hand. Natural-born doubting bastard I may be, but something rang very wrong with this scene.

Finally, the creature raised its head slowly, features still hidden by the ragged hood but within that shadow, pinpricks glared. Bright and fevered, raging with anger. I could feel it from all the way from where I stood, and the sense of danger notched up about twenty degrees.

"I ... I come to challenge. Challenge the despoilers. The ravagers. The betrayers. Those you call *Lords,* foul harridans you call *Ladies."* The creature's voice rasped in a sharp angry hiss, quiet enough so that it should have been lost in the large open space but somehow the words echoed round the arena. There was pain and venom in those words, my lycan senses picking up the timbre in the challenger's voice. And loss. Buckets of the stuff.

It's not difficult ... imagine how it sounds when a woman you know tells you that *nothing is wrong.* That sort of undertone but amplified.

High up and to my left, Lord Oberon slowly rose from his throne and stalked down to stand at the gold balustrade, flanked by guards of flame and ivory. His lion-like mane of hair hung down over massive shoulders, and today he was arrayed like some emperor of old, in armour moulded to follow his inhuman musculature. A wrap of ivory cloth finished the ensemble, as the ruler of Ivory Court laid his broad hands on the gilt barrier and glared down.

"Who dares call my Lady such things? Who dares throw such a spurious challenge at our feet, at my cousin's feet, without revealing themselves? What manner of craven creature are you, to utter vile lies and bitter claims yet cling to the shadows in so cowardly a manner?" Oberon paused a moment, and looked directly across to where Madb waited, shrugging his shoulders and grinning ruefully. "No offense meant, cousin."

On her throne of bare bones, Madb smiled sweetly, dark veins shifting like snakes under her skin.

"None taken, cousin. This is no thing of mine. Not a child of the shadow. I too desire to know the identity of the one standing below, casting such accusations at us on this day." Madb stepped lightly down to match Oberon across the way, shadows oozing and flowing around her as she peered intently down. "Show yourself, so we may know of your nature ... if we are to hear any more of your words. Otherwise begone back to the hole from whence you came."

The figure shivered, shrinking down under the withering attention of two of the most powerful immortals in the Real. Then, finding some inner strength, it slowly straightened with the break and crunch of joints unknotting. Hands slipped from ragged sleeves, and fingers slowly grasped the stained hood before inching it back.

"Lies? You say I speak *lies*?" The creature rasped, as it pushed it's hood down. "Look on me and know the *truth*!"

Revealed, I was surprised to see the thing standing before was ... well ... it was an elf, one of the fae, but unlike any I'd seen before. It was emaciated to the point that its bones pressed tightly against skin the colour of ash. Not like the vibrant Shadow fae I'd seen, this thing's skin was dull and chalky, and it looked about as brittle as a twig. Its face was gaunt, jawbone tightly stretched with tendons, whilst its eyes were massive within their sockets and lit with that fire I'd noted. Its sparse hair adorned a scarred and knobbled skull, but what strands remained were silver in colour and fixed with glittering charms. The figure stepped out of its tattered robe, revealing a body just as thin as its features, with its ribcage bowing out beneath taught skin. A ragged strip of cloth gave the thing what little dignity remained, hanging off sharply defined hip bones, and its legs were bowed and bent.

Two things struck me as I looked at the wasted, gaunt figure opposite us.

First, the creature bore chains and manacles, rune scribed and weighted to hamper its movements. Hence the shuffling gait and bent-form under the heaviness of its bonds. The skin around the manacles was scarred and rough, and I guessed it had been wearing the chains for long enough to carve a deep mark into the prisoner's flesh. What little there was of it.

The second was its stench. Not the smell of imprisonment, the clinging odour and reek that came hand in hand with being locked up someplace without the base needs provided for waste removal. No, this was entirely different and wholly unexpected. It took me a moment to place the smell, so out of place was it here, in this place.

The reek of the Veil.

Somehow, this thing smelt of that hellish barrier between the mortal realm and the Real.

Revealed, the creature rose to stand as tall as it could whilst still hampered by the chains, glaring up and around the arena. Oberon glared back, silent but tight lipped, his expression suddenly closed. Behind the Lord of Ivory, Titania was a little less discreet, shock showing for a second on those gorgeous pin-up features before she hid away behind a fan.

Madb didn't bother trying to pretend she wasn't shocked, but after a moment of thought, that curving knife-thin smile split her dreadful features as she nodded to herself. Then she turned and walked back up to her throne, settling back down to watch even as one of her fae servants handed her a steaming cup.

"Speak on then, if you will." Were her only words.

A hiss came from beside me, and I snapped my attention back to find Manisha glaring at the challenger with almost human surprise, and more than a little shock. Given how used I'd gotten to fae keeping their real emotions under wrap, this struck me as a trifle odd. Worrying, even.

"What's the problem?" I whispered, as the prisoner slowly turned, taking in all those ranged above it. It raised its emaciated limbs, rattling the chains in an all too meaningful display.

The captain of the Ivory Court guard looked back at me, eyes narrowing, obviously fighting to get herself back under control. She nodded to the prisoner, drawing a short breath before letting it go like a sigh.

"There are rumours ... Whispers amongst my folk. But I had not thought ..." She spoke quietly, eyes fixed on the prisoners. I bit back on voicing my thoughts on just how frustrating that sort of half arsed answer was, instead simply growling out.

"Go on? What rumours?"

But it was the Bayun Cat who replied, sliding through the air like some psychotic furry shark swimming through water. It eyed me mockingly and gave me that all too wide smile.

"That there was a third family of the fae. One even older than the Ljósálfar and Dökkálfar. Another Court, dwellers in a distant land who yet were kith and kin to your Lord and Ladies now. Which once stood between Light and Shadow. That of ..."

"Twilight."

At its words, Manisha shuddered, jerking her attention away from the prisoner, shaking her head.

"Just childish stories we tell ourselves. There was no proof ..."

"Oh, dear child, I think the proof stands before you. And is more real than some simple campfire story." The Bayun yawned as it drifted around us, seemingly unconcerned at the swelling sense of threat filling the arena. Above us, Oberon's expression was now thunderous, and one hand reached out to point at the prisoner. High above, storm clouds swirled and birthed thunderheads which boomed with growling lightning, flashing through the darkening sky.

"Who has done this? What deceit is this?" Oberon snarled, leaning forward. "Take this ... *thing* away, before it utters any more lies. It has no place here!"

"No place? No place?" The Twilight fae shrieked, its own anger blazing out like an inferno to crackle over its wasted form, violet flames shimmering over its skin. "And why is that, oh mighty Oberon? Where is my place, the place of my people?"

The stench of the Veil grew stronger as the prisoner turned round slowly, manacled hands raised, eyes blazing with uncontrolled fury.

"You *took* my home from me. You killed my people by the hundreds and turned those that survived into *monsters*! You made of our home a wasteland of death and destruction. You failed to rule there, so you made it a place where *none* could live. You, oh *mighty Oberon*, you and your Lady, your cousins of Shadow. I carry the stench of my home with me forever, whilst you blithely pass to and fro through it with nary a single regret, any sign of the guilt you *all* bear."

The prisoner's shoulders slumped and his head bowed, as emotion choked his cracked tones.

"My home. Ivory stole the light which brightened my people's eyes, their dark cousin now rules the Shadows which were ours to command. Once a place of song and merriment, now my home is but a simple tool, used to ward the *mortals* of all peoples, to protect them from your poisoned touch. A place of ruin and woe, filled with the things you made from those I call kith and kin."

"My home."

Shit, I eloquently thought, as the creature's words sunk in. A place of death and destruction, filled with monsters, protecting the mortal Realm.

The bastard meant the Veil.

"Enough!! I demand you be silenced!" Oberon raged, slamming his hands down on the balustrade so hard that the wood and stone shattered, as lightning stabbed down from on high. Thunder roiled like the boom of a thousand cannons, as he stabbed his finger again at the prisoner. "Take him away! Throw him back into the hole he crawled from, and bring me the one who thought to taunt us with this one's vile tongue! Who so dares?!"

The golem facing our little group swung round and laid a massive hand down on the Twilight fae as if to action the Lord of Ivory's words. But instead of crumbling under the weight, the prisoner straightened and reached up to entwine its fingers around the massive metal hand. A bitter smile split those bloodless lips.

"And so, as you took from me and mine, so I will take from you. This Beltane, this day of truths, I lay challenge at the feet of the champions gathered here to decide who rules. Let your pitiful few fight to keep your shame and guilt buried. Mine will fight for retribution. And for the blood-debt owed my people."

The Veil stink surged up around the fae as he spoke, as grey smoke oozed from the prisoner's skin. It wrapped around the golem's fingers as they held his shoulder, tentacles of writhing smog lashing out to strike each of the other metal statues. The smoke writhed with some form of life, pulsing akin to a heartbeat, probing and testing their defences as the nearest golem clumsily scraped at the clinging murk. But its fingers simply shredded the stuff and passed right through without doing any seeming harm. The viscous smoke roiled then sank into the flexible joints and gaps in the metal gargantuan, the golem immediately beginning to shake as if suffering some sort of fit. Rasping groans slipped from the faceless mask, filled with metallic agony.

That was enough for me. I wasn't about to stand idly waiting for the shit to royally hit the fan. Slapping a hand on Manisha's shoulder, I sprang forward, sword raised and already swinging.

My own views on the right and wrong of whatever the fuck had happened to this particular fae didn't matter, at least not right now. I just needed this to be done and dusted, the whole stupidity dealt with so I could get back to things that mattered.

Short sighted, maybe, but the fae could argue till the end of times over what had or hadn't been done.

It wasn't my fight.

I covered the space between the fae and me in a single breath, aiming for the prisoner. Take him down, knock him unconscious if he'd let me, drop him if not ... Stop whatever crap he was trying. Simple plan, simple solution.

I have *got* to learn sometime.

Simple never, ever works with me.

Chapter 14

Now, us lycan are pretty quick when we want to be. Forget all the heavy muscle and bone we carry, the fact is we're no lightweights in any way. When we want to get somewhere, we get there fast.

Unfortunately, the fist made of fluid metal slamming into me pretty much ruined that plan.

Thrown through the air, I curled in on myself and rolled, somehow missing spiking myself on my own sword, to come to a stop spitting sand. Springing back to my feet, I faced off where the attack had come from, but reigned back my instinctive urge to go for the bastard's throat … only coz I'd probably end up spitting teeth if I tried.

The golem kept its arm cocked and ready for another punch, greyness bleeding over the metal like oil over water. Where before an inferno had raged in its eye sockets, now a sickly flame roiled, grey and tainted, and its fist bled the same inferno. Veins of the grey infection ran through its once-shining metal body, pulsing and writhing with unnatural life.

Nope, the bastard was no longer in charge of itself, and definitely now a threat.

Risking a quick glance, I spat a curse seeing the seven other golem all similarly infected. Whatever the Twilight fae had done, the enchanted guardians were now under its command, lock, stock and smoking barrel. Which were pointed directly at the three of us. Happy days!

"Now! Now my family will be avenged with the blood of the betrayers!" The prisoner howled, pointing upwards to the Ivory and Shadow boxes. "Beat these champions into the dirt and bring me the heads of those false Lords and Ladies!"

Four of the golem strode forward, the one who had slapped me down and three of its brethren. The other four split into pairs, and each double started towards the arena walls. It seemed the prisoner wanted to cause as much carnage as possible, and wasn't waiting for the outcome of the challenge before getting in some good old-fashioned payback.

Cries and shouts filled the air, as the gathered host belatedly realised this was not part of the entertainment. Oberon was bellowing for his guards, as Titania joined him, grabbing his arm and attempting to drag him back and away. Ivory fae warriors slid between their Lord and Lady, forming up to face off against the oncoming golem, weapons raised and ready. Across the arena, I caught sight of Madb watching the outcome from behind a bristling wall of shadows, the Morrigan and her Crow guards already moving to protect their Queen alongside her own Knights. For now, everyone seemed to be taking things in their stride.

Leaving us, down in the arena, facing off against four maddened and possessed golem. Not *exactly* the kind of fight I'd wanted but it had been a long time since Santa brought me anything on my wish-list.

I strode back to where Manisha and the Bayun Cat still waited. Ignoring the Wyld champion's sardonic chuckle, I nodded toward our looming foes.

"Any suggestions?" I asked lightly, as the Ivory captain rolled her shoulders, spear held ready. "There some manual that comes with these things that tells you where the off-switch is?"

"Don't get killed?" She quipped back. "The golem are supposed proof against any and all enchantment, and most mortal weapons. Before this day, I would have said this be an impossibility."

"Ain't it nice to be proven wrong, just once in a while?" I couldn't help myself, earning myself a solid glare from the Ivory champion.

"If you two *children* are aiming to flirt much more, I will take myself away and let you mate in peace." The Bayun Cat drawled, earning an even more fierce glare from Manisha, and a single finger from me. "Whatever. If you would cast your attention to our foes, you will see they are not *exactly* themselves. Whatever has been done to them, it looks not to have done them much good. In fact, decidedly the opposite."

The Cat was right. Checking the golem over, I caught the faint shivers and shakes in all of the possessed statues, twitches that in anyone else I would have thought indicated severe mental problems. With them, it was more like they were fighting themselves, fighting for control. So maybe they weren't completely at the Twilight fae's beck and call. Still meant they could easily finish us, those big-arse swords wide enough to cut any of us in two, let alone their fists heavy enough to pulp us into the sand and who knew if they still had their innate powers to cook us where we stood. But they were slower, less indestructible.

Hell, if it was the only edge we got, I'd take it.

"If you will listen to good advice earned from many Hunts, I suggest we split them, keep them from coming at us together." The Bayun drawled. "I can … I believe the mortal phrase is *tank* them whilst you pick them off one at a time. It is how the Hunt is done, and has proven most *effective.*"

With that, the Wyld champion shimmered and flashed away, a streak of crackly fury that slammed like a bowling ball amongst the golem. Metal shrieked as those claws gouged jagged lines in their bodies, as the mighty metal guardians turned, swords lashing out with inhuman strength. But slow, far too slow to catch the Cat.

"Fuck it. You know, he's probably right." I shrugged, seeing the Ivory fae nod in reply. "Might as well see if the fuzzball's plan works. I haven't got any better ideas."

"Indeed. Also, I suggest our foes warrant your *full* strength." Manisha told me bluntly, without any real need. Herne knew I was here, knew what I was and the bastard didn't seem too keen on making me one of his hounds at the present moment. So, what the hell.

Full suit it was.

The Change ripped up through me, melting my bones, shifting my body as I let the beast out to play. My senses blazed with energy, sight, hearing, smell and taste lit with lightning. I could now *see* the energy wrapping the golems, see how it was actually alive, something from the Veil and as such poison to anything it touched. But also obvious were the cracks splitting the metal bodies, the shaking as they fought this vile intrusion. Might as well have painted arrows and "Hit me here" on the poor bastards.

Ivory and Shadow, champions both, we raced into the fight. Manisha's spear was a blurring shaft of roaring fire, batting aside the sweeping strikes the golem threw at her, point slamming again and again into the metal statues. I dove and rolled, following the trails of pulsing energy that each golem left, feeling their hammering blows a heartbeat before they happened from the sickened auras. A length of sharpened metal slammed down beside me as I rolled, kicking out and hammering the metal leg closest to me so that it buckled and gave with a screeching groan.

The golem roared, staggering and falling. One of its brethren surged to defend it, grey fire wreathing it as it threw itself at us both, but Manisha held it at bay with skilful thrusts of her lance. I wasn't going to waste the opportunity and rolled back over onto the fallen golem. It grabbed at me with its massive hands but I dodged and reared up, sword held like a big arsed knife.

The point slammed down between the grey fire pouring from its eyes, and I put all my lycan strength behind the blow. With a shriek, the point punched through and I twisted it as hard as I could. Smog and muck blasted up like a sickly geyser, spilling out of the golem as its frantic motions slowed. Stilled and stopped, the metal losing any glimmer of energy, slumping down into a cold lifeless statue without a head.

One down. Three to g...

I had that much time to think before I was hurled to one side, the blow catching me in the side and sending me sprawling again across the sand. The kick felt like a sledgehammer blow, pain burning as my ribs creaked but thankfully held.

Snarling, I dragged myself up, sword lost somewhere out of reach. Turning, I found two of the golem still engaged with trying to slap the Bayun Cat down as the psycho kitty howled and clawed between them. The third, the one Manisha was engaged with, had managed to grab her spear and as I watched, with one sweeping wrench it threw her across the arena to slam into the wall. Hard. Grey fire roared up and ate into the weapon, shattering it into pieces. It cast the fragments aside, sword rising and grey fire blazing up in its metal orbs as it looked for its next victim.

"Come get some." I growled out the words, my lycan jaw mangling them almost to incomprehensibility but I didn't care. I ripped out a pair of long knives, my claws curving over my clenched fists, and I threw myself at the golem. Time to pay back that kick.

The massive sword swept down, narrowly missing taking my legs off as I twisted and rolled. Following my senses as they led me on, I hammered at the thing's wrist where a junction of the grey veins were knotted. One knife bent and broke with a sharp retort, but the second cracked the metal shell, digging in deep. Whether the infused spirit within felt the pain from cold iron or not, its hand spasmed and the sword crashed to the sand with a resounding thud.

The golem howled, its undamaged hand slapping down at me to smear me all over the arena floor. Grey fire blazed and burned at me, so I snarled and dodged, forcing the scorching pain aside. I'd deal with it later, but for now, it just got in the way. Tossing my knife aside, my claws screeched as I pounded at the thing, feeling metal dent and buckle under my inhuman strength. The golem brought up its forearms together like a prize fighter in the ring, weathering the blows as I ripped at its possessed shell. All it needed do was wait me out, let me get tired, then ... splat goes the lycan.

Thankfully, that was only if it had been the two of us fighting. The golem focused fully on little ol' me, didn't sense Manisha's approach until the last minute, sand crunching under the Knight's booted charge. Spear gone, she'd unsheathed her equally large sword and now slammed this home in a savage strike. The golem, metal hide sliding to meet the new attack, raised one damaged arm, expecting an overhand strike. But Manisha was a skilled warrior, a survivor from many battlefields, and she read its counter and instead dipped low, slamming the point of her sword home through a crazed spread of cracks below its molten ribcage.

The statue howled and stumbled back from the force of the blow, dragging itself off the sword spitting it with a shriek of metal. Grey fire bled from the wound, but the golem somehow still snatched up its sword from the sand and heaved a blow at the Ivory champion, forcing her to either block or dodge.

This time she wasn't so smart, and went for the block.

The swords rang as they met, but the golem outweighed the fae many many times over with its simple mass, and physics won out. Manisha bellowed a curse out as her sword was slammed down into the sand, bones in her arms creaking almost to breaking point. A backhand blow came from nowhere, the golem flipping her head over heels to crash into the dirt, somehow still gripping her sword as she crunched down hard into the sand.

Roaring, the possessed statue reared up, foot raised and towering over the fallen Ivory Knight's head. All that weight concentrated in one single stomp ... the fae would be pancaked to a smear before she even knew what hit her.

Enter stage left, lil' ol me again.

Throwing myself across the sand, I grabbed that raised foot and bellowed, roaring with all my savage might as I heaved against the golem. Grey fire and poison ripped at me, so I cursed and spat at the pain, but I focused on one thing and pushed all else aside, keeping the bastard off balance. The golem tottered, trying to swing its sword at me but I spun the bastard, keeping it moving until I got the proper leverage. Then I gritted my fangs and threw my considerable muscle behind one heave, spine crunching in protest, those muscles of mine shrieking with agony. The golem gave a forlorn groan as it was lifted up and hurled from its feet, sailing through the air to slam back into the arena wall and the nearest massive spike. Metal shrieked as the point punched through, shattering its chest and letting grey murk spill free as the statue jerked and writhed on its impalement.

"Behind you!" The Ivory fae's voice rang out in warning.

I spun to find one of the remaining golem towering over me, sword raised to strike. I hadn't heard the big bastard approach, and for that one second, didn't know what the fuck to do as the keen edge slammed down on me like end of the world.

Game over for lil' ol me.

Chapter 15

Except … the Bayun Cat saved me.

Man, I was never going to hear that end of that.

Like a growling thunderbolt, the Wyld champion appeared between the golem and me, its claws carving through the metal of the possessed guard with a shrieking howl. Both wrists shattered under the assault, the sword slamming down to land point first beside me, as the golem staggered back, grey fire and murk gushing from the broken limbs.

The Wyld champion looked at me with those bright, fever-fire eyes, and smiled widely.

"Do I need to clean up for you as well, little pup? Mayhap attire you in a new diaper if you have soiled yourself just now?" It snarled, as it shifted through the air and sped off again.

"Fucker." I snarled, throwing myself at the damaged golem even as grey fire and muck bled from the wounds and reformed into rough digits like the ones it had lost. I slapped those burning fingers aside and hammered my claws into the thing's face, ripping it's scratched and riven metal features until the metal gave under my blows and the golem collapsed under me, pumping grey smoke like blood.

One last golem was on its feet, but so badly torn from the Bayun Cat's attack that it lurched and groaned with every move it made. Metal shrieked, one arm torn almost completely free, the other lashing out in drunken blows the Wyld champion easily slipped past like … well, smoke.

Seeing the Cat happily playing with its victim, I spun round at the shriek of metal and a slow fading groan, to find Manisha standing beside the golem I'd felled, sword embedded deep in its head. Metal had exploded out amongst the shreds of smoke and fire, and the statue lay still and silent now. She nodded down to the fallen foe, as she jerked her sword free.

"Know you not the simple truth - never leave an enemy alive at your back, no matter how damaged you think they are?" She asked me bluntly. "Finish it. Or die."

"Thanks, mom!" I growled, knowing a lecture when I heard one.

A final crash signalled the end of the last golem as it splintered and fell under the Bayun Cat's violent assault. Grey fire writhed across the sand, sucked back into the Twilight fae as the prisoner writhed in the grip of whatever sorcery it had conjured. It glared across at us, heaving great breaths, tendons creaking as its jaw worked but no words came.

Leaving the challenger to glare all he liked for a moment, I checked on the state of play around us.

The other possessed golem had mounted the walls of the arena using those handy spikes as ladders, a pair each heading for the Ivory and Shadow enclaves. Bodies strewn around them gave testament to their desire to reach their targets, but as we'd found, whatever the Twilight fae had done had severely weakened them.

On the Ivory side, fire lashed the two statues whilst armoured fae darted in to hammer and strike at their foes. Cracks all over the golem bodies showed from the damage they were taking, and they had ground to a halt halfway up the stairway, blackened and fire-crazed.

On the other side, where Madb waited, shadows had risen like a mass of sharpened spikes which lashed out at the golem, spearing through them with inhuman strength. Crow guards and Shadow Knights darted amongst the shifting gloom, halberds chewing into the weakened metal, leaving one golem already down and its brother partially dismembered under their assault.

All in all, the two Courts seemed to have things well in hand, or at least enough for me not to be unduly bothered. So I turned back to face the prisoner, even as I let the Change take me. Talking with a mouthful of fangs and beast's head just isn't a great option for a two-way conversation, and the danger was obviously passed.

"Looks like that's about it. You tried, you lost." I offered the fae a shrug, toeing a piece of shattered golem in the sand aside. "I reckon you'd better prepare your ass to be slung right back to whatever hellhole you crawled from. No offense, but if you could give me the name of who was behind this little farce, I'd really appreciate closing the loop."

The fae gave a cackling laugh, made all the worse as it shook the creature's emaciated body.

"This? You think I cared if you beat these mindless automatons?" The fae shook in the grip of its own anger, foam dripping from its cracked lips, eyes blazing with the strength of its rage. "They were nothing."

It snarled a laugh.

"Just the diversion."

Oh fuck.

Chapter 16

The Twilight fae was shaking even harder, as the stench of the Veil thickened around us. I looked over at Manisha, who shrugged and hefted her sword into a guard stance, taking a step toward the challenger. Looked like we still had one final fight to complete, before we closed the book on today … and I voted burning the bloody thing.

Grey fire and muck flared up around the fae, darkening and roiling into a viscous smog as more thunder split the heavens. Out of the fog, a tentacle … a frikkin' tentacle … lashed out and slammed into the Ivory champion, tossing her aside like a leaf in a gale. The Twilight fae cackled, arms raised and thin strands of hair streaming in the sudden howling maelstrom.

A storm ripped right from the Veil.

The fucker was opening a Way, a rip in the Real but not leading to the mortal realm this time. This was just a passage straight into the Veil itself, opening for the horrors which lurked in the barrier between realms. And he meant to let them loose right into our laps, the bastard.

Manisha had rolled to her feet, bounding back with sword raised high. The Bayun Cat twisted through the air, jaws gaping far wider than should be possible, claws gleaming in the lash of lightning. And I bounded forward, my own fists raised as I focused intently on the centre of the boiling fog.

"I don't have bloody time for this!" I shouted as I crossed the sand … just as a forest of razor tipped tentacles burst out of the mucky smoke, lashing out everywhere. Something gave a bellowing roar, as the pillar of grey fire shot upwards, lashing the sky and ripping the air as the tear stretched and widened.

I dodged and rolled, ducked and weaved, slimy scaled limbs coming at me from every side. Manisha hewed about her with inhuman strength and speed, bits of the intruder's limbs splashing through the air, and for a moment the hidden creature focused on her.

Not one to miss an opportunity, I dived forward on the hard sandy floor, skidding under the flurry of writhing tentacular horror to find myself facing the Twilight fae. Its body was in the grip of its own summons, shaking and writhing as it fed whatever magic it was using with its own life, so that its skin grew ever more grey and desiccated. Blisters had already opened on much of its exposed flesh, weeping grey smoke as it howled its anger and pain.

"You've gotta stop this shit!" I shouted over the bellows of the beast and the shriek of the Veil, but the fae shook its head in violent negation.

"Never! This is my chance! I was freed for this one thing, swore I would make them pay, even if it cost me my life! They … you *all* must pay! The blood I spill here feeds those wretched monsters, all that are left of my people! And their hunger is *endless!*" It ranted, obviously lost in the grip of its own madness and sorrow.

Now, normally I'm open to seeing both sides of the argument, playing the devil's advocate, hearing everyone's view. Normally. But right now, Felix was locked up somewhere dark, all alone and terrified, and I'd promised to keep her safe. And this shit was keeping me from finding her.

Enough was enough.

"For fuck's sake! This ends now!" I bellowed in frustration as I searched my battered brain for a way to stop the mad bastard in his tracks. And it just so happened being a Knight of Shadow gave me a little something-something perfect for this. I'd used it to stop Terrigyle when the mad little fucker tried blowing us all up, and here I was again, another lunatic to deal with.

Awkwardly reaching inside myself, I searched for that weird thing, the feeling of bitter ice and glacial frost I'd been bestowed. My anger, my frustration, my simple desire to pound this bastard's head into the sand so I could go find Felix's kidnapper and put them down too. All of it, dumped into the freezing centre of shadow at my very core.

"Just bloody freeze!" I should, lashing out with my hand.

It felt like the magic or whatever it was stuttered like a waking engine, tried to spark to life but found itself blocked. Hell, I was no expert ... maybe I wasn't doing this right. There hadn't been a handbook I'd been given with the bloody thing, but I was too stubborn to quit. I threw everything I had into imagining the prisoner freezing in place, encased in ice and locked safely away. "For the love of ... Freeze, you bastard!!"

The magic lashed out, leaving me so suddenly I collapsed to my knees, almost ready to faint again. In the sand. Dry, dry sand. In a dry, dry arena. With no water nearby, is what my hindbrain decided to finally make clear to me, right there and then.

"Ah, balls!"

The grey fire guttered and died, the stink of the Veil shredding like the smell of a takeaway after someone opened a window. The howling tentacles pulsed and bulged, then exploded in great gouts of muck and slime that liberally splattered the nearest of us with gore … namely me … leaving only the dismembered remains littering the sandy floor, pools of purple-blue blood soaking the sand underfoot. Overhead, the sky slowly cleared of thunderclouds and lightning, revealing once more the swirling ocean-blue of the Real … a colour far too vivid for the mortal realm without very strong narcotics. Oh, and the triple moons on show this day, shining in full glory

Manisha leaned on her greatsword as she rested its point in a pool of ichor, immaculate having somehow dodged the shower of crap as the tentacles exploded. She looked over at me as she took a slow steadying breath, and I could read the grin all the way through her helmet. Checking what stood before me, she cocked her head for a long moment and then, finally, shrugged her armoured shoulders.

"Well, I guess that completes the Challenge." I spoke slowly, wiping muck from my face and hair. The purple blood dripped off me, and it reeked of the Veil and dead things. Oh so pleasant. "Would've been nice to question the bastard, find out who sent him. But hell, omelette and eggs, I guess."

The Bayun Cat drifted to my side, its features once more normal sized, eyes bright with feral amusement.

"You do so entertain, Knight of Shadows." It told me as it examined the prisoner, drifting around to gaze upon it from every side. "Life around you certainly promises to be ... *far* from boring. Do try to keep it so!"

Then it slowly faded from view, leaving only a vague outline of glowing eyes and a very wide mouth. Full of sharp teeth.

Sighing, I decided it was time to face facts. Me and magic, we aren't best suited. I guess I needed to think more and not just shotgun it. Unless I wanted to be left with this sort of mess to clean up. Or clean off me, more like.

When I'd summoned the ice, I'd thought to freeze the Twilight fae in place. Lock it down, contain whatever madness it was summoning in the ice with it until someone ... anyone more powerful than me could deal with it. Hell, the thing had ripped the Veil open, so I was betting we were due a visit from the Furies sometime real soon. They'd have handed the bastard its innards for this particular trick.

But ice needs water, no matter how little the measure. Last time I'd used it, I was standing knee deep in sewer-water the Mistress had kindly pulled up from the noisome depths of London's pipes to lock my pack mates and I down. This time, I was standing on dry sand. So when I'd forced the magic, it had gone for the only water it could find.

I guess I hadn't put much thought into whether mortals and fae shared any sort of biological similarities, but it seemed both are made up of quite a bit of the old wet stuff. In the Twilight fae's case, the magic had taken all the water in its body and converted it in the blink of an eye. And when ice appears like that, it's never pretty.

Jagged spikes had erupted through and out of the prisoner's body, as it had contorted and writhed in the grip of the Veil's summoning. Its head was probably the worst, as the ice had burst this open like a ripe melon, leaving a spiky ball of gory remains atop its body ... like some sort of crazed hedgehog that had been dipped in frozen gunk. A lone eyeball pushed out on a thin spike glared at me with all the fae's hate and rage.

Guess I probably need to think these things through a little more, or at least experiment some before just calling it up ... but c'mon, this ain't Harry Potter and I'm no wizard. Not even if Hagrid appeared behind me with a cake and an umbrella to announce the fact.

Still, the danger was over. The last of the golems were a pile of burning or shredded metal atop the arena's tiered seats and it looked like no real hard had come to either of the Courts. We'd met and vanquished the challenger, and caused as little mayhem and property destruction as possible along the way.

And I had all my limbs roughly still attached.

All in all, for my first Beltane tournament, I was calling it a win.

Chapter 17

Dryads, fauns, satyrs and all the Wyld types of nature spirits have long since quit the Mortal realm, driven from their natural environs with the encroachment of cities, agriculture and all the other 'advancements' mortal laud over their need for more land, more space to cover. Most affected are the spirits of the trees, the children of the forests who used to ward their charges with their lives and sorcery. Mortals used to respect forests, knowing that a stray axe blow or mis-placed fire would be rewarded by a visit from something truly enchanting, yet keen to deliver retribution with the sharpness of their knives or teeth.

The Morrigan met me as I trudged out of the main gates of the arena, held open by a pair of silent but thankfully uncorrupted golem. I'd thought about taking the flight of stairs back up to the Shadow Court's enclosure, but then decided simply 'Fuck that' and made for the nearest ground floor exit. I'd been bounced around enough times in the last hour to warrant giving my legs a break.

The Mistress of War stood off to one side, in a calm void amidst the chaos of the tourney, since despite all the confusion, none were brave enough to approach her. She watched as I alone headed in her direction, dripping Veil-creature blood.

I had lost my last companion shortly after the clean-up crew arrived to square away the mess we'd left. Manisha had clapped me on one shoulder, harder than was probably necessary, and headed off to rejoin the Ivory Court and whatever merriment the Lord and Lady of Ivory had planned. I'll give them this, fae bounce back from near certain tragedy with the speed and resilience of a three-year-old. Of course, the fae Knight showed no fatigue from the fight, bouncing lightly up the steps with inhuman speed.

Good for her. I was happy to keep things at a slower trudge.

The spectators had mostly left the stands by this point, those that could walk having beat a hasty retreat. Shimmering bursts of power amongst the shattered seating indicated where the more gravely injured were being seen to by whatever medic was near to hand, whilst the less critically hurt were escorted off-site by amour-clad fae. If not for the flares of magic and the obvious inhuman-ness of the victims as they lay strewn in the wreckage, the scene could've been from any one of recent news-reel horrors back in the mortal realm, from a multitude of tragedies inflicted in the name of religion or politics or some other insanity.

Me a cynic? Nah.

For her part, the Morrigan simply stood and waited on me as I limped my merry way out of the crime scene. Real residents were all too aware of her nature and wove a space around her and the traffic from the arena, affording us a little privacy.

"So, job's done. Your little issue is sorted. Now can I get the fuck out of here?" I growled as I rolled my shoulder against a bone-deep ache I knew would linger for a while. Inhuman healing, yes, but the body still wilfully reminds me when I do it damage. You'd think I'd learn to be nicer to myself.

"I bring word from our Queen of Shadows." The Morrigan replied quietly, and I ground my teeth as I settled onto the soles of my feet, breathing a slow sigh. Fae are all about formality, pushing it to the point where even a mortal Japanese veteran of that country's history would've called them anal-idiots. But you just can't rush the bastards.

"Ok, let me have it. Did I deliver as expected or do we need to drag the dead challenger back from the grave so I can try pummelling it better next time?" I snarled a joke, then remembered who I was talking to. "Scratch that. Please don't say that's an option. Once was bloody enough."

"Be appeased, Sir Pup. The prisoner is beyond even our arts to bring back, and all its secrets lost with it. Including the name of the one who set it up and released it from its deep prison." The fae shook her head so that her braids clicked, then smiled coldly. "Your use of your burgeoning gift proved equal to the task, as we expected. Our Queen has only words of praise for your actions, indeed your ... ah ... flair for the dramatic. I believe it is one of the reasons she chose you for the role."

"Fine then. She's welcome. The clock's ticking and I've done what you asked. Now can I just *please* get out of here?" I know I sounded a little whiney, but hell, this was as painful as trying to get Jacob to explain something. Twice over. So I was letting my 'get the fuck over it' instinct guide me and do whatever it took to get back on track.

"Whilst my Queen has little more need to delay you, delay you I must. One desires a word, before we release you." The Morrigan told me bluntly, just as those hairs on my neck did their merry dance and my senses lit with the stench of beast and blood. I didn't even bother reaching for a weapon this time, just took a step back and held up one hand, swear words rising like knives in my mouth.

Herne melted into the foreground, the Hunter appearing from thin air with the same skill as the Bayun Cat. Given his titanic size and almost overwhelming aura, that was one hell of a feat. Still clad in darkened fur and gnarled leather, hood hiding his bestial features and leaning on a gnarled and carven spear ... the Wyld Lord of the Hunt stared down at me from the dark folds shrouding his face, the force of his attention a lighter touch than before. As if he were restraining himself. I just put all my pissed-off feelings and general belligerence into a glare and faced him off.

"If you're even *thinking* about making me one of your bloody Hunt, Hounds I'll chew your throat out before you take one more breath." I spat, tiredness melting aside on a river of rage. And maybe just a touch of fear.

For a long moment, the Hunter held my gaze with his hidden eyes, then the Wyld Lord nodded once and growled out.

"The task was well done. I will grant your boon."

"Oh, you know where you can go shove your ...!" I started to snarl, but snapped silent as the Morrigan shot me an icy glance that sent shivers of frost through the brand on my skin, and held up one wode-entwined hand to forestall me.

"Sir Pup, learn the wisdom of silence. Or mayhap the grave will yet teach you." She snapped, and stepped up to stand in front of me, locking gazes with Herne. "Lord, as offered, we will gladly accept your sacrifice."

Herne snorted from within the confines of his leather hood, a snarling cough that still managed to sound oh so human in its sarcastic tone. He nodded once, to me, then turned on one booted heel.

"Hunt well, pup. We will meet anon."

With that, the Hunter melted away once more, the lingering stench fading like stray strands of a truly god-awful dream.

"What the fuck what that all about? And what boon? I never asked the bastard for anything!" I snarled, not caring how petulant I might sound, and that I was throwing my arrogance at an immortal who could wipe the floor with me without breaking sweat. "Enough of the bullshit already!"

"The Hunter judged you worthy enough to stand as Champion to offer one of its own to stand with you in the Challenge." The Morrigan replied bluntly, leaning on her staff and eying me with those bottomless bloody orbs of hers. "I am not surprised that you missed the obviousness here, so as my last act in your service, I shall explain. The challenger levelled its charges at the Courts of Ivory and Shadow. Alone. The Wyld Court had no call nor need to stand with you, and did so only on the whim of its Lord."

I let the grey cells kick in for a moment, damping down my anger as logic worked its magic. Yup, the bloody fae was right. The Twilight prisoner had failed to mention anything of the Wyld, keeping its accusations limited to Oberon, Titania and Madb. I hadn't even bothered to notice, but then I had been rather busy dodging possessed golem and tentacled monsters from the Veil. Cut me a little slack, huh?

"As for the boon, that was a matter you were not involved with and had no knowledge of simply because I wished it so. Get used to that, Sir Pup. Call it a … *wager* of sorts between Courts." The Morrigan smiled coldly. "Had you lost, and the Courts been overturned, I had given Herne my word to offer my services to him and take a place in the Wyld for a time. As it happens, you muddled your way through, so the boon he offered in return was mine to accept."

"What, you get Herne as your personal manservant for now? Opening doors, handing you a skull of hot cocoa to drink before bedtime, rubbing your tootsies when they ache from all the skulls you crush? Or is he going to keep you warm some other way? If you know what I mean?"

I waggled my eyebrows in what I thought was a suggestive manner, and tried a mocking leer, but the Morrigan just shut me down with one simple withering look.

"Nothing so … *trite*, though it surprises me not that is where your thoughts immediately go. So infantile. No, Herne agreed to release any of your brethren that he currently … *employs* in the Hunt, and to look elsewhere for his hounds for a period of my choosing. You have been granted, tooth and nail, immunity from his call for a year and a day. *That* is the measure of his boon, Sir Pup."

I gotta say I found myself struck dumb, so surprised at the gesture and the full weight of the gift the fae had dumped in my lap. I think I may have mentioned how afraid we lycans tend to be in the Real, Herne and his bloody Hunt always looming large over our shoulders To know we had a free pass, even if it came with a Best Before date ... well, halle-fucking-lujah!

"Your silence is enough thanks, so please do not ruin the moment with words." The Morrigan told me as I struggled to out voice to my thoughts, so I clamped down hard on my mouth and any unwise jest I *might* have been about to make.

"Uh, ok. Uh, thanks?" I finally tried, receiving a short nod from the ancient fae.

"Indeed. Wisdom may yet be yours, pup, if you continue to heed the words of your betters." The Morrigan smiled impishly as I scowled. Nothing like a backhanded compliment to finish things off. "My Queen made clear her thanks be expressed, for your actions today duly prove her choice of you as Knight of Shadow a wise decision. There will be other times she may and will call on you, for services such as this. But for now, she is happy to release you back to your own hunt."

"Finally!" I growled, letting the frustration show just a touch. Thankfully, the fae chose to ignore my outburst. "How much time have I lost?"

The Morrigan gestured, and the air swirled between us, forming in an archaic hour-glass with sands pouring between the two bulbs.

"Six of your hours have passed in the Mortal Realm, which means I believe the time nears midnight." She held up a hand as I let loose another frustrated growl. Too long, hours that could have been used better than this stupid challenge. "Your pack have used the time wisely, and only await your return to pay a visit on this family your companion fears have his daughter."

"But ..." She stopped me, reaching up to tap my nose once. "As I have already alluded. Your suspicions are of worthy merit, pup. Whatever you may uncover in this den of mortal criminality, I believe your search for the child Felicity leads elsewhere. Your instincts carry weight. Return to the place where knowledge is locked and bound away, where mortals fritter away years filling their minds yet emptying them as well. Seek there once more, and follow those who you mistrust the most. This is your Hunt, and your quarry is closer than you may think."

"Gods, more fucking riddles!" I swore without a care but swallowed all that anger and desire to pound the arena wall, let alone the mystical Yoda standing before me. It wouldn't do Felix any good.

Instead, I decided to adult it. I took a deep breath, loosed it and then gave the Morrigan a short bow.

"Thanks for the update. Now, if we are all done, could I trouble you for a way home? Back to the office or nearby, if it isn't too much bother?"

The Morrigan smiled like winter's ice, her eyes dancing.

"But of course, Sir Pup. All you needed do was *ask.*"

I tried hard not to show how hard I was grinding my teeth at that little quip, and instead just grinned with as little pain as I could manage. That just made the fae smile even wider.

I'd expected the Morrigan to take me out of the fayre, given how we'd had to walk to reach the place in the first place. But I guess with the Challenge done, the rules had changed. Greyness writhed and split in the air before the pair of us. The stink of the Veil, so recently loosed with dire consequence, sent the nearest Real fayre-goers scrabbling away with shrieks and curses.

The Morrigan simply laughed scornfully at their fear.

As the Veil tore open and the hole to the mortal realm gaped wide with the customary wails and screams, I took a breath and went to duck into the way between. The cold touch of the Morrigan's hand on my arm stopped me, and I swung round to find her looking up at me, eyes hooded.

"One last word, 'ere you leave." The fae spoke quietly, her words only for me this time. "Be wary of mockery, in your words *and* deeds. The Courts are interwoven and changeable like the seasons, and many have walked another Court at one time or other. We are a fickle folk. Your intimations before, about what service Herne might supply me? Unknowing you may be, but the Hunter is but a youth of the Wyld and has not seen the many aeons as have I and my Queen. And as every child must have a mother, so the Hunter has one too. So understand why your jest was most unwise, and why he may have granted such a boon to me and none other. Consider, and choose your words more wisely."

With that, the Morrigan turned away, as the way started to close between us. Not wanting to waste any more time or chance being trapped in the Veil, I shoved the surprise aside and dove through.

Time enough later to dwell on what the fae had said, and why.

But fuck me, the Morrigan? Herne's mother?! Like ... what the bloody hell?

You just can't make this shit up!

Chapter 18

True to her word, the Morrigan dropped me right back in the office of Good Deeds. Cue flaring fires and alarms shrieking as she tripped every ward all over again, just to prove a point. Likewise, I should have expected something extra after my crack about her and Herne, so I found the way between had opened in our largest ornamental fountain.

She probably thought it would help wash off the crap I was covered with. Yeah, definitely that was what she was thinking.

So here was I, back in the mortal realm, soaking my ass in the chilled water and watching it turn a disgusting hue of slurry, painted in all the tripping lights from the wards. With at least six lycan packmates surrounding me with weapons raised or talons bared.

It had been one of those days, so the best I could manage was a rueful shrug, raising my hands with only a small wince, and a "Honey, I'm home!"

Twenty minutes later, I was sat in a comfy office chair, cradling a steaming mug of coffee and in a spare set of dry clothes. My blood-soaked and muck-covered attire and armour had been dumped in the cleaning room, along with the remaining undamaged weapons I'd managed to salvage from the tourney. I was down one short sword and two knives, but given the arsenal we kept on site as well as my personal hoard back at home, I wasn't unduly worried.

Thomas, a ginger-haired and freckled member of Jacob's crash-team filled me in on the details of the ongoing investigation into the Carteloni family whilst I waited on both Jessica and Elspeth to appear. My Alpha, so I could give her the lowdown on the tournament, and the witch so she could check me over for anything I might've picked up in the Real. Fleas, lice, the odd malignant charm … that sort of thing.

I'd already been run through the standard decontamination process, which consisted of stripping me naked and dumping a pot of cold iron filings over me before making me shower in cold running water. Old-school magic prevention one-oh-one from the days when mortals had to live alongside the Real and deal with the fallout from that sort of madness. It works by grounding the unlucky sod to the mortal Realm, then washing away any residue charms or the like. However, the stronger types of workings could survive this "*kills 99.9% of bacteria*" general cleanse which is why I was waiting on Elspeth … especially after my last encounter with the Ivory Court, and subsequent property damage.

So, it turned out the Carteloni family were in the phone book, so to speak. Nice offices in Mayfair, a family business running – of all things – family planning and medical research into birth control. Supposedly had clinics in the US as well as across Europe and were doing a roaring trade in the pharmaceutical business. Drugs by any other name …

Anyhow. Jessica had turned up the sort of quiet ongoing investigations into the business and individuals which made me think more than local law enforcement might be keeping tabs on them, which made our involvement tricky. We had no reason to be leaning on them, no connection except the one given us by Danny. And I'd already handed that bundle over to the Met Police, so if we were caught sticking our noses in, I was seeing a cease-and-desist order being slapped my way pretty bloody quick.

To be fair, I didn't really give two fucks if that ended up being the case, as I had serious doubts they were caught up in the whole Felix kidnap. But I remembered the unmarked car parked outside Danny's house which had burned rubber as I approached, and the second one parked outside my own home shortly after.

Too much coincidence, what with the timing and all. So it was a lead that needed following.

Drowning myself in coffee to restore some of my sapped energy, I perked up as soon as I felt our Alpha and consultant arrive. I was guessing Jessica must have picked up Ellie on the way, since the witch still travelled by bicycle and muscle power, and unless I could start calling her Elliot and making cracks about "*E.T. phone home*", there was no way she'd made it on her own steam.

And if the Elliot comment is a mystery, go buy a box of Kleenex and watch the movie. You'll need the tissues.

If you were wondering, Jessica appearing on my senses was like someone powering up one of those old-fashioned light bulbs... where you see the circuit glow copper-hot and flare with light. For Elspeth, it was more someone had just opened a window and let in the fresh air, with cut grass and trees after a storm all mixed in. When you have the supped up hyper senses of a lycan, it all makes sense, I promise.

"Alright, Morgan, ah know time is ticking. So let us keep this brief." My Alpha reassured me as she strode up the stairs and into her office. Dressed immaculately for half past midnight, she could have stepped out of a board meeting or from a fancy cocktail bar reception without a trace Jessica had been sleeping or disturbed. The joys of being an Alpha, with no need for the millions wasted by mortals on dubious creams and beauty tips to stay fresh.

Jessica motioned Elspeth to complete her examination first, even as Sam, another packmate, pressed a large mug of coffee into the witch's hands.

"Goddess bless you, child." Elspeth quipped, then eyed me carefully. "So, Morgan dear. Do I need another circle of protection, or have you been a good boy?"

"I thought you only had to worry about protection round strangers?" I attempted a vague stab at humour, and thankfully she smiled a little at the gesture.

"Oh Morgan, you know you are the strangest one here. Quite positively. But I think I will take the risk." She stepped up to me and gently took my head in her free hand, tipping my chin up and staring into my eyes. "Your aura's taken a battering but there's no intrusion or recurrence of whatever was from earlier. No chunks missing from your life force, so you can rest a little better. And rest, I mean it. I prescribe a solid dose of sleep and avoiding violence for the next ... oh thirty minutes or so is the best I'll probably get from you, right?"

"Thanks doc. I'll try." I clasped her hand and gave the back a quick peck of a kiss, earning a warmer smile. Sometimes, rarely, I know the right thing to do around women. Not enough to have salvaged my relationship but hell, there had been bigger problems. Much bigger.

With our resident witch's sign off done, I steeled myself, draining the last of my coffee as Jessica settled down onto the chair opposite me.

With caffeine fuelling me, I launched into a full de-brief of the tournament, keeping to the details as best I could, biting back my desire to rush. Yeah, the clock was ticking, but my Alpha deserved my undivided attention at this precise moment. Something I did or didn't say might fuck things up for a packmate, for us all, later down the line ... and I trust Jessica a whole lot more than any fac or immortal. She deserved my patience.

For her part, my Alpha let me muddle through without interruption, jotting down notes on a sleek slim electronic pad. At mention of Herne's involvement, the rest of my packmates chimed in with the customary and totally deserved swearing and anger, but all I got from Jessica was a tightening around her eyes and a nod to continue. She had nothing to say about the fight itself, the revelation of a third now-defunct Court, not counting the Wyld, and its home somehow transformed into the Veil between Realms only earning a saddened sigh from her lips.

But she made me go over the prisoner's words twice, forcing me to recall exactly what he'd said word for word, before moving me on.

Then I was wrapping up and reached my second meeting with Herne.

As I explained what the Morrigan had done, what Herne had agreed to, Jessica closed her eyes and sat tapping one finger against her digital pad's screen. Knowing her well enough after all the years as part of the Pack, I shut up, waiting with the rest of the crew, watching for her reaction.

The seconds drew out, everyone else within earshot completely silenced. Even Elspeth seemed lost for a quick response.

"Um, Jess, I know I probably should've refused another debt to the Court." I offered up, knowing despite this being a great thing for our Pack and any other lycan working in the Real, I'd ended up further in debt to the Courts. I'd crossed a line, one that existed for very good reasons.

First I'd been made a Knight of the Shadow Court, now I'd been given a boon by the Wyld ... I could kind of see how my Alpha might be a wee bit peeved with me.

"I've gone over it in my head. There was no mention of a bet or boon when the bastard confronted me that first time. Just told me I'd do, then fucked off. And I *tried* to turn it down ..."

"Oh Morgan. Ah am glad, this time, the Morrigan forestalled yer instincts." Our Alpha finally answered me, opening her eyes and smiling warmly. Then, with no warning, she rose to her feet and stepped up close to me. Before I knew or could react, she had leaned in and laid a soft and gentle kiss on my forehead. It was so unexpected I almost jerked back, but she laid a hand on my shoulder, with a reassuring grip, before settling back into her chair.

"Ah know you have some ken what this means for our brethren, but in truth, probably nae understanding the good you've done here. The threat of Herne calling us tae Hunt has been an ill inflicted upon us fer centuries as you well ken. Yet without desire nor forethought, you've given us a reprieve of a year and a day from this. You'll nae be beholden tae the Wyld for this boon, so dinnae worry yerself." Jess gave me a short nod, but the sense of her feelings filled the room, so strong the link between us as Pack that none of us could have missed this. Made me feel a whole lot better, to be fair! "There will be time later tae talk this over properly, but know you have the gratitude of the Pack, an' mah own personal thanks fer yer boon this day."

"Um, ok?" I managed, as ever eloquent in my conversational repertoire.

Behind me, Sam and Thomas grabbed each other and roughly hugged, slapping each other on the back. David threw me a big thumbs up, whilst Elspeth cut me a low curtsey. Of course, Jacob was nowhere to be seen … just my luck he'd miss it when I actually did something good!

Oh well, seems I'd not managed to fuck things up totally this time. Go me!

The revelation the Morrigan and Herne were mother and son ended up being fairly anticlimactical after that, with Jessica simply jotting the fact down on her pad for use later. I did suddenly wonder about those poor bastards who'd been let loose through the deal with Herne. We hadn't lost anyone ourselves recently, but there were bound to be some lycan dumped back into the mortal real who would need careful handling. The Hunt was not kind on our kith and kin.

"Ah will pass the word round before the Blooding, fer our kin tae know of yer deeds." Jessica reassured me as she slipped the cover back over her pad. "Ah will need to review our case files, an' see those Accord breakers we can now chase with impunity in the Real, with nae worry for Herne's attention. Those freed from his Hunt will nae be themselves, but we should be ready to welcome them back. But fer now, I have a fear these troubles at the tourney are nae isolated. The fae's words, they speak of assistance, that he did nae act alone. So who freed him? What did they desire from this challenge? Ah fear we are still in the dark too much, an' there be more troubles tae come."

I thought back to just after the events at the Natural History Museum, when the Morrigan had appeared like some twisted Mary Poppins and delivered a file with blacked out details she thought would help with my search for my parents. Even the immortal had suggested that something was wrong with the crazed Lady of the Lake's behaviour. That she may have had help, that her plan was not the sort of thing she could've dreamt up herself. I hadn't had a chance to share with my Alpha this little nugget of information, given how everything had then blown up with Felix's kidnapping ... but now it seemed a whole lot more than just suspicions, and the ancient fae jumping at shadows.

Before I could speak up, however, the heavy clomp of feet and a vague thundercloud on my senses announced the arrival of Jacob Moon.

Clad in a heavy biker jacket and fatigues, he loomed as he came up the stairs, calm expression slowly taking in the scene. I guess he'd been parking the 4x4 battle cruiser out back, or just been loitering downstairs to see if his team could handle whatever came through the Veil themselves. That might sound like him passing the buck, but he takes safeguarding seriously. Every lycan on his team is expected to be able to handle themselves against all manner of supernatural nasties that come a-knocking, and he is constantly testing them to make sure every Pack member's fit to throw down with the worst of them. Pampering just isn't in his nature or temperament.

"Ah, Jacob. Right on time." Jessica nodded at his approach and gestured towards me. "Morgan is ready tae join you, as ah believe you have an appointment to meet the Cartelonis at their Mayfair residence? They should be settling in fer a night of whatever criminality is best done at these wee hours."

"Coming, squirt?" Jacob grunted at me, and I realised I'd missed my chance to debrief Jessica. I'd catch up with her soon enough to pass on the Morrigan's suspicions, but for now, it was time to go pay a visit on Danny's ex-employers and find out how the hell this lot were mixed up in this shitstorm. Maybe not at all, but I'd keep my suspicions burning until the slippery bastards proved otherwise … oh and agreed to pull the team off my home, and Danny's place.

I'm decent like that.

The drive to Mayfair gave me time to knock back another flask full of coffee that Jacob had passed me in the 4x4, as well as chow down on a couple of pastrami and gherkin bagels fresh from the store. For that, I could have kissed my packmate … well, gripped his shoulder quite firmly, maybe even fist bumped him. Trust me, it translates.

Mayfair at gone midnight is the polar opposite of Mile End. Less like the set of an apocalypse movie, and more like the aging ruins of an old mausoleum. The buildings are ornate and loom high overhead, the streets wide and deserted. Not a vagrant to be seen, no rubbish strewn in the gutter. An echo back to London of olden day when the city was fresh and clean, before … well, mortals trashed it. You lot came along, and treated it like some old rock band making the most of their hotel rooms before checking out the next morning.

Do I sound jaded? Go take a walk around your home city sometime, then check out some of the history books at how it *used* to look. Then tell me I'm mistaken.

Arlington Street is tucked round the back from Green Park, just a spitting distance from The Ritz and, surprisingly Dukes Hotel where I had found Jessica in what seemed an age ago on my hunt for Excalibur. Just goes to show Evil and Good can live hand in hand, round the corner and comfortable in each other's company without squabbling overly much.

The address we had for this particular den of evil was a large mansion building, solid grey stone and glass doors, four stories in height and, as lairs go, pretty innocuous. But good ol' lycan senses crackled to life as we pulled into the empty street, both Jacob and I instantly alert to the threat of the place.

Wards had been crafted and set discreetly enough so as not to trigger by the day to day passers-by, but powerful enough for us both to sense them straight off. So not some novice spell-splunker, but sloppy enough work to be laughable. That sort of idiotic nonchalance usually pointed directly to something from the Real ... given the run of the mill immortals' natural ability to manage subtlety like a five-year-old mortal child.

Number 23 Arlington Avenue was easy to spot as Jacob and I slid from our ride and strode down the lamp-lit street. As I said, it was a massive grey mansion that would've graced any Batman movie for downtown Gotham, but what set it apart from the other buildings at this hour of the night were the two large and heavily clothed gentlemen standing alert by the front doors.

The pair had *goon* written all over them, as they stood in long black coats barely fitted over straining muscles, buzz-saw hair-cuts and solid jaws standing out as they cast their gaze slowly and meaningfully in our direction. This being London, not New

York, I wasn't too fussed about checking for suspicious bulges under their arms or at their waists, but I was betting the bastards had weapons near to hand. Far enough to disavow if we were law enforcement but near enough to grab if we were idiot yobs chancing a hit.

"Can we help you ... *gentlemen*?" The goon on the right asked as his partner stepped down to the pavement and discreetly to my left. The guy was a mortal, stinking of stale cigarette smoke, a light patina of sweat and some over-rich cologne that he probably thought made him irresistible to women. What it did for me was turn my stomach *but* also kick my hackles into overdrive. I'd smelt that stuff twice before, a whiff of it on the air as I had aggressively approached a car outside Danny's house. The second time outside my own home, when I found a suspicious vehicle parked outside.

What were the chances?

"Yeah, maybe." I jumped in before Jacob could speak, ignoring goon one, looking over at the guy trying to flank me. "I was wondering. If I wanted to lurk outside someone's home and do a truly piss poor job of it, could you give me some pointers? Pass on your wisdom, that sort of thing?"

I felt the weight of Jacob's hand on my shoulder, my packmate making his thoughts clear with no need of words. We weren't here to start a fight, and no matter my personal feelings, we'd be playing this one by those rules. At least till someone else threw the first punch. Then all bets were off.

For his part, goon number two did a decent job of hiding his reaction to finding a mark suddenly opposite him outside his own office. Most mortals would have flinched, started breathing rapidly or just released a cloud of pheromones as the fight or flight instinct kicked in. This guy was at least a little professional, and all I got from him was a small muscle twitching along his overly-thick jawline and his eyes narrowing slightly. Good for him.

"Got an appointment with Mr Carteloni." Jacob interjected. "Jessica Walker's party. We're expected."

Goon one scowled and cupped his hand over his ear, whispering into the mike hidden in his sleeve. I would've loved to tell him describing us as *two wise guys from the circus* wasn't exactly good customer service, but that would mean admitting my hearing wasn't anything near normal, and tipping them off.

Nor would it have helped looking up and waving at the very discreet security camera that zoomed in on us from a fake brick set above the front door. But that I couldn't help doing, flashing the security detail behind the lenses a lopsided grin.

Jacob rolled his eyes and grunted his disapproval but I just shrugged. He knew me, he knew what to expect.

The response to goon one's query came a heartbeat later, and the pair of us found ourselves ushered in through the main entrance without any further intimidation or small talk.

The lobby was deserted, but the sort of scanner you find in airports and governmental buildings awaited us, requiring Jacob to dig out keys, loose change and all the usual metallic crap that ends up in pockets without you remembering you had it there. I'd left my stuff back in the office with the rest of my gear, to be picked up when I was sure it was clean from malignant charms. Lucky me.

Goon number one followed us in, leaving my good friend and personal stalker outside. He pointed us to the lifts once we'd cleared the scanner, two on each side of the lobby, and politely informed us we'd be met on floor six. High enough to be above the hustle and bustle of normal street life, but leaving, if my estimation was correct, another three floors above for whatever the Italian crime family cum fertility sponsors didn't want the authorities to know about.

"Behave." Jacob grunted to me as we waited patiently in the pretty box taking us up. Background music played something European through hidden speakers, probably from around the time when the Rat pack were still a bunch of well-meaning boozing mortals singing crooning tunes, instead of now near immortal legends across most of the US and "*ROW*".

I'd busted a rib when I'd heard those acronyms for the United States of America and then Rest Of World. That was the type of thinking I'd expect from the Courts, but was happy to find mortals following hand in hand with that kind of backward, prehistoric border defining mentality.

"What, moi? You wound me." I told my packmate, oozing sincerity. "All I'm after is a nice little chat with some lowlife scum who may or may not be involved in the kidnap of my friend's daughter. And who by lucky chance has had his goons stake out my home, which by the way I'm not all that happy about. Nothing to be worried about."

As I spoke, I looked up, directly into the second security camera disguised as a piece of ornamentation in the lift's ceiling. It wasn't the operator's fault, you just can't use that sort of kit and not start ringing alarm bells for us lycan. Something about being watched, I guess.

"Oh and I politely suggest you pull anyone else sat outside my home, whoever you got to replace the idiot you have on the door downstairs. Before I decide to take *direct* action. Call it a friendly warning." I smiled again, keeping things pleasant. Not causing trouble at all.

Jacob just grunted another sigh and rolled his shoulders, obviously bracing for things to go south fairly rapidly.

Floor Six pinged on the counter and the lift doors hissed open. This time we were met by a dangerously attractive young woman, dressed professionally in a pin-stripe suit and matching skirt and obviously no sort of threat to two burly well-built men like us. She wore a glamour like a second skin, obviously meant to throw us off our game and leave us ogling her instead of thinking straight. Yeah, right.

She introduced herself as Valeria, Mr Carteloni's personal assistant, and asked if we would follow her. Gentlemen that we were, Jacob and I let her lead us through a set of oak double doors and down a corridor lined with expensive looking paintings and deep thick carpet underfoot. As Valeria politely enquired if we'd like to leave our coats in the coat room (*No thanks*) and whether either of us would like some refreshments at this late hour *(Tempting but Jacob's scowl put paid to me asking for a very expensive bottle of red wine)*, both of us let our hyped senses roam over our surroundings, and my packmate gave a quick nod upwards as we both felt the wards checking us over.

Someone was definitely in our line of business, and the fact the Cartelonis had a player from the Real in-house made me doubt my misgivings over their involvement in Felix's kidnapping. Maybe the murders too.

Valeria pushed open a second double set of doors, leading us into a large state room. On the far side, curtains were pulled back and light filtered in from outside to alleviate the gloom of the interior. Dim crystal spheres lit the walls from inset niches on every side, and the floor was covered by more rich carpet so that the whole atmosphere of the place felt muffled. Probably meant to make whoever was shown in feel more at ease, less prone to aggression. It's amazing what you can do with simple furnishings.

A large desk was set in front of the floor to ceiling windows, a thing of dark oak and solidity that spoke old school craftsmanship. No Ikea job this, the thing looked like it weighed half a ton and wasn't made to be moved. Behind this, a large, heavily muscled and well boned man sat in a high-backed chair, fingers steepled and eyes half closed as he watched us enter. Another three men lounged to one side, two seated on a plush sofa and one propped against the wall, seemingly thoroughly disinterested in our presence yet wired for action despite their appearance.

So, time to meet the Boss, and his thugs.

"That will be all, Miss Artemi." The man behind the desk pushed himself up and out of his seat, stepping round the wooden monstrosity and leaning against it as he studied us. "I'm Charles Carteloni. I believe your ... ah ... boss? Ms Jessica Walker, she wished for us to talk? But I am a little unclear about the subject. You don't have the look of our usual clients ..."

"Oh that's easy." I let my big mouth get the jump on Jacob, going for a reaction. "We just want to know which one of you fuckers kidnapped a young woman of our acquaintance, and where the fuck you're holding her so we can cut to the bit where we hand you your inbred, fuckwit asses. Simple, really."

Jacob gave me a long, hard look and loosed one last, deep sigh.

Chapter 19

Djinn, genies, marid and the assortment of spirits epitomised by Arabian Nights or Aladdin exist, but the truth is far darker. Find an enchanted item, a lamp or ring or such, and contained within you may find a being of extraordinary might and sorcery. Yet their only desire is freedom, their only wish to turn upon their masters and see them suffer as they suffer in turn., Any creature that has been locked away, their powers crippled and only of use to serve another ... these are creatures you should not trust to have your best intentions at heart. Instead, your heart, possibly, their only intent.

The response I'd wanted from the various criminal elements in the room was at once entirely predictable and at the same time, nothing like I'd expected. Yeah, I know how that sounds, but still.

Mr Carteloni remained where he half sat against the desk, the perfect up-and-coming god-father figure in a very expensive suit as he smiled a cold, thin smile. You could have chilled ice off him, he was so cool and collected.

The three resident goons were the ones to react to my words, the pair leaping up from the couch where they had lounged, muscling up in front of us whilst the last one slipped along the wall and slid nicely behind us. Between us and the door, as if we were even thinking about running. All big muscle and aggression. Typical watch dogs let off the leash.

What surprised me was the raw emotion the three exuded, their face contorting with animalistic rage. I kid you not, foam actually flecked one of the pair's mouth facing us down, the guy's eyes mere slits but still filled with inhuman anger. I'd thought watchdogs, and the image stuck ... barking, slavering Dobermans in suits surrounding us, just waiting for the word to go for our jugulars. And if that seems harsh, one of the pair actually *growled* at Jacob. Full on, guard dog style.

"I would advise taking a more respectful tone, and a better choice of words, Mr Black." Charles Carteloni replied with even tones, no trace of ire or anything in that chill voice. He indicated his men with a brief nod. "My ... *boys* here, they don't like it when you disrespect me. This can be a perfectly pleasant talk, or not so much. The decision is yours."

Before I could open my mouth to tell him where he could shove his pleasantness, and just how far up, Jacob gripped my arm. Hard. I bit back my response, as my packmate took one step forward. Into the face of the nearest goon, the one growling at him.

"Back. Down." He told the man, the two words heavy with threat and ending with a growl of his own that was all lycan. The goon, he of the foaming mouth and angry disposition, snarled ... actually snarled, and his hand twitched to his open jacket and a nice suspicious bulge that waited there.

Jacob didn't bother with a second warning, just looking round at Charles as he simply laid his hand on the other man's chest and *pushed*. He didn't bother hitting him, as mortals don't tend to fare too well when smacked by any of us, but a simple shove tends to make a point. In this case, the point was the goon flying across the room and slamming into the glass window with a suitably solid crunch.

The second goon of the pair took exception to Jacob's shove, barking out a weird kind of half assed roar as he swung a punch that was heavily weighted by a solid set of knuckle-dusters. Jacob spared the idiot a withering glance before he grabbed hold of the man's expensive looking jacket, pulling him close and smiling into the rage-infused thug's face. Then with no sign of effort, he sent the idiot crashing through the air to crumple down beside his colleague.

The last man standing, goon three, jumped at me whilst Jacob was having fun. Jumped, as in leaped like some sort of monkey swinging in the trees on a BBC documentary. He'd pulled a short stick from his belt, lashing it out into a full-fledged truncheon with a practised flick of his wrist. This he then sent crashing towards my head, obviously thinking I was the sort of idiot to expect a chest blow or strike between the legs from an opponent jumping me from behind. All the while hooting out some sort of angry sound that made me think baboon. *Idiot* baboon, but still bloody weird.

Grabbing my attacker's arms, I stopped his monkey-ass jump, watching his face as it reddened with exertion from trying to free himself, then tossed him back against the wall to land in a heap on the sofa. The crunch as he landed was eminently satisfying.

Then we both turned back to Charles Carteloni, the only uninjured mortal remaining in the room.

Who had conjured a gun from somewhere, and now had the big ass barrel trained on Jacob. I'm not an expert on firearms, but the thing was large enough to suggest it might be do serious damage to an elephant. Which didn't mean a thing to either of us, except for who would have the bruises to show for tonight's fun.

"Are we supposed to be worried by that thing?" I asked, seeing him still smiling that cold smile that was beginning to grate on my nerves. "Got any more idiots on crack you want tossed around the room before we get down to business?"

"These? Oh these weren't meant to be anything other than ... well, a test to be honest." Charles drawled, as his free hand tapped something hidden on the desktop. "And I would have to say, yes, I have *lots* more idiots but I doubt you will find these next ones so easy to manhandle. For a pair of *lycan*."

I shot a look at Jacob, just to check I hadn't misheard the last word.

At that moment, the doors behind us crashed open and a dozen more men stormed into the room, coming to a halt in a semi-circle with us at its epicentre. This lot were a different level of goon to the three we'd just dealt with. Firstly they were in full tactical armour, faces hidden behind darkened goggles under full-face helmets, and armoured like some futuristic Neo-Nazi militant unit. No designer suits to be seen. And secondly, they cradled ... well, not guns as I'd expected, but freakin' crossbows, siege bows almost of a size to turn any Safari-hunt into just so much schitz-kabob..

But the clincher was the stink coming from those medieval weapons, the tips of each of the dozen of sharpened heads dripping with a viscous liquid. One I'd had the displeasure of being dosed with not so long ago.

"They've got fucking *wolfsbane,* Jacob. Why the fuck do they have that shit?" I complained aloud, as Jacob cracked his neck and rolled his shoulders.

He didn't bother responding, since it was obvious the bastards knew what we were and had prepared accordingly. Despite the fact wolfsbane was on a prohibited list of substances, the ownership of which carrying a stiff penalty within the Courts, and a much more painful one if any of us lycan caught the bearer alone.

So, twelve heavily armoured and armed guards, with enough 'bane to do both of us serious harm. Mr clever-dick Carteloni still had his hand cannon trained on us, and that smile had slipped into something much nastier. More jackal-like.

All that was left was something pithy to say before we got on with the blood spilling and pain.

"How about you take the flunkies, and I go have a chat with Mr Carteloni up close and personal like, ok?" I offered Jacob, ever the consideratory pack member.

"Maybe he's got a kitten he wants finding. Go check, an' let me know." My packmate grinned sharply back at me, shifting his weight onto his back foot. Ready to turn these goons into so much wallpaper.

Man, was I ever going to hear the end about that bloody kitten?

A slow clapping came from the wide-open doors, as we were joined by a third and final member of the Scooby Villain gang. The personal assistant stepped demurely back into the room, stopping behind the wall of goons. Valerie smiled sweetly as she peeked between the shoulders of two guards, dark eyes twinkling.

"Oh aren't you both just so *butch*! Typical Redcloaks ... Thief takers, hounds on the hunt for any dare who break one of those asinine Accords." The PA shook her head, dark locks framing that slim face as she set one finger to her lips. "But, lo, what do we have here? I see no Accord breaker present, no threat to the Realms levelled at Mr Carteloni's feet? What *could* be going on here? Surely nothing ... *personal?*"

"You know, I'm guessing the whole *personal assistant to Mr Carteloni* line was bullshit, Miss." I tried, facts grinding into place with glacial speed. "Someone put a shitload of wards around this building to keep prying eyes away, and then there's whatever is wrong with the goons here ... the way these idiots are acting, I'd call them more animal than mortal. And finally someone's handed out a proscribed substance which I *know* for a fact takes a witch to make, having had the details explained to me at wearying detail by one. So ... pardon my French but who the royal fuck are you really?"

Valerie's smile widened, her dark eyes dancing as she stepped lightly between the armoured guards and faced the pair of us.

"Oh, you're taking all the fun out of this. Can't you at least try and guess? The clues are all here for you, slapping you in the face if you would just use the few braincells kicking round that thick skull of yours. Evil witchcraft, men turned into their animal-selves, a beautiful yet deadly woman at the centre of it all. Would it help if I mentioned Greek tragedy?"

I shrugged, bone-tiredness and adrenaline warring inside from too little sleep, too much fighting and the ever-burning anger over Felix's kidnapping.

"Sorry, lady. I must have missed the movie. I got bored right after you started flapping those lips of yours. Why not make it easy and just tell me who you think you are, before we cuff you for creating shitty '*bane*' for mortal use?"

The witch, for there was no other thing she could be, tightened those aforementioned lips, eyes narrowing from dark amusement to waspish irritation in a flash. I can have that effect on people, my ex was happy to inform me.

"Mark me, lycan. All I hear is a childish pup yapping when a wiser decision would be to still your foolish tongue and think for a moment. You admit to knowing one of the Sisterhood, so you should know how thin the ice you are treading is right now." Anger bled from her like crackling flashes of lightning, earthing in the thick carpet and on the solid doors behind her. The guards had enough common sense to step discreetly away from her, whilst keeping their weapons trained on us two ... but me, I was undeterred, caution having thrown in the towel and slunk back to the bar for a shot.

"Fuck the ice. You want to throw down right here and now? Bring it." I snarled, but then Jacob gripped my shoulder with enough force to tell me to back down. My packmate shook his head once, then looked back across at little Miss Attitude.

"Cerce. Recorded in Homer's *Odyssey* as marooned on one of the lost isles, with a habit of turning foolish sailors into animals. One-time minor goddess of change, before you fell in love with Odysseus and sacrificed your god-hood for his love ... which he foolishly spurned. You then cursed him to wander for seven more years upon the oceans before he ever found his home and the wife he had left there."

I honest to god had never known Jacob string together that many sentences in one go, and use that many words in all the time we'd been in the Pack. It was like he'd been saving up just for such an occasion. And Greek mythology? I *so* would not have pegged him as a myth-nut.

"Time for the adults to talk." He told me with a broad grin, and I snapped it shut, biting back on the *what the fuck* I so wanted to let loose.

"Well guessed, Redcloak." Cerce gave a shallow curtsy, "It is so nice to be remembered in this day and age. But you sadly have been misled on a few points. Not surprising given the Greeks wrote the fables, and were ahead of their time on hyping up their heroes at the cost of the truth."

She stepped closer, raising a hand and honest to Gods, ran one finger down Jacob's arm. Was she flirting with him?

"I'd be *happy* to enlighten you, on those little facts?"

So with the change in pace, standing in the lair of a crime family, surrounded by armed guards and now with a centuries old witch and once-goddess flirting with my packmate ... I was feeling decidedly thrown. Only thing I had left was my skills of diplomacy, coughing hard to interrupt the pair.

"Um, wolfbane? Pointed at us?" I nodded to the guards, who had frozen in place, weapons held ready. In fact, even Mr

Carteloni has shut down with Cerce's entrance, almost like she had thrown a switch.

"Oh, silly me. I would never have let them *use* the stuff on you." Cerce drawled. "Think of this as more just a demonstration of my ... *our* good faith and trustworthiness."

She clapped her hands once, and the guards instantly shifted like a well-oiled machine. Those siege bows dipped, wooden bolts snapped free from their cradles and dropped to the floor, as the soldiers all stepped back a pace. I couldn't read their expressions from behind those full-fitting facemasks, but the sensation I got from the dozen men and women was akin to a bunch of watchdogs who had just been told "Sit."

Cerce stepped round the pair of us, joining Charles at his desk. Laying a hand on his arm, she guided him as his expression slipped into a blank mask, all anger and smugness disappearing away like so much smoke. He slid the large handgun back into its hidden holster, and moved to take his seat in the high-backed chair, reaching up to take the witch's hand as she stood at his shoulder.

"There, you see? Nothing to be kicking up a fuss about. We are all adults here ... well most of us, present company of one excluded." Cerce shot me a sharp look, then smiled back as she focused on Jacob. "I'm sure we can comfortably discuss the matter which brings Redcloaks to our door at such a late hour without any further violence. It is the whereabouts of the young lady you know as Felicity Price you came for, correct?"

Still getting my head round the shift of dynamics in the room, my *fight* instincts hotwiring rational thought, all I could do was nod.

"I thought as much. Well, gentlemen, I am sorry to say you have had a wasted journey this night." Cerce held out her hand, the picture of sincerity. "You see, despite whatever grief-stricken home-truths the young lady's father must have supplied, we have *no* clue as to Soshana's … ah, Felicity's current location nor the reason for which she was taken. The Carteloni family, in this matter, are frankly blameless, and as eager as you to locate her."

Chapter 20

Many fabled immortals from mythology are simply Real denizens seeking the rewards worship by ignorant mortals offer. Many "gods" or "goddesses" are simply creatures who were smart enough to notice a niche, and carve their way to power for as long as they could hold it. If you doubt, look at how many Gods and Goddesses seem the very same individual just by another name, from one generation to the next. Immortal denizens of the Real are simple in their need for followers, and averse to changing a good thing if it is working.

"And we should believe you, exactly *why*?" I was not having any of this "concerned family" bull this witch seemed to think she could peddle. There was something really weird going on here, and I still had that feeling Felix sat at the centre of it.

"Because, quite frankly, I *could* have had you shot full of wolfsbane and dumped in the Thames before you set one foot inside this building." Cerce answered bluntly. "Even right now, I have you at my mercy. As your colleague would tell you if he could. And yet I have not acted upon the fact."

Jacob. I realised he hadn't spoken since telling me to shut the fuck up, since Cerce had then addressed him and been weirdly flirting … enough to touch him. Shit. Checking across, I saw his expression gnarled with frustration, hands clenched and veins popping where his muscles strained to move … without any visible success.

"What the fuck have you done to him?" I snarled, but Cerce just shook her head, wholly unintimidated.

"He will be fine. The paralysis should fade by the time we have finished speaking, and apart from a mild headache, your colleague should be right as rain afterwards." The witch rubbed her thumb and finger together. "Just one of the many products I specialise in these days, And just the thing to deal with an annoyingly magic-proof lycan when I need to."

"Why him? Why didn't you just dose us both and have us dumped someplace far away?" I truly didn't think the reason indicated any positive thoughts the witch had toward me, and was pleased to be proved right when she smiled coldly.

"Oh, don't think I didn't consider the possibility *most* thoroughly." Then she shook her head. "But no, you both disappearing would just have meant more scrutiny upon the Cartelonis, more lycan tramping their great feet all over our business … and we are already under investigation by the mortal law, as I am sure you well know. No, I wanted to talk to *you*, as you are the most involved here. You are acquainted with by Daniel Price and his daughter, and so I must reason with you."

"More scrutiny, huh? So what are you into these days that you need to keep so secret?" I gestured to Charles Carteloni. "The company you're keeping doesn't lend credibility to you being all nice and legal, mortal or Real."

"These? They are just tools, a means to an end." Cerce shrugged, as she stepped away from the large desk and towards me. Conscious that she had somehow bewitched Jacob with a simple touch, I kept an eye on her hands, ready to react if she tried the same thing on me. Trust her, hell no, no matter what she said.

"Let me show you what I am currently involved with, and why it would make no sense risking the wrath of the police or you lycan by going after the errant daughter of the 'family'." She noted my wariness and smiled that shark-toothed smile, gesturing for me to follow her. "If you would?"

"Uh, if you think I'm leaving my mate here whilst we go traipsing who the fucks knows where, you're more batshit crazy than I thought." I told her bluntly, but Cerce ignored my insults, instead just shaking her head.

"Your packmate is safe, lycan. None here will make a move unless I so will it." She nodded to the guards, then across to Charles, all who had not moved a muscle since we'd begun talking. "They are, as I said, tools … and tools do not act without the hand which wields them. *Witch* indeed. Now come."

Shooting a glance at Jacob, I weighed up our options. I shouldn't leave him alone, not when he was defenceless but then again we really needed answers, and that looked like I'd have to play along with Cerce some more. Whatever it was she felt she had to show me, was it worth risking my packmate's life over? Probably not … but I couldn't take that chance.

Knowing I was in for one hell of a dressing down as soon as Jessica heard what happened here I folded my arms instead, playing the stubborn bastard card. It's one I know very well.

"We'll go see whatever you want, but not until you undo whatever the fuck you did to Jacob. I'm not leaving him here like this, no matter what you say."

"Tsk, you lycans are so pack-bound." The witch sighed, then shrugged. "Fine. I will loosen the bonds which bind him, but he will not thank you for this. If you had waited and let this happen naturally, the headache, as I mentioned, would have been but an annoyance. Now … not so much."

She dipped her hand into her jacket and withdrew a small glass phial, like some expensive perfume bottle. This she opened and, using the stopper's end, dosed her thumb and forefinger with whatever was inside the bottle. Then she simply stepped to Jacob's frozen side and ran her digits over his bare skin above the collarbone.

Breath exploded out as Jacob snarled, one hand rising up to hold against his head as he screwed his eyes shut against whatever shitstorm of headache he'd just been hit with. Cerce stepped away before he could lash out, obviously expecting him to seek retribution. But Jacob just waved her off, looking across at me with one screwed up eye.

"Go find out what she wants. I'll be fine here. And don't let her touch you." He grimaced, but I knew that Jacob, even at half strength, could wipe the floor with most things. And I could tell he wasn't feeling too bad if the sod felt the need to point out the blindingly obvious, for my own benefit.

"Come. This will not take long, but I prefer we deal with this matter so you can be gone all the sooner." The witch told me as she walked past the guards, and to the double door.

Shooting a last look at Jacob, who gave me a reassuring nod, I followed her out.

With Cerce in the lead, we made our way back through the short corridor to the lifts. To my surprise, instead of sending us up to the penthouse where I had reckoned they did their nefarious crime-stuff, Cerce chose down. I kept my questions in check though, knowing time was ticking, and definitely against me. If the Cartelonis were not involved in the kidnapping, this was a complete waste of my time, and I'd rather be chasing down those three suspicious students instead.

Of course, I was also worried a little bit about leaving Jacob alone … I'm not a complete arse!

When the lift finally arrived, Cerce motioned me in and followed me after, waiting till the doors slide shut before reaching for the number pad. With that know-it-all smile plastered over her face, she jabbed "B" three times, causing the light to change from green to red, and another button to appear as if by magic below the Basement setting. This she only stabbed once, making it light up green, and the lift slid smoothly into motion.

"Am I getting a tour of your private dungeon? Gee, and it's only the first date." I quipped, feeling the silence between us wasn't proving that helpful. "If all you want to show me is your whips and cuffs, I'll pass, thanks."

"Across the ages, many mortal and immortal men have performed great acts and valiant deeds for the mere chance of such delights, lycan," Cerce just snipped back, her expression imperious and mocking. "You I wouldn't even consider wasting one impassioned breath over, let alone a good use of batteries. You have the reek of Shadow about you, their mark upon you. You are not my toy to play with."

"I'm no-one's toy." I growled back, then stopped and thought for a second. "Wait, batteries? Not getting the sort of attention you were used to, huh? Suitors a little thin on the ground these days? Is there a select line of merchandise for once-Goddesses?"

My remarks simply earned me a chilling stare, but I'd faced down the Morrigan, and weathered the ire of the Bitch of Battle. Cerce wasn't even in the same league.

Before I could think up any more personal questions to ask, the lift slid to a stop, and the doors swished open.

"*Welcome to my lair, said the spider to the fly.* Won't you come this way?" The witch asked me as she lightly stepped out, holding out a hand as if to offer to take mine. Not falling for that trick, I just motioned her on with a grunt. This fly was wise to the spider, and fully intended on getting the hell out of here under his own wings.

Chapter 21

Cold, clinical light bathed us as we stepped out into a large, open plan sub-basement. Glass dividers sectioned off small units like office pods, but I did a quick calculation and realised the dimensions of the place didn't fit with the building above. Either Cerce had charmed the place like a troll-hole, or the Cartelonis had been busy little diggers and burrowed under a lot of other real estate in the neighbourhood.

Rows upon rows of metal benches ran throughout the enlarged room, set upon what looked like mesh rubber matting. Overhead, a myriad of copper-hued pipes ran on delicate hangers to form a bizarre puzzle ending in nozzled tubes over each bench, and what they bore.

Plants. A veritable jungle of green leaves, delicate stems and bowing flowers met my gaze as I looked around me. Rich scents of loam and vegetation filled my nose, so out of place in this brick and glass underground lair that I had to shake my head, for an instant thinking Cerce was just spinning another sort of glamour. But nope, definitely no masking going on here. What I was smelling, seeing … was a garden. Weird-ass and freaky, but definitely long on the green fingers and short on the obvious criminality. Unless …

"Oh please, don't tell me you're running the weed business in the neighbourhood? Seriously, if this is what you're up to, we can stop right here." I cast around, but nothing shouted cannabis to me immediately, the little I knew from pictures and the odd news-case I'd caught covering the most recent drug-bust in the city.

Illegal drugs for mortals were so not our beat. It might be big money for those involved, but none of it ever threatened the balance of existence or causality, and the Accords were fine with mortals rotting their brains on such stuff, just so long as they left Reality alone.

"Nothing so trite." Cerce walked out into the herbarium, gesturing around her. "What you are seeing here is the cultivation of centuries of lore, years of trials and failures. I used to waste my powers turning mortals into animals … Entertaining though that was, there was never much progress to be had in that sector. Man to pig. The pig could then be nothing but a pig, with a man's mind trapped inside. But this … this, is far, far different and much, much more satisfying."

"Get to the point. You want this over with as much as I do." I told her as I followed her into the greenery. Water had dripped from the plant holders, hence the need for absorbent material underfoot, but I wished I'd known we'd be taking a trip through Eden. I would have brought my wellies.

Cerce waved to two white-suited goons, dressed in the sort of outfits you normally see in crime scene sequences … all gloved, booted and masked. They had been working at a bank of computers, pretty high tech to my ignorant mind, which illuminated rows of script running faster than the eye could follow. Images of gene-sequences … I'd seen a documentary once so I can at least recognise the picture, plus I've watched all the latest Spidermen movies and they all have the same sort of graphics. Gene-splicing and matching, whether it's with a mortal kid and a nuclear spider, or plant genetics or whatever they have, it all looks terribly complex.

By the way, I still think Sony should have stuck with Garfield as ol' Spidey. Personal viewpoint, I know, but hey, I liked him.

Anyhow, at the signal from Cerce, the pair melted away, sent off without even a word. That thing again, it just wasn't normal behaviour no matter how well trained your average mortal is. They must have gone to goon training-school, and learned all the non-verbal commands … I almost snorted a laugh thinking of the witch batting them over the nose with a rolled newspaper when they disobeyed. Almost.

"The point, you ignorant furball, is that I have moved on from base physically transformation. That is *so* last century, and never really agreed with the mortals I chose to change." The witch tapped something into the nearest keyboard, and the linked large screen changed. Now it displayed slowly revolving men and women, full length images, with small script scrolling beneath each. Some of it was highlighted in red, but I'd have needed the vision of an eagle to know what it said. My eyes are good, but not that good, ok?

"No, what we specialise in now is the *inward metamorphosis* of the subject whilst leaving them outwardly as they were born. With the right herbs, the correct dosage, I can change a mortal to have no fear, no sense of pain or injury no matter the damage they sustain. On the other hand, I can remove any and all violent instincts from a subject, effectively pacifying them with none of the messiness mortal doctors still attempt with scalpels and needles. I have unlocked Pandora's box, the mortal's emotional control mechanisms … and they are mine to, well, *adjust* as required. Now I can make a mortal be an animal in all but form, be that a pig, a wolf, a lion or lamb. I take all that confusion these little people let fill their heads, cloud their judgement … and remove it with a simple touch, a drop or two of my elixirs. Far simpler than before."

I let that sink in for a second, then jerked my head upwards, back the way we had come.

"So that little display with Charles Carteloni and his guards, that was just you showing off, huh? Got them all under your spell. I didn't think they were acting right."

"Charles had an unfortunate *medicinal* habit from his youth which was draining the family wealth, and threatening to provide opportunities for the mortal law to close in on their business interests. I was approached, offered whatever I so desired if I could cure him and set him straight from that moment on." Cerce smiled coldly as she thought back. "I *may* have added my own little twist to the mix, leaving me with all the resources I needed for my own work, and a completely loyal mortal to front me as an added bonus. But the family seemed pleased with the new-improved Charles, and dares not complain."

"So, you're playing God ... Goddess again, monkeying with peoples' heads, how they think?" I shook my head, even a thick lycan like me seeing the obvious consequences of such experimentation. Mortal history is full of it ... hypnosis, mind control, mind altering drugs ... hell, conspiracy theorists lived for this sort of shit. "Do you *know* the shitstorm of trouble you are messing with here? How badly this can go wrong?"

"We abide strictly by Accord rules, and *most* of the more sensible mortal regulations." Cerce responded snippily. "For now, my work is focused on mortal fertility, and the myriad issues such a stupidly simple process is plagued by that have nothing to do with biology. Gods, even monkeys can make babies but your average mortal? Beset by issues and complications at every turn. And so much of it is down to the mess they have going on in their heads. With the right herbs, the correct plan, I can alleviate their stress, invigorate their passions and strengthen their unions so things progress much more smoothly. What is so wrong with that?"

I wandered through the rows of greenery, still trying to get my head round what was going on here.

Cerce wasn't the first mythological figure that had had to move with the times, or face fading into nothingness this side of the Veil. Most had called it quits after trying out various new gigs, only a few immortals able to keep the sort of belief and following going that made all the other crap worthwhile. The Lady of the Lake at least had the excuse of being banished here, rather than sticking it out by choice, but still not a good enough reason for her going bat-shit crazy.

But fertility. Baby-making. Seriously?

Thankfully, something caught my eye as I let the facts line up in my head. Just a flash, something vaguely familiar, as I zeroed in on one specific glass unit.

"Please don't touch. The plants in the cases are not from the mortal realm, and as such, need care and attention to thrive here." Cerce told me as I stopped by the box in question.

Yup, very familiar. Red poppy-like but with bells.

"What's this one?" I tapped the glass, half hoping to trigger some sort of alarm. I'm a kid like that.

"*Papaver Somnumorium.* The Sleeping Poppy." Cerce told me, one eyebrow raised. "Not to be confused with *Papaver Somniferum,* the Opium Poppy. This one only grows in the Wyld woods of the Real. You can't get drugs from it, if that's what you are worried about. I use it for it's effects on mortals … a relaxant of mind and spirit, it forms a base for the elixir to then work without resistance. I believe a mortal writer used it in an old movie … *The Wizard of Oz,* I believe … to put the characters to sleep just from walking through a field of the stuff. Farcical fictional myth, but that's mortals for you."

"Hate to burst your bubble, but that's not the first time I've seen it this side of the Veil, and in a shitload more numbers than these." I faced her, suspicions flaring bright and hot. "Are you importing Real flora and selling it onto mortals without warning them? Coz that *IS* a pretty fundamental breach of Accords!"

"Do you take me for a cretin?" She asked, then held up a hand to forestall my instinctive response. "Hold your tongue and childish jibes. I have just finished explaining my efforts to remain discreet and within the law of both Accord and mortal writ, to then flaunt evidence of a breach so obviously to a Redcloak? Think with those few brain cells you yet retain. My mortal clients only ever receive the finished elixirs, never the ingredients. I have a few *select* individuals who I might supply with certain stock, but they are definitely within the Accords' purview. And I most certainly do not involve myself in … *horticulture.*"

Sadly, despite my wanting to make it stick, it didn't add up. There was no reason for Cerce to be selling Real plants to then have them planted in a university grounds of all bloody places, doing nothing but …. What? Pretty the place up? But what the hell were they doing there then?

"If I knew somewhere where a shitload of this stuff was, around a load of mortals … what sort of harm could I expect these things to be doing?" I asked, knowing on a hunch it was usually bad news when the Real intruded on the mortal realm, but Cerce shook her head.

"You have admitted you have contacts in the sisterhood. Ask whoever has the patience for your endless and infantile questions." The witch stepped away from the computer, facing me as she picked up a fat folder which she held out for me. "You came here seeking evidence that Soshana Carteloni … *Felicity Price* as you know her, was kidnapped back by her family, to seek revenge on Daniel Price. Petty mortal business. Exactly the sort of stupidity I would not condone, nor allow to happen."

"What's this?" I couldn't help asking another infantile question, just to see her frown deepen.

"Evidence that the concerned party has known of Daniel Price's return to this country from the moment he stepped onto English soil. The Carteloni family also knew of his travels abroad and have tracked both his and his daughter's progress most thoroughly over the years. I had Charles extract all the information from that time up until the present day, the moment we were alerted that she had been taken. There has been ample opportunity for an intervention to take place but the honest truth is, lycan … they just don't care." Cerce waggled the folder, and I reluctantly took it. "I have met the girl's mother, and she is further gone than Charles ever was on chemical stimulants and narcotics. I doubt much she remembers that she *has* a daughter, let alone feels any need to take her back into the family. The girl's grandfather was the only member who truly cared what Daniel did, and he only lasted a few years after the abscondment. Charles inherited the business, and I have explained the mess he was in when I intervened. Daniel Price has been kept under discreet surveillance all this time, purely to make sure he did not decide to make good on his threat and reveal old deals, pertinent details that could damage the Cartelonis. Having kept his side of the bargain, they did and still do feel that the matter is settled and closed."

"So the watchers on his house. On my house?" I pushed, hearing the ring of truth in Cerce's voice but not wanting to fully believe her. They were a frikkin' crime family … this sort of shit is what they did.

"The men on Mr Price's house? Call it paranoia. Call it protecting the family's own investment in Daniel's continued silence. Call it whatever you wish. I care not." The witch told me bluntly, tapping the folder then pointing at me. "I was made aware of this history shortly after I was … ah *consulted*, and the involvement of a Redcloak as a casual acquaintance of Daniel Price was not something I chose to ignore. I have thoroughly interviewed all members of the family, and I can *guarantee* their total truth on this matter. The girl is not with us, and no one knows where she is, or who took her. The men I suggested keep a watch on *your* home were ornamental and obvious, an offering for you to spot, to follow the trail back here and for us to have this meeting. We have, and that is all I have left to say on the matter."

Crap.

"Now, the hour is indeed late, and we are done here." Cerce motioned for me to leave back the way we had come. Clutching the folder, with no other evidence to counter her with, I had no other option than to comply. As I turned to go, Cerce unclipped a slim phone and tapped a quick number, cocking her head as it was answered.

"Please advise Mr Moon that we will join him in the lobby, and that his companion is safe and well." She ordered whoever was at the other end, in that professional manner that sounds like a request but clearly never is.

The ride up in the lift was held in silence, me wracking my brain for anything she had said which sounded contrary to her testimony, whilst for her part Cerce pointedly ignored me with the accustomed aloofness we thief takers normally get from immortals. I think they take lessons from mortal gentry – nothing like generations of inbreeding to hone that particular talent.

The doors slid open and I was cheered a little to find Jacob in one piece and scowling like a chunk of granite. The way he was surrounded by six of the armoured guards, all standing outside of immediate reach, told me he'd been having fun without me … I'd not known anyone like him to psych out whatever unlucky sod he was irritated with, with just a scowl and a presence that conveyed all manner of unspoken threat. I'd seen mortals turn on their heel and walk in the opposite direction after sensing him coming down the other end of a street when he was in a particularly bad mood.

I also couldn't help but wonder if all six had squeezed down with him in the lifts, and how *that* must have gone!

"So. Our business this night is concluded." Cerce told the pair of us, motioning with a casual flick of one hand to the door out. "You can compare notes when you are off private property, but I am sure you will find we've been obliging enough for you to turn your attention elsewhere for Miss Price's whereabouts."

Jacob looked across at me, and I had nothing better than a shrug and nod, idly waving the fat folder in my hand. He grunted a sigh, then faced the witch.

"We will decide when the matter is done. For now, we'll leave … with the rest of your supply of wolfsbane. That is not a request." He kept his voice neutral, no threatening or raised tone, but the certainty was there this was not a matter up for discussion.

"Of course. I would not have expected otherwise." Cerce clicked two fingers sharply, and a seventh armoured guardian appeared, gods knew where he'd been lurking. He carried the sort of container you normally see used to transport radioactive materials, along with a smaller crate that held, from what I could see, the collected crossbow bolts that had been aimed at us in the conference room. I'll give the b...*witch* this, she definitely was prepared. "Take them and dispose of the substance as you will."

"And of course, this *is* your only stock of the substance, and you *will not* be reproducing any more. Correct?" Jacob nodded to me, and like a good little sidekick I collected the case. To be fair, he'd taken the paralysing hit from Cerce whilst I got to chinwag with her in her herb garden, so I figured I owed him that at the least.

"On my honour, Redcloak." She smiled right back in his face, the lie blatant but of course, completely un-provable.

"Then, we're done." Jacob smiled right back, and beckoned me to go ahead with the poisonous cargo. We'd reached the doors, the two goons from outside ever so helpfully opening them for us to get us the hell out as quickly as possible, when he stopped and turned.

"Oh, and we *will* be in touch for your client list for this stuff. It *is* illegal to manufacture and sell a proscribed substance in the mortal realm, whether to mortal or immortal alike, and we have at least one accord-breaker in custody who I am sure will be happy to provide the name of their supplier, and details of where the delivery took place." Jacob grinned nastily, knowing like I did that there was every possibility Cerce had supplied the Mistress with the nasty shit she'd given her shape-shifter to use on me. And that must have taken place here, given the immortal's inability to travel without Court leave or her pet patsy, Artur. Pedalling this sort of shit in the Real was out of our remit, but on home turf? Not on our watch.

"That will require a writ of proof that we are in any way linked to such actions." Cerce shook her head, an old hand at this game herself. Despite the fact I was literally carrying the evidence of her guilt in my hands. However I was at least pleased to see the smug smile slip from her lips, replaced by just an ounce of concern. "I am *sure* your Alpha will arrange for such a document to be delivered before you come calling again."

"Depend on it." Jacob gave a short bow, mocking in its brevity. Then we left the building.

Chapter 22

Mythology is littered with creatures that defy logic, rally against the natural order of the universe. Centaurs ... half mortal, half horse. Sphinxes, both mortal women, lions and scorpions with dragons' wings. Manticores ... Chimeras ... the list is endless. All this really shows is that in the Real, whatever can be, will be. No matter the logic nor the seemingly lack of sense to a creatures' origin. All you can truly be sure of is, the creatures of this strange menagerie are one and all rumoured to have little patience, and vast appetites. You have been warned.

So. That had been a royal bloody waste of our time.

Jacob and I headed back to our vehicle in silence, ignoring the weighted attention of the goons who had followed us out as we started up the engine and drove slowly past the Carteloni's residence. Ok, so I *may* have waved cheerily like a child as we passed my personal stalker-goon, but then no one had ever accused of me of being an adult much in my life, and I had to do something to stop myself swearing and kicking the shit out of a company car.

The Cartelonis were definitely a dead-end. I didn't need to bother flicking through the folder Cerce had so helpfully supplied. My instincts on this sort of thing were rarely wrong, and they were shouting at me to throw in the towel on this little escapade, and go hunt down my other lead. Those three students. They *must* know something ... otherwise, I truly had fuck all, and Felicity was as good as ...

"Stop thinking that." Jacob told me, eyes focused on the road but obviously easily picking up on my plummeting mood, and just as easily deducing the shit that was going through my head. "We've got other leads to follow up. This is just another case. Think anything else and you're doing her no good."

Yeah, just another case. Except I knew it wasn't. I could tell myself we'd had shitter leads, less to go on, far worse scenarios in the history of Good Deeds, but this was the first time someone's life who *I knew and cared about* was in my paws, someone who I called friend putting their trust in me to see their daughter safe from harm. Someone not Pack. Maybe it was the lack of sleep, the adrenaline burn from the Tourney, or just the upcoming Blooding, but I was seriously struggling to find anything zen to calm myself right now.

Checking my reclaimed watch, I saw we'd lost another hour finding out this lead led nowhere, making it half one in the morning. The streets were even more deserted as we rumbled down them, those late night party goers already slumped on the last tube home or up to no good in cheap hotel rooms.

This was the time the Real residents were up and about, however, making use of the short time their lives weren't cluttered with mortals underfoot.

Gazing out the window, I caught the odd flash of movement on high amongst the gutters and rooftops, signalling the stealthy cat and mouse games gargoyles played after sunset. More than one mortal had woken to find they'd gained a statue overhead that they could have sworn was not there the night before. Troll-kin, gnomes, dwarrow, gnolls … those averse to sunlight and its petrifying effects … they were easy to spot, cleaning up the streets of the crap mortals had dropped throughout the day, to make into all manner of shiny and precious items to sell back to those selfsame mortals on electronic sites like Wish or Etsy.

Hey, I'm not a complete technophobe. Besides, what did you really think all those knock-off items and *item may be different from the visual representation* purchases were made up of?!

Anyhow, I only realised where we were headed when we rumbled past Tower Bridge, lit against the dark with flickering lines to stop the many tall ships from crashing into her in the gloom … hey, that *used* to be the case, and since then, she's just looked pretty all lit up at night so I can't argue with the mortals wanting to stick that particular tradition.

"Um, aren't we supposed to head back to the office? Catch Jess up on the Cartelonis?" I asked Jacob, knowing our Pack Alpha wouldn't have gone to bed whilst we were out on business. "Not that I don't appreciate the ride home and all …"

"Nope. Got a text whilst you were off going through Cerce's *shrubbery*." Jacob grinned sharply at his attempt at innuendo, and I guessed I was in for a few weeks of jokes about going down with the witch and playing in her basement. "Those kids you wanted followed. They were spotted heading back onto the university grounds about a half hour ago. Jess thought it worth taking a look."

Students going back on campus at past one in the morning? No, nothing suspicious about that whatsoever! Of course, we'd have no valid reason for being on site either, and I guessed an expensive and historical site like the old Naval College wouldn't stint on security. But for a couple of big, bad lycans? No problem.

Jacob pulled up a street down from the university grounds, settling the big pack-tank in besides a rack of student cycles that miraculously hadn't been stolen. Slipping out and closing the door quietly … nothing like a slamming car door to wake up a sleepy security guard … I joined him at the boot. Trunk. Back of the vehicle, whatever you want to call it. From its cavernous depths, he pulled out a black balaclava and a heavy-duty truncheon which he handed to me. Perfect tool to tap any curious mortal on the head with to make their troubles all go away. The hood I rolled up and slipped on like a cap, ready to pull down and disguise my features but not so obvious that I shouted *lawbreaker* to anyone I might pass on the way in.

"Jess wants this to go nice and quietly." My packmate told me as he closed up the door. "In, find the students, ask them what they know. Anyone interferes, it becomes a snatch and grab. Get 'em out and we'll head back to the office and interrogate them there. Got it?"

I bounced the truncheon in my palm, feeling its solid weight.

"Uh, I know it's just three kids, but what are you going to be doing whilst I'm breaking in and doing all the legwork?" I couldn't help but ask.

"Your case, Jess is happy for you to take the lead." Jacob grinned, then nodded at a package on the backseat of the big vehicle. I'd thought I'd detected the smell of meat when we'd been riding to the Carteloni residence but the fact hadn't seem that important at the time. "'Sides, Alpha was worried your dog might be missing you, so I'm off to go feed the bloody thing whilst you play with the mortals. But don't worry, you ain't going in alone."

At the same moment, I caught that familiar whiff of spring freshness, and turned to see, of all people, Elspeth walking slowly down the street towards us. The witch had swapped her normal gypsy colours to more utilitarian grey combat pants and a loose black top, wrapping up her red locks with some sort of dark headscarf so she looked a little like a new age ninja.

"My, Morgan, is that a cosh in your hand or are you just pleased to see me?" She grinned as she joined us, as Jacob grunted a laugh. Seems I was due to be the butt of all jokes this evening … morning … whatever.

"Fancied some breaking and entering to liven up your boring day job?" I shot back, but she shook her head, pointing one slim finger at me.

"Last time you went into this place, you came out with a chunk of your soul weakened, and if I recall rightly, ended up in a circle of protection somewhat out of sorts." The witch shrugged. "Jessica felt the risk worth taking again, however this time you should have backup and maybe someone professional along to ware your tender spirit. In case the big bad decides to take another bite out of you."

My Alpha, thinking three steps ahead as always. I hadn't even thought about whatever had fucked me up last time I was on the grounds, yet Jessica had already assigned our consultant expert to safeguard me. And I *was* a little worried how Bear was coping, given he'd only been out the once since this whole shitstorm kicked off. Asking Jacob to head over and play chew-toy to the trollhound, so he didn't eat the whole of my furniture in defiance, was a nice touch, Just goes to show how much she cared for her Pack and all those linked to each of us. Even big, slobbery hounds with more attitude than an all-girl high school year.

"Speaking of which …" Our resident consultant nimbly reached up and shucked off my rolled-up balaclava, looking at it with a sardonic smile. "Ah, these things are so old school. And totally useless for the matter at hand."

Tossing it to Jacob, she slipped something from her pocket and handed it over. I graciously accepted the offering, thumbing it open to find one of those close-fitting cycle masks, black and slightly futuristic looking with filters on either side of the mouth and totally enclosing the wearer's nose and lower face.

"I don't know exactly what caused your last episode, so had to hazard a few guesses as to the root of the problem." Elspeth held up an identical mask, though hers was a cheerier rose colour. "I've charmed these to filter out anything that might be in the air, and most of the more generic charms and hexes linked to souls. I'm flying blind, but you *should* be better prepared than last time wearing that."

"Funny you should say root …" I realised we hadn't had a chance to share our intel from the Cartelonis, and especially what I'd found in Cerce's basement. Knowing we were working against the clock, and hanging round jawing at this early hour risked drawing attention to ourselves, I quickly gave Elspeth the shortened version of the poppies, and what Cerce had said about them.

"Sleeping poppies? Here? That makes no sense." The witch pursed her lips, tapping one finger against them as she digested the new information. "I'll need to get a sample, see what's been done to them. There is no way they should be growing healthily in mortal soil, and in such numbers. They *could* be used as a base for a crafting but … this changes things. I'd thought this to be a creature's power, something like the lamias of Asia or somesuch. Spirit drinkers, like your run of the mill vampires but much worse. But the poppies? That could mean …"

Jacob and I waited but Elspeth didn't finish, instead just turning away to look towards the university with a thoughtful expression. I cleared my throat but she just made that shushing gesture to mean she was busy, and mere lycans wouldn't understand.

"Fine. Call me when you're done, or when it all goes tits up and you're running from the big bad poppy monster." Jacob told us both as he slid into the driver's seat and started up the tank. With that vote of confidence, he drove off, leaving the pair of us standing in the silence of Greenwich.

Elspeth finally broke her thoughts, shaking her head and turning to face me. I didn't bother asking her what conclusion she's come to … I'd find out when the surprise was probably trying to tear my face off. That sort of thing.

"So, Dorothy. Shall we go knock on the door and ask the Wizard to gift you a brain?" She linked her arm though mine, obviously having made up her mind, steering me round so we faced the Old Naval college rising up in the early morning gloom.

"What, not courage? Thought I'd be more the cowardly lion." I asked as I slipped the cycle mask round my neck to hang loosely, ready when I needed it. We walked slowly, taking the scenic route along the Thames path. Getting in was going to be the least of our problems, given the number of handily scalable walls and fences around the buildings. CCTV was most certainly an issue, as well as any foot patrols, but now that I had a handy witch along to jinx up the security footage, I was less worried about a starring role on Breaking Into College.

Elspeth snorted a quiet laugh.

"The last thing you are short on, my dear Morgan, is courage." She told me as we strolled like a couple out for a walk along the edge of the Thames. "No, definitely common sense, I think. Even the good inept Wizard could hardly make you any worse than you are."

"Stop sweet-talking me, or I'll think you're trying to get me into bed!" I joked back, earning a rolling of her eyes and a world-weary smile.

The walls here were far too high for scaling, and too exposed anyhow to casual observers let alone interested parties with phone lines to the police. No, I was already thinking we'd try the far side, with its street running parallel to the grounds and a much handier lower wall to navigate. It was the far exit for anyone driving through the college, and had a manned station which we'd need to take care of … but that posed little problem for a witch and lycan tag team.

True enough, there was a wide-awake and fairly alert watchman inside his little booth, outfitted with a flask of coffee from the smell of it and a nice view of the comings and goings around the college entrance.

I stopped as if to tie a shoelace, whilst Elspeth spun in a few lazy circles like a much younger girl, hands outstretched, enjoying the night air. Nothing to see, just two tourists out late and taking in the grandness of their surroundings. It certainly helped to cover her hands moving in rather specific gestures, and the spill of streetlights spoiled the sudden emerald illumination as she called on her Craft.

The guard, oblivious to what was going on, immediately slumped on his seat as the witch's weaving sent him off to cloud cuckoo land, and her follow-up jinx caused the camera to spark and short out. Then it was just a case of calmly slipping around the pole barring the entrance, and me remembering to reach inside to turn the guard's handset off, just on the off chance it beeped or did anything to disturb his happy slumber.

With that, we were in.

Elspeth stopped me a foot onto the grounds, nodding to my mask. I hooked the thing up and over my mouth, taking an experimental breath … finding the night air sharp and clean to my nose and definitely lacking the energy-sapping sensation I'd felt the last time I'd visited the site.

Though, and this I realised with the next breath, whatever charm she'd used wasn't perfect.

"Uh, Ellie. I can't smell anything."

"Ah, yes. Sorry about that." The witch whispered as we made for the nearest building and its handy shadows. "Like I've told you so many times, there's always a balance when using the craft. I could block out all manner of nasties and stop you breathing in anything latent in the air, but I had to stop a lot of other things as well. Like smells. As long as you wear the mask, you won't get any scents or anything. Just lungfuls of good clean air."

Great, so no jinxes taking chunks out of my soul, but I'd just been crippled, lost one of my most important senses. I wouldn't smell anyone approaching, pick up on any hinky scents or get the sharp nudge of danger I was so used to until it literally hit me in the face. Taking another breath, the air lacked all those flavours I took for granted, as well as the crap you mortals fill it with. I reckon it was like trying the caffeine-free, sugar-free Coca-Cola I'd seen in the shops instead of the far unhealthier but fuller flavoured version I was used to.

Still, all I was here for were three mortal kids. Whatever the big bad was, whatever the thing with the poppies, that wasn't my concern. Get to the kids, make them talk and follow up on wherever that led. Simple. What could go wrong?

"Morgan, I'm going to need to spend some time here. Collect some samples, work out what the hell is going on here. You ok to find the students yourself?" Elspeth whispered as she eyed the banks of flowers standing in bight clumps despite the gloomy light.

"Yeah, no worries. Scream if you need me to come running." I grunted, figuring the witch was safer staying topside and able to make a quick break for freedom if anyone stumbled over her. Plus, a lone woman was going to elicit a whole less suspicion from most security guards than if they discovered us both wandering around the joint.
Call it sexist bull or father-instinct nurturing but it's a well-known fact. Ask anyone.

So, all on my lonesome, lurking round the university grounds. Thankfully I'd made a note of the security cameras on my last visit, their presence shouting to me despite all the attempts to keep them concealed in fake fascia. Dodging through the wide concourse, making use of all the long shadows and handy walls to hide behind, I worked my way into the university grounds without attracting any undue attention. Well, apart from startling one lonesome pigeon, and getting the evil eye from a passing cat ... but that's almost a requirement when doing any proper lurking.

Where would I go if I were highly suspicious students with a terrible secret, who had broken back into their university? This didn't strike me as a prank or chance to go party, no, those three had freaked in the class when their mate ... Adrian? No, it was him, Gregory and Samantha who made the trio.

Gary, that was it. Gary Weatherby. When the goth girl had called him out as missing too, that was when the three had freaked. Whatever their secret was, it linked to what all four of them were into. And the immediate conclusion which sprung to mind was their class, occultism. Maybe they'd met there, or known each other before, but that was where they'd spent time together ... and where Felix had crossed their path. So, let's start there, shall we?

Getting to the classroom proved surprisingly easy. The security for the place seemed to be focused more on the Great Hall and more grandeur buildings, so the fact that Professor Plum and his School for Witchcraft and Wizardry had been delegated to the basements made things oh so much simpler. I didn't even need to knock a single security guard out with my handy little cosh, which almost seemed a waste of a good tool.

The classroom door was ajar, and I took a moment to listen in through the gap. Regular run of the mill silence greeted me, just what you'd expect from an empty room ... except just on the border of my hearing, the sounds of muted voices. Two very distinctive one man, one woman. Possibly cleaners doing their thing but then, possibly not.

I slid into the room, keeping the door from announcing my presence with its customary creaking groan. And found it empty, the tables and chairs set ready for the next batch of young hopefuls' backsides to fill. The blackboard had been wiped clean of whatever occult symbolism Professor Knox had been trying to imprint in his classes' grey matter, and even the sleeping poppies in their vases had been removed.

So, no evil monster lurking in the basement ready to pounce on me. No troubled teenagers poking needles into voodoo dolls, or crones cackling over a burning cauldron. Nothing that you wouldn't expect to find in a hundred classrooms across the world out of hours.

Except the dwarf door.

That *definitely* did not belong.

Dwarrow tend to be worse than trolls for keeping their front doors as secure and lacking hospitality as possible. Once you'd made it in through the portal, you could expect a dwarf's forge to be a much more welcoming place given you most likely had business with the owner and were therefore a source of the fabled wealth the little bastards were known to hoard. However, they'd long learned that treasure seekers, disgruntled clients and the run of the mill inquisitive mortals had a habit of a'coming knocking and disturbing their privacy. Quite often to drop off pamphlets for the local pizza parlour or PII re-claimers offering their services for that magical word "free.

Anyhow, Dwarrow were renowned as masters of the invisible door, runes used to mask a portal's presence unless the proper sequence was used. Breaking through the intricate crafting usually set off all manner of nasty counter measures, so thieves tended to leave the things alone and instead take on less painful and risky schemes. The things were used, therefore, by mages to guard their laboratories, Dragons to hide away their hoards, even evil villains to ward their collections of stuffed toys or childhood photo-albums.

Not universities, or professors wanting to decorate boring old classrooms. Or to lock up the chalk. Talk about overkill.

Whomever had opened the dwarrow door had helpfully not closed it behind them, so the thing was outlined in the ruddy light of the activated runes, taking up most of the space behind the teaching lectern, and partially hidden behind the blackboard. I could see the thing had been set on hinges, to swing out and allow access to the portal, just another little detail to show someone *really* didn't want the entrance discovered.

So. Mysterious door in the same classroom where occultism was taught. I didn't need my sense of smell to tell me how hinky this was. Voices drifted through the open portal, definitely a guy and girl in very agitated states. Carefully and quietly approaching the dwarrow door, I took a moment to listen in, just to get a sense of what lay ahead.

"... *Shouldn't have come back here! You know he said never to* ..."

"...*Gary's the cause of this! Never meant* ..."

"...*can't we just stop? It's gotten so crazy* ..."

"...*Adrian, he's got Felix! That man who came round asking, he knew* ..."

That last bit did it for me. The three of them were wrapped up in this whole stinking mess, and they knew something about Felix. Time enough for the softly-softly approach, now I just wanted answers.

I went through the door like a police unit raiding an illegal's safehouse, yanking it wide open and barrelling through. The room beyond was far larger than the classroom, set with shelves and cupboards, hanging bundles of herbs amidst caged skeletons and other bizarre paraphernalia. Some sort of large apparatus had been set up on a wooden platform, glass glinting in convoluted bulbous configurations through which some sort of glowing liquid slowly passed. All very weird, all very ominous in a *what the fuck was this doing in the university basement* kinda way. Light was cast by glimmering stones set in sconces on the bare walls, definitely *not* running off the grounds' electricity and more fitting to some Victorian style dungeon than a modern-day centre of learning.

I took all this in with a quick glance, also noting three other doors set in the walls leading Gods knew where. However, my attention quickly settled on the two figures huddled off to my right, crouched down by a large chest that looked some sort of old pirate-booty holder. Blackened iron bound, scarred timber and large crafted handles. The guy … Greg or Adrian, had frozen in mid shove, pushing some sort of furry object past the girl's resisting hands … Samantha. He already had something similar wrapped around his waist.

"What the hell are you…?" Greg / Adrian started, but I shut him down by simply grabbing hold of his jacket, bunching it up and hurling him off his feet to sprawl on the floor. Samantha skittered back, one hand clutching at whatever her friend had given her, eyes grown wide with fright.

"Shut. The. Fuck. Up." I rasped, pointing a finger firstly at him, then her. "All I want to hear from either of you is … where the fuck is Felix."

"You were the dad? You came to class today … Who are you?" Samantha stammered, shock and fear warring inside for control of her vocal chords. Greg / Adrian pushed himself up but I just knocked him back down with a casual backhand, seeing blood spill from a split lip as he cried out.

"Whatever shit you are up to, ends now. Before I get *really* angry, I'll ask again! Where's Felix?"

"You've got no right … You *hit* me!" Greg / Adrian blubbered from the cold floor, staring at the blood on his fingers as he checked his face.

"I'm going to do a lot more than just hit you, if you keep jerking me around!" I snarled, then decided enough was enough. These kids were fooling around with the occult, so maybe it was time for it to bite back a little. So I Changed.

Samantha went white as my mask deformed and stretched against my muzzle, seeing my claws slide with sinister snicks from their sheaths. I held one gnarled fist up and let the strange gemstone light glint off the four points, staring with my awakened eyes down at the pair.

"Now talk." I growled.

That's when things went – as Jacob predicted – completely tits up.

Chapter 23

Hexed items have, throughout the ages, enabled their users to take on different forms. Hexenwolfen changing to beasts, cloaks to enshroud and change their wearers, armour that once adorned transforms the owner into a mighty warrior or foul creature of unspeakable might. The one truth with all these items is that they feed from those that use them, transforming them from the mortals they once were to beings of lesser will, with themselves lost to the enchantment. For any word of warning, JRR Tolkien wrote it best in that the wearer of the One Ring would always become a lesser shade, under the rule of Sauron. Never truth an enchantment.

There is always a price to pay.

To my awakened senses, the furry belt that Adrian / Greg wore, and that Samantha now clutched protectively to her, glowed with a malignance I hadn't been able to see with my day-wear form. Off to the side, the mad scientist's apparatus now thrummed with some weird vestige of life, like the stuff flowing through the tubes had a pulse or something.

But that was only a momentary distraction, as I *felt* the sudden surge of magic, a virulence I had sensed before. In Felix's room. Weaker, definitely, but of the same brand of mad-ass mage-fuckery.

And before my eyes, the interchangeable Adrian / Greg himself Changed.

Where before had been a lanky, weak chinned and acne ridden youth with mussed up hair and the sort of skin colour normally attributed to milk gone sour, now I faced … well … frankly a wolfen. Not a proper lycan, but this thing was a damned spitting image to the cheap monster-movie guest stars gracing late-night tv. Coarse fur sprouted like quills from exposed skin, and his face was deformed to allow for a mangle of snaggle sharp fangs. He'd bulked out too, as he crouched and snarled at me, muscle-mass straining the thin shirt and trousers he'd worn for this late night whatever.

"What the fuck?" I growled eloquently, as my mask finally gave up and slipped free. Instantly I felt that weird-shit weakness clawing at me, trying to chew a piece of me all over again, as I staggered from its aggressive assault. The Changed student launched himself at me, lashing with jagged claws, but even off-balance I'd easily read his intention and simply dodged the clumsy attack. I hooked the collar of his shirt and spun him, ramming him hard into a stack of crates which exploded around him in a burst of glassware and wooden shrapnel.

"Stay down." I snarled, adding a kick to the side of his head to keep him from getting up. Normally I'd have treated mortals with a lot more TLC, used the rubber cosh Jacob had given me for just this sort of encounter, but I reckoned that the bastard on the floor now could handle more damage than normal. What with the way he still writhed amongst the wreckage of the crates, and was spitting with fury.

Turning, I faced Samantha, who still remained her normal self despite clutching the totem that I now recognised for what it was now. Definitely bad juju, the sort of witchcraft that in the middle ages had quite rightly had its users burned at the stake or drowned, whilst unfortunately missing the real villain of the crime. The bastard that had crafted the item itself.

Hexenwolfen. A totem, like the magic rings from Tolkien, or the invisibility cloak in Harry Potter, that allowed its user to be something or do something supernatural, whether they were Real, mortal or had any talent whatsoever. In this case, the skin taken from a true lycan, dipped in the blood of a witch and then cursed under a full moon to allow its wearer to change into a beast.

Pagan druids used to grant them to their protectors, Viking *berserkers* would oft-times use them to change into bear-like beasts in battle … these things had a habit of popping up throughout history, and in each and every case, it never ended well for the wearer. Wonder why *hex* is in the title? It's a cursed item, and is powered by the spirit and emotion of the user … the more they changed, the less they had of themselves until they were simply beasts without the natural intelligence of animals or morality of mortals. Blood drinkers, flesh eaters, the users always needed hunting down and slaying eventually as they gave into the addiction of being the *other,* the freedom it granted them from their own lives.

And let's circle back to the point it takes the *skin* of a lycan to make. So these students were wearing the dead flesh of one of my kith and kin, possibly.

"Don't be stupid." I told the young woman, even as she pulled the belt tighter around her waist. "Just tell me who the fuck gave you those things, and where Felix is. This doesn't have to end badly."

Which was a total lie, given they'd been using hexed-totems for Gods knew how long, and were most likely scarred for the rest of their lives from the damage it would have done them. But I wasn't about to brighten up her day with that reality check.

"Y…you're … you're one of them. A *real* lycan." Samantha panted, the war she was going through flitting across her features. Anger … fear … rage … fear … back and forth like a seesaw. "*He* said you'd come if we were stupid … Gary couldn't stop himself … we *didn't* mean for this to happen! He's one of them, Greg!"

Her voice rose to almost a shriek as she backed up, pedalling her legs like she had any place to go. And then I realised she was looking over my shoulder.

Fuck. *Three* students. I'd heard two voices from outside but there had been the three of them together in the classroom, and Jacob had said they'd all been sighted breaking back into the university. Without my sense of smell, I hadn't picked up on who was or wasn't in the room, and like a true dumb-ass I'd assumed on seeing two of them, that was all there was.

Greg, now that Samantha had named him, barrelled into me from either one of the doors I'd spotted and dismissed or from wherever he'd been hiding. The bastard had already Changed, snarling and spitting from a mouth full of fangs as he threw me off Adrian. I felt talons score through my clothing flashes of sharp pain from the shallow cuts making me snarl in reply.

Lashing out, I grabbed the third student by the throat and lifted him off me, as we tumbled through another packing crate. Glass and other materials shattered and crunched under me as I rolled, heaving the furious *hexenwulf* up and pounding his stupid-ass face with one fist. I didn't want to kill the fucker, so I kept my claws clear, but made sure I hit hard enough to smear blood and broken teeth across his face as he screamed in pain.

Pain erupted in my left leg, as I rolled to find my feet. Adrian had jumped me whilst I dealt with Greg, biting into my thigh and worrying me like some crazed rabid dog. His Changed teeth were sharp enough to slash into muscle, and I pounded his thick skull without a care until he dropped away. He yelped and tumbled away, shaking his head, but quickly found his feet and snarled at me … as Greg joined him, circling to try and take me from either side. Pack mentality, the way weaker predators take down a strong prey.

That's when I felt Samantha jump onto my shoulders, wrapping her legs round me. I twisted, trying to buck her off, imagining her Changed teeth trying to chew through my neck and spine any moment, but she still seemed to be herself.

"*He* said you'd come! Said the only way to stop you. Got to stop you!" She whined, definitely unhinged, but the next moment I felt her hand cover my mouth and nose with something like cloth. And a vicious, noxious smell I had grown to *hate.*

Wolfsbane.

I tried not to breathe, to wrestle her off me and grab the fucking cloth off my face, but her two accomplices hammered into me, thumping hard into my chest and throat so I couldn't do anything but gasp reflexively ... and take a huge dose of that bloody stuff inside. It ran down my throat like acid, burning so I choked and stumbled. Samantha threw herself off, backing away as I stumbled on sudden-weak legs, everything growing fuzzy as the shit kicked in.

A shape loomed in front of me, and I feebly raised an arm, but felt it brushed away.

"Tha's fer my teef." Someone spat ... probably Greg from the spit and bloody froth I felt shower me, then his fist slammed hard into my head and it was goodnight for me.

"*Go see if anyone came with him ...*"

Voices drifted to me as I lay on the floor, more than a little surprised to find I was still breathing. A fuzzy through sparked through me ... *Elspeth* ... but there was fuck all I could do about it, as the wolfsbane worked its charm on me. When this was over, if I lived to see it through, Cerce had some *serious* fucking explaining to do ... my thoughts bounced around my head. Supplying mortal students with this shit ... someone had warned them ... *Him,* Samantha had said. Told them what I was, how to deal with me. Bastard ...

"There was someone, but the bitch threw something in my face. Got away." Another voice bounced into my ears, and I couldn't but give a snarl of joy. The witch had gotten clear.

"Shit. He's still awake!" I think it was Samantha, but then all of them were girly sounding to my ears. Balls hadn't dropped for the two of 'em, probably why they'd gotten mixed up in the *Hexenwolfen* shit. Made to feel stronger, more Alpha. Fuckwits.

"Can't deal with him here. He'd kill us when he finds out. Take him to the Park. We can bury him up there."

Oh good, I was going for a ride. The park sounded nice … grass, fresh air, and a very own hole for me to lie in and wait for this shit to be over. My thoughts tumbled and spun, images of Felix and Danny causing me to wince, knowing I'd probably fucked things for them royally.

Then someone's foot connected with my jaw, and I was out again.

The stink of him filled her nostrils, jerking her up as she scrambled to her feet. Still blindfolded, Felix lashed out trying to strike him … she could feel him close to her, watching …

"Let me go, you bastard!" She screamed, voice raw, tears running down her face uncaring.

Silence answered her except for the heaviness of his breathing, that rank smell she'd first in the alley, that night when … god, when he'd murdered that poor man. And then in her room … and now down here, wherever he had taken her.

"Let me go!" She yelled and felt something brush her face. Throwing a punch, missing, feeling the touch stain her skin like oil and shit.

"I never wanted this." The voice was harsh and rough, sounding oddly broken … but still familiar. Terribly familiar. "I just wanted you to … to notice me."

"Gary? Gary! Let me go!" She screamed, as she felt him there, so close and yet beyond reach. Watching her.

Sobbing, she crashed to her knees, dirt smearing through her clothes to chill her skin.

"I just want to go home!"

No one answered.

Chapter 24

It is often wondered at the allure mermaids … part mortal woman, part fish … have upon mortal men. With their upper torso so brazenly on display, it is easy to see how sailors far from home, far from those they love and cherish, might be bewitched. Yet all know that beneath the waves lie only cold slippery scales, the touch and feel of the fish. So why are they drawn time after time to through themselves into a watery grave? The answer is … mortal men. Who really knows.

I woke to my surroundings slowly, the punch and kick to the head definitely sapping my ability to bounce back, almost as bad as the crap they'd dosed me with. Too many injuries over too short a time, with wolfsbane doubly dosed to make things that much worse.

We were definitely out of the university grounds. Whatever shit was going on with those poppies was a fading memory, easily overtaken by the long list of other injuries and damage I'd taken. The fresh scent of grass, the whisper of leaves, all pointed to the fact we'd relocated. And given the three students would have had to cart me along between them, I guessed they hadn't thought to go far.

Greenwich Park sprawls behind the town, rolling over high hills and deep dells, and was a popular haunt for students, locals and visitors alike. Normally the place would be ankle deep in children playing ball games, cyclists dodging slower moving joggers with the occasional screech of brakes and shouted swear words, and teenage boys tanning their muscles in the sun whilst their female companions gossiped over who was the most fit of them all. Or visa versa these days.

But this early in the morning, the only people in theory out in the Park would be the park rangers on their patrols, and the drifters and down-and-outs looking for a tree to sleep under. For three enterprising students neck deep in occultist shit, and the ability to change form into beasts with better hearing and smell, it was a piece of cake to dodge these and find a nice secluded spot to dump me. As was their plan.

As I lay on the crushed grass, I could hear the rhythmic grunting and hiss of breath that normally would have had me walking away, and leaving whatever couple were … well, coupling to their business. The crunch of dirt however gave away the fact at least two of them were digging, not anything else, and most likely their intent being something deep enough to dump my body for it to remain undetected for a long while. Typical mortal reaction … shit hits the fan, find the nearest hole and try to hide the crap.

Thankfully, they weren't aware of a couple of things, both of which I was betting on saving my ass. However, lying here waiting wasn't going to help anyone, so I'd best at least string this along as long as I could.

Rolling slowly, feeling the world wobble around me, I prised open my eyes … blinking them against the feeling of needles stabbing repeatedly into them. Dawn light was slowly cutting through the night's murk, making me think it had taken them longer to drag me here undetected that they'd probably wanted … another point in my favour.

Samantha stood off to one side, thankfully still herself though she wore the *hexen* belt and stroked it possessively without thinking. Maybe the thing didn't have its claws all the way inside her, maybe there was hope for her.

Just at my line of sight, I could see the Changed forms of Adrian and Greg ducking and hewing at a large hole they'd dug with their claws. They were going at it enthusiastically, heaving dirt onto a pile off to one side, ready to be pushed back over me. Given what I could see of them, they were already a good five feet down, so I probably had a little breathing space before they finished the job. Not much, but maybe enough.

Checking myself carefully over, I realised they'd searched me, my pockets ripped and flapping, contents probably dumped. The bastards had been clever enough to use the cable ties I kept on me as sturdy hand cuffs, lashing my arms behind me. No way I could use my claws to sever them … whatever you see in the movies, no one is that flexible. Plus I'd Changed whilst unconscious, slipping back into my mortal suit. If I shifted whilst cuffed, I risked the chance of those tough-as-steel cables cutting through my wrists …maybe I'd snap the cords, maybe I'd end up with severely fucked up hands. Not worth risking it.

Instead, I settled on shifting into an upright position, fighting the nausea of the poison, fixing my eyes on the three. Samantha caught my movements, taking a further step back from me and flapping a hand towards her two friends. Black-spiky haired and ugly clawed its way up out of the hole, eyeing me with those fever-crazed eyes of his. Adrian, I remembered. Greg remained in the hole, digging with great heaves of his arms, but his crumpled face with the damage I'd done with my fist glared at me from over the grave's lip.

"Whoa, hold on." I told them as Adrian snarled and raised one clawed hand to slap me back into unconsciousness. "I'm not going to put up a struggle. You got me, fair and square. Just wanted some answers before you bury me."

"Why should we care?" Samantha told me bluntly, face still far too pale to be healthy, hand twitching on the furry belt. "We don't owe you anything …"

"Nope, you don't. But you owe Felix Price something. She's been taken by your buddy … Gary. Gary Weatherby." I told them slowly, fixing each one of them with my gaze, looking for it.

The flicker of guilt, the shred of mortal shame and what had happened. In the hole, Greg snorted and carried on digging, but Adrian checked his attack, arm lowering slightly and monster head looking across at Samantha. For her part, she ducked her face and shook her head, as if denying the fact.

"He's killed, murdered at least six men, maybe more we don't know about." I ground out the facts, every moment I delayed, the better the chance I had. "The *hexenwulf* is in control of him, he's lost himself. And if that's true, then there is nothing good coming out of him having Felix. She didn't do anything to deserve that sort of end."

"It's not his fault." Samantha half whispered, still shaking her head. "He never … We never meant for anything like this to happen. It was just a game, something we did. Being *different*, not stuck with these clumsy awkward bodies." She gestured down at herself, at Adrian with his bulging muscles. "When he showed us how to change, it was like … Christmas!"

"He? I'm guessing your Professor? Knox?" I hazarded, but breathed a sigh when she gave a quick nod. "I'm guessing it started small, lessons after class … him seeing something in you four. He wanted to show you it was all real, not just boring shit in old books or theoretical crap, right?"

"He took us up here." She gestured to the park around her, the trees standing ghostlike in the pre-dawn. "Said he wanted to show us something real, something true. Not to be scared … but something we could all share in."

"And he changed into a wolfen. You probably wanted to run away, but he didn't attack you or anything. Just let you get used to him?"

Samantha looked up, a spark cutting through the fear, the shame.

"Run away? Are you kidding?" She pointed at herself, then Adrian again. "I was bullied all through school for being so weak, so gawky. Girls used to rip my hair and slap me in the toilets just for the fun of it. Adrian was put in hospital by one of his school bullies. Three broken ribs from being kicked like a football."

"We were weak! Told to put up with it, to move on. It's just a phase every kid goes through." Adrian mangled the words through his toothy jaws, but I'd grown used to hearing speech from non-mortal mouths, let alone my own kin speaking to me whilst Changed.

"And so when the good ol' Professor showed you how you could be strong, be bigger and better than anyone who'd bullied you, you leapt at the chance." I sighed, knowing the ease at which the man had manipulated the four youths. Preyed on their weakness, made them feel special, like they deserved this special treatment. Gods, sometimes I truly do wonder how the mortal race has survived so long when you're basically a bunch of furless lemmings shown a cliff …

"What about Gary? Am guessing he was bullied too?"

Samantha shied away, then sighed.

"His dad. Mr Weatherby worked on the river. Used to pull barges and rubbish floats up and down for a living. He drank, something he'd picked up in the Navy." She caressed the fur belt, seeking some comfort from it. "He used to beat Gary, hit him hard. *To make him a man*, he'd say. I grew up with him, saw what his dad did to him. Humiliated him, treated him like dirt. Blamed him for killing his mother, when she died in child-birth. It wasn't fair!"

A poisonous home-life, plenty of damage thrown in and a truly fucked up relationship from a dead mother, no proper contact apart from Samantha here to teach little Gary Weatherby about men and women. Add a little seasoning of *Hexenwolfen*, and no wonder the guy had gone postal. He'd probably been headed for some sort of breakdown, probably due to break some mortal law and en-route to life behind bars when he'd crossed paths with

Robert Knox, or whomever the hell the guy was. And he'd seen all that pent-up darkness, that anger and fury, and decided to give it a little nudge in the very wrong direction.

"It was just fun. We would ... change, come up here and run around. Stalk the deer and just enjoy not being *ourselves.*" She went on, and I guessed where this was headed. "But then Gary ... he didn't mean to hurt the old man. He was homeless, sleeping out rough and drunk. I think he reminded him of his dad. Started shouting and screaming, he tried to run away and Gary just ... oh god there was so much blood ..."

"So you buried the body, pretended it never happened, and didn't think it had any effect on your friend? You never thought he might have *liked* killing the guy? That he would want more?" I choked back a laugh, just at the sheer stupidity of people. The naivety. Just because it appalled one of them, *of course* it would be bad for them all.

"He started disappearing. Turning up late for class like he hadn't slept. The Professor took him aside, spoke to him, but we never knew what about." She whispered, ringing her hands now. At least it was a good sign, her stopping touching that bloody belt. "When he started sending notes to Felix ... I thought it was a good sign. Something nice, not anything to do with his dad ... that tramp. Maybe he'd get over this, come back to us ..."

"So you encouraged him. Told him he should do something, make Felix see him?" I read the truth in the way her shoulders shook, the guilt running like water from her. "Must have pissed him off when she started passing his love notes to those other girls in the class? She told me someone was writing her in runic script, said she gave it to the goths who loved that sort of thing. Felix wasn't into that sort of silliness ... if you'd just spoken to her ..."

"Spoken to her?" She whipped her head up, eyes narrowing as anger sparked. "She was just like those girls in the school. Always better than me … prettier than me … She didn't want to have anything to do with us. Just ignored him, Like he … he … ignored me …"

Oh crap. And there was the crux of it. Samantha had had a crush on Gary, probably always wanted them to be together. The young woman had shared his pain, known his past, and dreamt that she would be the one to heal him. And he'd gone after another woman, someone who reminded her of the girls who had bullied and tormented her … and who, I was pretty sure without any real understanding … had not even seen him, or them. The world Felix lived in was just so different, so untouched by the level of damage this small group had experienced.

"So you told him to do something. *Make* her see him." I told her slowly, the anger snarling inside, fighting against the shit pumping through me. The hot flame of righteous kick-ass fury baying to be let loose. The sheer fucking stupidity of it all …

"I went to Professor Knox when he stopped coming to class." She stuck her chin out, defiant despite her guilt. "I told him, told him everything. He said I hadn't done anything wrong. That Gary just needed some time to think. He warned me that people like you might come sniffing if we did anything rash, like try and find him. Best to leave him alone, let him come back in his own time …"

Either Professor Knox was a prize one idiot, or he'd guessed Gary had gone off the reservation and for whatever reason, actually wanted that to happen. It made no sense to my poison fugged head, too many facts lining up that needed sorting through.

"And that shit around the university? The poppies?" I asked, but drew a blank from both her and her monster friend. They could be lying, they might know the whole weird shit story of whatever that crap was in the hidden room, but I guessed not.

The professor hadn't needed to share those details, happy enough to let them play monster instead.

"Enough!" Greg growled, pushing himself out of the now fairly deep hole. He glared at me, his muzzle skewed and broken, still bloody from my punch. That was the thing with *Hexenwolfen* … it was inferior magic to true lycanthropy. He'd heal, eventually, but the magic fed off the spirit of the user, and these three were still fairly weak mortals. Yes, they'd gotten the drop on me but I was exhausted, had been in multiple fights and had just been getting over being poisoned when they dosed me up all over again. Toe to toe, I'd have handed them their panties in normal circumstances.

And, if my ears were there to be believed, I'd be seeing that fairly soon. The sounds I'd been hoping for, let alone the scents now slipping through to me, were as welcome as a cold beer after a long hard day.

"You've got your answers." Greg growled, stepping past his friends and looming over me. "Your fault for poking your fucking nose in. Now you'll pay."

"Oh, I'm not going to argue. This was entirely my fault," I told him blandly, seeing the surprise in his maddened eyes as I didn't try to fight or beg. "Thing is, though. It wasn't just my nose that got poked into your shit."

And that was when twenty-five stone of truly pissed trollhound hammered out of the undergrowth, roaring like the end of the world itself.

Bear, bristling and enraged, slammed through Greg like he was made of sticks. The *hexenwolfen* spun as my faithful hound bounded past, blood arcing in a sticky spray as the hound slapped him aside with one clawed paw. Adrian howled, leaping to attack, but Bear took him in his massive maw and shook him, slamming him from side to side as the *wolfen*'s claws tried to cut through his thick spiky fur.

Samantha stumbled back, as I pushed myself up onto my knees and then feet, facing her.

"Tell them to stay down, and I'll stop him from doing too much damage." I told her gently, even as Adrian screamed as something crunched under Bear's impressive jaws. "Tell them now, or ..."

Oh fuck. She Changed.

Snarling, she sprang at me, claws reaching for my throat and maw spitting hate as she sought to take me down. Stop her friends getting hurt. All reason had fled her crazed eyes, the student had finally given in to the belt's call. I fell back, lashing out with my feet ... but no need.

Jacob had been a step behind Bear, Changed and a powerhouse as he crossed the space between the edge of the clearing and us. Even as she realised her mistake, Samantha tried to twist and lash out at the newcomer, but he simply grabbed her arm and spun her, letting her own bodyweight do the work.

A sickening crack resounded through the glade, and she gave a choking scream as her arm flopped in his hand. Probably not a clean break, as he ground the injured limb between his gnarled fingers, eliciting further choking gasps from her as she dropped.

Bear dropped Adrian, a crumpled mess making groaning sobs, and rounded on Greg who was stumbling from where he had landed, one clawed hand gripping his bloody stomach. There was still fight in the bastard, but I didn't want this to end in any corpses where possible. Besides, there were answers I still needed.

"Jacob!" I shouted, as he gave Samantha a solid kick to the head, silencing her muted screams. "*Hexenwolfen*. The bastards' belts."

"Guessed that." He growled back, reaching down and ripping the thing from Samantha's waist. She instantly shifted back, a slight and very damaged young woman, thankfully unconscious given the angle her arm lay at.

"Bear! Leave him alone!" I shouted, even as the trollhound easily dodged the stumbling *wolfen*, shoulders bunched and ready to strike. He shot me a look of downright disappointment, jaws bared and bloody, but padded back as the student crumpled to his knees. Jacob was there a moment later, batting aside the snapping jaws and yanking off the furry belt.

"You do know how to make a mess." Elspeth's voice sounded behind me, as she joined the merry gathering. Still clad in her dark greys from the break in, she quickly stepped to my side, peering into my eyes. "Goddess, Morgan, did you get yourself poisoned *again*?"

I held out my bound wrists behind me, shaking them suggestively.

"There were three of them, and I didn't think …"

"No, dear, you didn't. That seems to be a common thread with you." She sighed, even as she sliced through the binding cords with a small knife she slipped from a pocket. Then she snapped open two vials, mixing the contents in one hand. "Here, swallow."

The sharp taste of raw garlic hit me as I swallowed down the handful, mixed with some sort of herbal extract. Instantly I felt the wolfsbane diminish, the nausea seeping away and strength flooding back through my ache-a-minute body. I straightened, drawing a deep breath and grinned.

"Thanks for the save. When did you guess things had gone to shit?"

The witch shrugged, pointing at the prone figure of Adrian.

"That one came looking for me but I disinclined to accept his invitation. Dosed him with a nice face full of silver thistle but I wisely decided I needed some help to come find out what trouble you were in." She nodded across at Jacob, who was bagging the fur-belts, having shifted back to his stone-faced mortal form. "He suggested bringing your dog, and he it was who picked up your scent and led us here. Then Jacob kept us waiting within reach until he judged you were out of time."

"Told you it'd go to tits up." My packmate happily grinned at me, and I just gave a weak shrug.

"What can I say? I hate to disappoint you." I gave him the point. I'd be hearing of this for months to come.

"Can you do anything for them?" I asked Elspeth, who cocked her head and looked at me with a judging eye.

"They were going to kill you, Morgan. And I heard enough to know they covered up at least one murder on this very ground too. Why should I waste the Goddess's gifts on such as these?"

"Coz they're just fucked up kids, Ellie. Led astray by the real bastard of the story." I argued, guessing she was just testing me but giving her the truth of it. "They're the ones always at the end of a bully's fist, always made to feel like they are worth shit. And that bastard knew it, and took advantage of them."

"Plus," I added. "I need at least one of them able to speak so I can go find Felix. This isn't over."

"All good points, and since you asked so sweetly, of course I will aid them." She tapped my cheek and smiled. "Jessica will of course cover the costs of my fee for healing up three mortals not on her payroll."

Great. Another bill I was landing in my Alpha's lap. Between this and the taxi fares, I'd be looking at some serious payback from any jobs I took for the next year.

It only took the witch a moment to judge, of the three, that Adrian was the least damaged despite my trollhound's mauling. Bear hadn't really applied much strength to his bite, otherwise the student would have been easily separated in half, and had inflicted only flesh wounds and possibly a cracked rib or two. So whilst Elspeth shot Jacob a withering look as she inspected the mess he'd made of Samantha's arm, I settled down by the groaning student and slapped him back into consciousness.

He stared up at me, eyes wide with fear and pain, as I leaned in close.

"It's over. Your friends are still alive, and we'll work on keeping them that way. And I'll try to forget you were going to kill me and dump me in a fucking hole." I growled under my breath. "For that, you'll tell me where Gary's gone. Where he's taken Felix. And then, when she's safe, everything about this Professor Knox. Now, spill."

It probably helped that Bear padded over and leaned against my shoulder, lowering his maw to Adrian's face and snarling deep and throatily down at him. Nothing reverberates like a trollhound ... which isn't a great thing when you realise this also counts for how loud the fuckers snore. I mean ... we're talking thunderous.

"I don't ... don't know." He stammered but I cut him off, thinking back to what the Morrigan had hinted at outside Danny's house ...

Seek your answers at a place where knowledge is worshipped and yet enslaved, and over water where things be out of sight and forgotten

The first bit was obviously meant to point me to the university, to these three bastards and Gary. But the second bit ... *Over water where things be out of sight and forgotten ...*

"Samantha said Gary's dad used to work on the Thames. What happened?"

Adrian shook his head, trying to clear his thoughts.

"Damn it, kid. Spit it out!" I snarled, pressing down on his wounded chest and eliciting a gasping howl. I felt Elspeth's disapproval, but I'd take it. This kid knew something.

"I ... Gary told us there was an accident. His dad, he got drunk. Slipped and fell. Hit his head and drowned." Adrian gasped as I lifted my hand. "They had a place down on the docks, down Deptford Creek. It's a small canal off the main waterway. He used to take us down there to smoke weed and drink … his Dad's boat is there. Used to say it was where he could get away from it all, shut everything out …"

"Out of sight and forgotten. Perfect." I grinned savagely and pushed myself up.

"Got what you need?" Jacob asked, as I tousled Bear's head and drew strength from the trollhound's closeness. He might be an absolute sod at times, and murder to any squirrel or fast-moving animal in a mile wide radiance of our home, but I'd go through fire for the furry behemoth, and he felt the same. Anything for an extra sausage or five.

"Think I know where the fucker is. Going to go get Felix." I told him bluntly, then nodded towards the students.

"Jessica needs to talk to these three." I nodded to the bag he had fastened to his belt, containing the hex-belts. "They know more about this Professor Knox, and there's a room down in the university. Dwarrow door built in, but with some weird-shit equipment that might make sense to Elspeth. Explain what he's been up to."

Neither of us even tried to guess what fate awaited the students. On one hand, they had been manipulated by their university professor, led down the path of using cursed items. On the other, the *hexenwolfen* had its claws in all three of them, and they couldn't be trusted not to go seeking the same feeling again. Like drug takers coming off their favourite high. They hadn't given up the things willingly, and it would eat away at them, risking the chance they'd go seeking the same thrill elsewhere. And there was no shortage of utter bastards from the Real willing to barter with weak-willed and desperate mortals.

"You going in alone?" Jacob eyed me up and down, in my ripped trousers with the pockets turned out, my top shredded from the *wolfens's* claws. The effects of the wolfsbane were severely diminished – whatever Elspeth had given leaps and bounds above the normal garlic cloves I'd crunched to help last time – but I still looked like a train wreck.

"I'll take Bear. Need his nose." I looked down, and took in my outfit's condition. I shrugged. "Too much to hope you have anything my size in the trunk?"

Chapter 25

Ghasts, gnolls, urid and other such creatures are known as feeders of the spoiled, creatures that haunt graveyards and battlefields to feast upon the flesh of the fallen. What is not so well known is that these creatures were, commonly, mortal men and women. Lost far from home, without the sustenance to sustain their vitals. Forced to survive by any means necessary. They are not devils, nor creatures of ill intent, simply damned souls bound to their misshapen bodies for the choice of life over morality.

Deptford Creek, also called Deep Creek, is a wide-ish estuary running off the Thames, just opposite the Isle of Dogs. It's a haven of old ship-builders' huts and decaying wooden runs into the water when the tide is high, large scale but abandoned warehouses which used to run as slaughterhouses when animals were brought up the Thames from the market, and these days a sanctuary for wild birds and whatever else managed to live amongst the muck and mire of the river. Despite it's presence in history, it definitely is a place of forgotten times, rusting old wrecks and pitted outbuildings slowly collapsing in on themselves in quiet ruin.

Jacob had probably guessed just how bad a mess I would get myself into, so when Elspeth had called him frantically after fleeing the *wolfen*, he'd grabbed one of my emergency bags from the flat as well as bundling up Bear to come hunting. So I'd been able to dump my shredded gear and change into comfortable clothes before calling a taxi for me and my dog. The bag also contained a small but suitably impressive armoury, most of which I'd left behind, but the shortsword of silvered steel now sat snuggly in a strap across my back, disguised as one of those courier-bag things. I'd added two boot knives and a chain of silver, all hidden about my person.

There had been one last item in the bag, picked up from where I'd left it after visiting Danny's place. No idea how Jacob had known it would be useful, but I was thankful all the same.

We were hunting a crazed *hexenwolfen* who had killed a handful of mortals, and had my friend's daughter locked up someplace in this decaying graveyard of old industry. Whether he came in peacefully, or made a fight of it, I wasn't walking away this time.

Bear bounded along the pathway leading into the Creek, as sea birds screamed overhead and the tide lapped at the muddy banks. Morning was finally breaking, and the river was slowly coming to life with the Thames Clippers churning up the waters with their first customers coming into or leaving the city, whilst the smaller tugboats wove slowly along its turgid length. Gary Weatherby's dad had probably been one of them once, idling up and down the river's length pulling who knows what crap from one end to the other. Boredom and frustration often drove mortals to drink, and that then led to violence towards those closest to them as the frustration ate away their normal morals … it was an old tale, and everyone involved walked away damaged in some shape or form.

Gary had just chosen a particularly nasty form to take.

Even in my mortal suit, I picked up the faint but unmistakeable taint on the morning air. Mortals wouldn't have thought it anything but maybe a rankness from those factories still working on this length of the Thames, or a spill from the refuse dumps further out, but I know it straight away. The same stink on the three student friends, and the one that had filled Danny Price's house only last morning.

Corrupt magic. *Hexenwolfen* and more.

As the cab had wended its way through the streets from Greenwich to Deptford, I'd thought on what Elspeth and I had found at Danny's place. And then on what Samantha had said, or not said, about Gary and Professor Knox. It was obvious the professor had done more with Gary than just gift him a *hexen* belt, given the jinx or curse that had knocked out the police guarding the house. This man, whoever he was, was obviously steeped in Real occultism, not the parlour tricks or rituals which fill most books in this realm. This man had either crossed over, or was connected to something from the Real, and was up to some weird shit at the university beyond teaching his most fucked up students how to wolf out.

And he'd done it under the radar, kept to himself until Gary blew his cover. That spoke of planning and a level of intelligence always worrying when dealing with Accord Breakers. Normally, any mortal wrapped up in this sort of shit is severely unbalanced, borderline mad and an obvious nutter. It helped when dealing with them to know the cost of their actions had been their sanity. This guy wasn't of their breed. He'd paid a different price. But what?

We passed a mortal jogger out taking in the fresh-ish air of the pathway, letting her speed on past and ignoring the predicable shocked expression as she passed my dog. As much as he tried to fit in, Bear just wasn't built to blend in on this side of the Veil. I think he found it funny, bounding along and seeing people almost leap over the nearest wall or climb the handiest tree before they realised he wasn't something escaped from the zoo or an experiment in war-beasts gotten loose.

Besides, it seems mortals focused on the less obvious animals to attempt to arm and use in their battles lately. Gone are the mighty armoured elephants and great jawed battle cats of decades past. Now, of all creatures … dolphins seem the next big thing for the world's military … probably coz no-one would believe anything that smiles so much could be lethal. I'd heard of a movie where the evil villain had wanted sharks fitted with laser beams on their heads. Like the bastards weren't lethal enough as it is.

Anyways, this early, the place was thankfully deserted which let me give Bear his head. I'd waited till we were dropped off by the ever silent and unquestioning cab driver, then pulled out that surprising item Jacob had packed in with all my kit. Felix's diary. Saturated with her scent, perfect for a Trollhound to get a bead on her trace.

I'd finally taken the chance to thumb through the thing as we'd driven over ... ignoring anything too personal and looking for clues about Gary. I'd found a few snippets, some threads I could use ... if the bastard was in a mood to listen.

If not, well then, that's why I had brought the sword.

Bear sniffed along the dirt path, then angled down a smaller canal that looked overgrown and disused. Brambles threatened to choke the way through, trash caught up in the plant's thorny embrace, and any buildings to be seen were grim and ruinous. The whole place reeked of *hexenwolfen*, growing stronger as we forced our way through the jungle, keeping as low a profile as possible so as not to announce our approach.

Steps led down from the walkway to the lower levels of buildings, obviously built to house the owner's boats when they were moored up and taken up from the Thames for service. The smell of mould and old water, rotting weed river mud, was strong ... stopping me for a moment as I realised it was the same stench I'd noted when sharing Felix's thought.

She was here, I was certain.

I hadn't planned much else than finding her and stopping Gary Weatherby, the two facts interlinked and unavoidable. The fact the police had an open case file and would be looking into her disappearance was an inconvenience to resolve later, when she was safe and back home with Danny. As for what to do with Gary, the best outcome I guessed he faced was him coming in quietly and being handed over to the Furies. They'd judge his punishment accordingly, but somehow I doubted we'd get to that.

Bear slipped quietly for a half ton mass of muscle and tooth down the steps and stalked between the buildings. I followed, keeping my eyes open and senses primed for Gary … the bastard liked to lurk in alleys for his kills, so was no stranger to ambushes.

Finally, the trollhound stopped by one stone and wood structure, and whined quietly.

"This the place?" I asked, and he cocked his head at an angle at the sheer stupidity of the question. "Fine, yeah, I get it. Ok, here's the deal. Felix is inside, and no matter, you guard her. Let me take the *hexenwolfen*. Just keep her safe."

Bear gave a couple of questioning chuffs, just loud enough to make it clear he thought my plan stank worse than our surroundings. But I was adamant on this.

"Guard. Felix."

He whined then shook his massive furry head, a sure sign he understood even if he didn't like it.

The door was unlocked, and I eased it open gently, wanting to keep the noise to a minimum. I didn't bother drawing the sword, knowing if Gary was inside then me showing up with a weapon in hand took most of the options off the table. And as much as I wanted him to make a fight of it, so I could deal out the punishment he was due, I had to at least try to bring him in the easy way.

Leastways so I could tell Jessica I tried.

The first room was a jumble of workbenches, old boat parts and the wreckage of old food wrappers and discarded bottles. An old faded calendar on the wall proclaimed it to be April 1998, the picture of a boat faded and riddled with holes.

Like someone had used it for dart practice. A cracked set of fluorescent bar lights ran overhead but there was enough light from the cracked and dirt smeared windows so I didn't need to flick them on. Instead, I carefully navigated the detritus littering the room, Bear padding along behind me, and made for the stone steps that led down into deeper shadow.

The steps led onto a small landing, with a small kitchen set off to one side, cluttered with old rubbish and piled up plates and mugs. The stench of mould and rotten food was strong here, almost bad enough that I thought maybe a gnoll or somesuch had taken up residence but I guessed it was just simple neglect that was the cause. A clear sign of Gary's instability, if he'd let things get this bad.

Another door led off to what looked a set of small bedrooms, both with tired-looking single mattresses and wash basins set amidst drifts of rubbish. Surprisingly, I didn't pick up any scent of rodents amongst the gathered rubbish, no scent of musky urine or scattered pellets where they had left their faeces, which was normal for any abandoned place along the riverside. Whatever lurked here had obviously scared even them away … animals quite often smarter than mortals when it comes to fleeing the really bad shit.

I left off investigating the other small door on the landing since my nose picked up mortal waste, and if the rest of the building was anything to go by, I really didn't fancy finding out how bad the toilet was. Instead, Bear and I took the second set of stairs which led down to what I guessed was river level. Coldness sank into me as we took the concrete steps quietly, a chill in the air from the pervading shadows but something more. The atmosphere of the building now crowded in on me, a sense of foreboding and fear thick in the air.

The bottom section of the ramshackle ruin may have been sectioned into workshops and other rooms, but the walls had been broken though so only jagged pillars braced the ceiling overhead. The floor was slick with mould and slime, obviously from where the Thames washed in. Windows set at small intervals should have lit the place with daylight, but someone had tacked old newspapers over the grimy panes, so that only the merest of illumination made it through. Shadows and cobwebs were everywhere, the stench of the *hexenwolfen* strong and foul as we stepped into the room.

Moving as carefully as possible, we still couldn't help but make quiet squelches as Bear and I stepped out into the wide-open space. I could see that the walls ended with two large, closed doors that must lead out onto the river. Built to allow a boat to be pulled inside when needing to be worked on out of the water, they were of a size to take up most of the side of the building. I could see a rusted chain and padlock draped over one, but something was off about them ... a vibe that set my teeth on edge. My ears instantly picked up the faint sounds of someone breathing quietly, sharp and fast, as a voice cracked through the silence.

"Is ... Is that you. Gary? Why won't you just let me go?" Felix's voice was riddled with exhaustion and fear, the last twenty-four hours obviously draining her of much of her strength. But there was still a spark of defiance. Anger. even. "This isn't you ... we can talk about stuff. Just, let me go. Please?"

Whatever else, Felix hadn't given up. Still the spunky women who loved to rip into me at any chance, hoping that somehow things would work out right.

Now, an amateur would have gone rushing over to her, focused on freeing the victim from her bonds and making sure she was safe and well. The sort of move any half decent bad guy would use to disable the hero and totally screw up any rescue attempt. Me, I knew how these things worked and had no illusions over my heroic status or the fact that Gary was lurking someplace close. The stench from his *wolfen* form was thick down here, whether from all the times he'd come down to taunt or watch his captive or just from him being really close by … I couldn't tell. But I wasn't about to play into his hands.

Also, I'm a suspicious bastard, and something was off about this place. I couldn't see anything beyond the grime and muck, but that dwarrow door hidden at the university had me thinking. What else was hidden, what had Gary done to prepare this place for Felix?

So I Changed. And that's when I saw just what the fucker had done.

The whole basement had been enscribed with runes, lit with ugly indigo fire that flickered and pulsed sickeningly to my eyes. The two doors were blocked with what looked like heavy-duty wards, any attempt to breach them most likely doing serious damage to whomever was unlucky enough to be caught up in their trap. But there were symbols here I didn't recognise, a level of intricacy that despite Gary's heavy clumsy strokes spoke of serious craft. Lines all converged like some weird ass spiders-web on the far corner, which had been cleared and set with a trio of occult circles.

At their centre, Felix huddled, painted by the glowing fire. It bathed her small form, and in some way seemed to be bleeding out of her … siphoning off her? This shit was far beyond anything I recognised, but I could guess that the light coming out of her wasn't anything good, and somehow Gary was draining her, keeping her weak. At his mercy, the sick fuck.

"Felix. It's Morgan." I spoke quietly, loudly enough so she could hear me as I checked around the floor. He'd warded the walls and exits, but thankfully the only other crafting seemed to be around his prisoner. Meant I didn't have to worry where I put my oversized feet. "I'm going to get you out of here. Just stay calm."

"Morgan? Oh god, Morgan, it's Gary … from my class! He …" Felix sobbed out the words, trying to alert me to a danger she didn't understand, couldn't know about. She probably thought she'd imagined everything, that Gary was just some messed up kid.

If only it was that simple.

"It's ok. I know. I've been to your house, seen the mess he made. It's what led us to his friends, those three from class." That I let slip with a little more volume, as I felt the atmosphere shift in the vile dankness of the room. Yep, the bastard was definitely down here with us, lurking nearby. I remembered he'd used a hex to cloud the minds of the police and Danny, and reckoned he was trying it now. Thinking to maze me, blindside me and deal with me quickly. Good luck with that, mate.

"Is … Is Danny …?" She stuttered, and I silently blessed her for worrying over the man she thought was her uncle, her own father, when she was the one bound up and hidden away in a shithole basement.

"Danny's fine. Just worried sick about you. I'm taking you back to him, just as soon as I've dealt with Gary. Isn't that right, mate?" I felt the rage piling up from off to my left, the threat of violence spiking as my words got the reaction I'd hoped for.

"Ain't taking her anywhere. She's staying with me!" Gary snarled out of the murk, the words slurring from a mangled, inhuman jaw. Bear growled in response, but I shushed him, motioning him off to the place I'd seen Felix huddled. Whatever went down, she'd need him warding her whilst I dealt with the twisted *hexenwolfen*.

"Look, kid, it's over. Felix's going home to her family, and as for you? Well, you ain't going to trouble her ever again." I drawled as I turned slowly, as if searching the room, seemingly blind to the slow approach even as his animalistic rage burned like a bonfire through the mystical fug. The lust was the same from Felix's room, out of control emotions raging through the adolescent's mind, overriding any good sense or morality. Sick with madness, longing, desire and self-hate … this kid stank of them all.

"We got your friends. They've told us everything, so might as well just give up." I growled out the lie as I stepped to one side, kicking a half empty vodka bottle with one foot to further advertise my position. Given his father had been a drunk, had beaten him when inebriated, I was surprised the kid had fallen down the same hole. But then mortals tend not to learn from mistakes all too well, and hell, the weakness might even be genetic. Cursed to want the same poison which killed his father. The stuff that started him down this dark and deadly road.

"Don't need them. Don't need anyone! Just Felix! Kill you, wolfman! Kill her dad! Kill every fucker!" He snarled and threw himself at me.

I'd expected something like Adrian or Greg, but Gary had gone far deeper into the *hexenwolfen*, given up more of himself to feed the beast. What hurled itself at me from a fog of blurring shadows was huge, bulging with gross muscles and scars, dark hair spiked and matted with blood and filth. Gary's face was almost bearlike in size, great jaws gaping and huge fangs snapping at me as he slashed with jagged claws, seeking to silence me with one rush.

I declined his invitation.

Diving into a roll I let him surge past, his taloned paws scrabbling and kicking up muck from the floor as he stumbled and tried to turn. Finding my feet, I ducked in and hammered blows into his oversized chest, barrel-like and bulging with arcs of massive bone. He'd grown into something truly bestial, his eyes crazed and bloodshot, as he drank down everything the cursed belt offered. He shrugged off my blows with grunts and snarls, lashing out again with those massive claws. I nimbly caught his misshapen wrists, feeling the inhuman strength in him as he struggled to break free. But I matched it with my own, holding him in place.

"Give it up, kid! Let go of the belt and we can help." I snarled at him as I spun him round, keeping him off balance. He snapped those massive jaws at my Changed face, trying to tear off my muzzle with his teeth, but I just jerked him around and sent him crashing into one of the brick pillars. Stone exploded, hammering at us both, as he howled with rage and fear, pulling himself free.

"He said you'd come! Said you'd take her from me! Jus' like my dad took everything from me!" He screamed, as his distorted and twisted form arched with dark fire. It was like the reverse of lightning, not bright and sharp but somehow darker than the gloom around us. Gary threw out his clawed paw, as if hurling something at me … and I felt the *hex* lash out, screaming through the air to chew through me, strike me down.

Lycan, remember? The magic lashed at me, flailing to find a grip and devour me … then sparked and faded. Grounded by my natural immunity.

"NO!" He screamed, conjuring more dark lightning and lashing it all around. Pillars of mortar and brick exploded, the dark magic chewing through stone like acid. I might be immune to its effects, but that didn't stop me snarling as chunks of stone shattered in the air, pelting me with fist size lumps, so I threw myself from my feet and away from the storm of foul craft.

Rolling amidst the muck, I gained my feet, feeling my own anger blazing up in response. I'd tried to get him to come quietly, to do the right thing but it was obvious he was too far gone, too much part of the totem he wore. Too steeped in the shit he had learned from Professor Knox. There really was only one way this could end.

Catching his lightning-lit claws, I jerked him toward me and slammed my thickened skull into his snarling jaws, hearing him shriek as teeth broke against my toughened skin. As he writhed and fought to break free, I bent his left wrist hard, then twisted it back as I threw him to his right, forcing his own inhuman body over in a sprawling tumble. The snap of bone was sharp in the basement, as were his shrieks as he sprawled out, left arm bent at an unnatural angle.

I drew my silver-bound sword with a steely hiss, light glinting off its razor edges, pointing it at him.

"Last chance, kid. Either you go down or I put you down!" I snarled at him, as he writhed on the floor and pushed himself back up. His broken arm flopped disgustingly for a moment, then he gave it a twist and it cracked back into place. Definitely stronger than his student friends, the muscles writhing like eels over the injury.

"Kill you!" He screamed, dark fire shattering the air all around me as he hurled more hexes at me. Whomever this professor really was, he'd taught the kid some pretty strong craft. Pity he hadn't taught him the sense not to use it on a naturally immune opponent with an extremely sharp weapon.

I ducked and spun, catching that just-healed forearm and clove through it with one massive blow, blood spraying as it spun free. Gary roared, backhanding me with his other fire-shrouded hand so I tumbled and rolled, smashing through another brick support. Overhead, the building gave an ominous creaking groan, dust and crap falling from overhead as things shifted. The place wasn't in the best of conditions, and us destroying its foundations wasn't helping.

"You'll never leave this place! Die here, like my dad!" He howled, and I caught a spike of shame shivering amidst his rage like a taint. Shame at something he'd done … something about his dad.

His dead dad.

"You killed him. Here, in this boatshed, didn't you Gary?" I guessed, sensing the guilt writhe in response, as he snarled and spat his hate. "Killed him and let people think he'd gotten drunk and drowned."

"Yes! Yes! Drowned the bastard. Held his head under and watched him kick like a baby. Now who'se the big fucking man, eh?" He howled as dark fire gathered in his paws. The hexes on the walls and door pulsed and flared with renewed life, feeding on the craft he was drawing. Fire lashed out in writing tentacles, crashing against the brickwork as the craft fed and grew. No way were we getting out that way ... one touch would do permanent damage to Bear, probably reduce Felix to dust. I'd have to get them back out the only way left open.

"You'll never leave here! Never!" He screamed, and then it happened.

The taint of the Veil, dust and ruin, rank and vile ... it swirled in the air as Gary drew the darkness between his paws. Garbled words tumbled from his jaws, whatever incantation he'd been taught to tear the protection of the mortal Realm, let loose the horror of the Veil. In this bloody basement.

"Gary!" I heard a choked cry, and twisted to find Felix up and on her feet, shreds of whatever had bound her half burned away from the lick of fire. Her blindfold had fallen round her neck like some sort of dirty scarf, and her eyes were wide with fear and disbelief at what she was seeing. Then her gaze fell on me.

"M...Morgan?" She stuttered, then all her energy drained from her and she crashed to the ground.

Shit. She wasn't meant to have seen me. Jessica came down truly hard on any of us exposing our reality to mortals. If I ever got out of this mess, I was due a serious dressing down.

I dove and rolled, coming up beside Bear as he loomed over Felix's body. The trollhound whined as fire raged like a storm around the *hexenwolfen,* Gary's own rage feeding whatever madness he was lost in now so that the Veil rippled in and out of sight, ready to spill through.

"Carry her." I dropped the sword for a moment, picking up her limp form and draping it over Bear like a ragdoll. His harness came with some handy clips and straps, useful for securing purchases on this side of the Real, and the odd trophy from the other side when we were hunting. In this case, they strapped Felix in securely. The trollhound didn't even grunt at her weight, just pawed the ground impatiently. "Wait!"

Gary's bellow forced me back to face him, as I stole my sword up from the ground. His bloody stump was already oozing some sort of blackish flesh, the *hexen* belt working to fix the damage with almost the same speed as a true lycan. There would be no separating them now, the thing was bound to whatever shreds were left of his soul. He'd shrug off anything but a true mortal injury, but that was looking more and more likely as he drew on more of the fire, the tear starting to widen between his paws.

My sword carved a furrow over his chest, spraying blood as I hammered a blow at him. He staggered back, snarling and spitting in bestial fury, but I followed, pushing him further as I slammed the silvered edge into his leg then jerked it free in another gush of gore.

"Gonna … hnh … kill … you!" He panted, jamming his stump into his leg wound as it tried to buckle under him. The Veil rent squirmed in the air as if alive, seeking to gain a foothold. But I just grinned my lycan face off.

"Bear. Out, now!"

I'd pushed Gary back from the staircase, turning him so his back was to the hex-warded door. And just so handily forced the way clear for my trollhound and his cargo. Bear gave a baying roar and burst into motion, carrying his cargo up the stairs and to freedom.

"NO!" Gary howled, flares of fire reaching out like writhing tentacles to drag his captive back. But I caught him by the throat, punching him in his bestial face with the pommel of the sword, eliciting a rewarding crunch of bone and flesh. His claws lashed at me, and I felt the sting of the cuts as he carved at my face but I shrugged it off. I'd heal.

He staggered, and I punched my free hand down, claws sharp and unyielding as I savaged his leg wound. The leg flopped and jerked, bloody thick like tar oozing out of the wound, and he howled again in agony.

The tear buckled, linked to him by a line of throbbing energy. He reached out for it, almost as if trying to grasp the thing. I'd no idea what he planned to do after opening the Way, no desire to find out if any further horrors waited on the other side. This had to end.

My sword punched through his neck, keen edges carving through distorted flesh and bone as his crazed eyes bugged with the horror of impending death. I threw my shoulder into his massive chest, driving the sword deeper ... and carrying him back.

Into the blazing fury of the hex covering the doorway. Into his own trap.

Silvered steel sparked like a blacksmith's smithy as the point punched into the nexus of the crafting. I didn't know enough about magic to understand the thing, but one thing I knew was that shoving silver into a rune crafted frame would disrupt it. And if it were powered up at the time, that disruption would be ... explosive.

Fury ripped out from the crafted lines, wrapping around Gary as he writhed, spitted on the length of metal stuck through his throat. I hurled myself back, feeling the fire burn and blacken my skin despite my protection, as purple hued flames spat and ate into the *hexenwolfen*. He writhed, crying out as he gripped at the thing holding him fast against the runes, his body bulging and malforming as it fought the destructive energies. But it was too much and with one final scream, he slumped and fell, body shivering into ash and ruin as the summoned energies ate through him.

The rent buckled for a moment, throbbing with unnatural life … then snapped shut, winking out like a candle flame snubbed.

I drew a shuddering breath, feeling my face sting from the claw-slashes, my body still smarting from the touch of foul magics. It was … finally … over.

Then the fucking building fell on me.

Chapter 26

It took me a good few minutes to dig myself out of the rubble. When a building falls on you, you're either instantly flattened or have the chance to get to the outer edge, missing out on the heavier bits of masonry in a frantic scramble. Thankfully I'd been by the door, so missed most of the central supports as they came crashing down. Leaving me with just half a ton of brick and shattered wood to dig through.

Shaking the last of the building from me, I staggered out of the rubble, blinking in the sunlight. I'd lost my sword down there too, burned and blackened from the unnatural fire, and my clothes were ripped and torn all over again, and smeared with Gods knew what muck and filth.

But I was out, in the fresh air. And the *hexenwolfen?* He'd paid the price for his actions.

That's when I heard the strangled gasp, and realised two things very quickly.

One, I hadn't Changed back to the mortal suit. It'd been easier to heave out of the mess we'd made of the Weatherby boathouse with the added strength the full Change lent me.

Two, Bear was sat waiting for me on the pathway, head cocked as if surprised it had taken me this long to get free. And standing beside him, free of the straps I'd bound her up in, smeared from head to toe with filth and dirt, clothes a ripped mess, stood Felix.

We locked gazes for a long drawn out moment, as the world seemed to pause round us. Then, knowing I'd now let her see my Real self twice in a row, all I could do was give a weary shrug and growl.

"It's over, kid. Let's get you back home."

Felix gave another stutter of breath, then collapsed in a heap by Bear. With a resounding thud that spoke of painful bruises she'd not enjoy waking up to.

"Bollocks." I soundly swore, then let the Change slide through me.

By the time Felix came round again, I was my mortal-friendly self again. I'd made an effort to clean off Gary's blood, as well as the worst crap I'd picked up in the outhouse, and I'd carried her a short ways from the ruins so that we were out of sight of the place.

"You ok kid?" I asked gently, as she woke with a start, scooting back across the gravelled path and gazing around frantically.

"Where … How? Where's … ?" She stuttered through the questions as her brain frantically tried to kickstart and make sense of things. "Morgan? I saw … You were … fuck, I don't know what …?"

"Slow down, kid." I tried a calming smile, as I sat back on my ass and took a slow breath. "It's all ok. We worked out where Gary was holding you, and I came to sort things out. He put up a fight, but I managed to get you out of the place just before it collapsed in on us. I got out, but Gary wasn't so lucky."

"But I saw …?" Felix shook her head, staring at me then flinching away, pressing her small fist to her forehead. "I don't know what I … There was … You were … ?"

"Felix, you've been tied up in someone's personal dungeon for the past twenty-four hours, without food or water I'm guessing. After what you've been through, I'm surprised you aren't seeing all manner of weird shit. But it's ok. It's over." I rationalised, knowing her good ol' mortal brain would already be fogging the details through trustworthy doubt and disbelief. She couldn't have seen Gary as a *hexenwolfen*, seen me standing there with a bestial head, covered in blood, with claws, sword and body Changed. That'd make no sense. She must have hit her head or something on the way out, possibly still been drugged from whatever he'd used on her at the house... I could see the thoughts bouncing round her head as they slowly settled into fact.

"Are we going home now?" She finally asked, exhaustion fighting its battel through the dregs of adrenaline she had left keeping her upright.

"Yup, but ... ah, I've got bad news." I told her with another shrug, then reached into one of my pockets. The mass of wire and twisted plastic that I drew out tumbled to the path, all that remained of the latest phone Jacob had given me. "It's a bit of a walk back to anywhere with a phone before I can call us a cab. Up for that?"

Felix gave a pained bark of a laugh, causing Bear to chuff out a cough too, as if joining in.

"Oh, Morgan! Only you could make a woman you just rescued from captivity bloody walk to freedom." She gave a small smile, a flicker of her old self showing through the exhaustion and pain. She held out her hand, and I carefully took it, pushing myself up and off the dirt.

"Piggyback?" I offered, and she leaned against my arm, weakly thumping it in reply.

And so, with Bear bounding up ahead, we headed home.

Chapter 27

So. I'd kept my promise and delivered Felix back into the loving arms of her father. Hero of the day saves princess and returns the lost child to her family. Queue the cheering.

Well, in more or less one piece.

Well, sort of delivered.

What, in fact, happened was we walked the canal path out of the Creek and were halfway back towards civilisation before I was able to flag down an early morning passer-by and borrow their phone to call one of the office cabs. I left the kind gentleman my home number and the promise to pay him back, whilst trying not to draw his attention to my ragged clothes, the state Felix was in and the enormity of Bear.

Bundled into a cab and racing back through the early morning traffic coming into London, I laid out the simple facts to Felix, who I'd expected to be unconscious by now but who had rallied and now seemed at least partially with it.

The fact that I'd been told by the police to stay out of the kidnapping. That I'd ignored them, gone looking for and yes, I'd ended up finding and freeing her but I'd basically messed with an ongoing police investigation. That sort of thing carried stiff penalties, not least because I'd possibly annoyed one or two officers at the Price residence not so long ago, and they might see this as a perfect way of balancing the books.

So, instead of me depositing Felix into Danny's hands, we agreed I'd drop her off at the café he owned, Buon Cibo. She knew where he kept a spare key to the back door and it would give her a chance to clean up and change into something fresher, whilst an anonymous caller would ring his house and say they'd seen her at the café. He'd rush over there with the police in tow, and she'd spin a story of how she'd been held captive by a classmate, a Gary Weatherby, but managed to escape from where he'd been holding her. She'd run to the first safe place she could think of, knowing Gary had already taken her from her own home.

Meanwhile, whilst Danny mother-henned her, and dependable DI Gregory Allen worked through her statement, I'd send Jacob and a small team round to the dockside ruin, retrieve the wreck of my sword and make sure there was no evidence to link Bear and I to the place. Random security cameras and the like that needed messing with ... just the sort of thing my Pack were used to doing. I was sure they wouldn't find any trace of Gary or the shit he'd been up to in his father's ruin, the way that hex had eaten through him ... but better safe than sorry.

Part of me felt uncomfortable after everything we'd gone through, leaving Felix alone. Even though I knew she'd be fine in the shop until the cavalry arrived. Gary wouldn't be coming for her, and since he'd been the mysterious killer she had wound up being a witness to, she was now doubly safe. His classmates wouldn't be a problem either, depending on how Jessica decided to handle their case ... either hand them over to the Furies to deal with, or let Elspeth try to remove as much of the taint from them as possible.

That just left Professor Robert Knox, and I was betting he'd already upped and vanished. Samantha had let slip he'd warned them about us lycans, that we'd come if they messed up, and I was betting he'd known me for what I was that time we met in the classroom. Whatever the fuck he'd been up to with the poppies, no way would he be stupid enough to hang around after his prized pupil had drawn the attention of the red cloaks.

So, hopefully she'd be fine hiding out until Danny showed up, and I could dodge any unfortunate police attention. I was already in enough trouble with Jessica as it was, without them focusing on me and the Pack, digging into our business.

Speaking of unfortunate …

"Hey, Felix." I was not the right person for this, but I couldn't let the chance pass. "When Danny gets to you … go easy on him? This whole thing, it's been extra hard on him. He's … look, there's something you should know …"

"What, that he's my dad?" She yawned massively, then leant against the cab window, pressing her head to the cool glass. "I did a DNA test years ago, and checked the results. No way was he my uncle by marriage or some shit like that. I figured we'd talk about it some day, just never really got round to it."

And that was Felix all over. Breezing through life with the ability to bounce off surprises like a rubber ball. Finding out her uncle had been keeping secrets from her, and was really her father … I could think of various ways that shit could've gone wrong. But she just shrugged it off and carried on.

"Ah, yeah. Ok well just be gentle with him." I lamely replied, totally wrongfooted. As said, I *so* was not the guy for that sort of thing.

"Morgan. It's not that he doesn't *want* a daughter, right?" She asked eventually, voice gone a little quiet.

I couldn't help but let loose a laugh, thinking back to the tale of woe Danny had laid out for me in his sitting room. The mistakes he'd made, the choices he'd made. The one overriding fact of the whole debacle had been the love he had for his baby.

"Trust me. He wants to be your dad." I told her gently. "Let him tell you the full story, but, kid, I'd be prepared to be a little surprised."

She nodded, then went back to looking out the window, but I could tell she was smiling. Just a little.

"Oh, and Felix?" I realised I'd best break all the news whilst she was in a frame of mind of to be forgiving. "There's something else. I kind of, well, I lost your diary. Sorry."

"What the hell, Morgan?! I mean, what the *hell?!*"

Pulling up a street down from the café, I popped the door for Felix but stopped her as she went to jump out.

"Listen, kid. You've been through hell. Get inside, take a moment and I don't know … break some plates or something. Just don't bottle that crap up." I told her, the wise sage of all things emotional for a young woman recently kidnapped and held in a basement at the whim of a severely fucked up madman.

She gave my arm a squeeze and hopped out onto the pavement. Turning to go, she stopped and held the door, looking back in at me.

"Morgan. I *saw* something. I can't explain it … but I didn't knock my head and I wasn't drugged." She told me bluntly, facing me with all the certainty she could muster. "When you're ready, I want to talk to you too. And get some answers. I think you owe me that. What with you losing my bloody diary."

Then she was gone, leaving me to look across at Bear and shrug.

"How the hell, after rescuing her, do I owe her? It was just one book?!"

The trollhound gave a grunting sigh and settled back on the floor.

The sensible thing for me to do next was call Jessica. Give her all the details, get Jacob and the team on the road to Gary's place. And probably for the first time ever, it's what I did. Thankfully the cab driver was used to our arrangement, and not only didn't ask questions but was happy to pass me his mobile to use to call Jessica's personal phone.

"Ahm' glad you are safe, and the young lass is too." My Alpha told me after I gave her the crib notes. No trace that I'd woken her, no sign to show that at such a silly hour of the morning she was anything but wide awake and alert. "Ah'd ask you tae stop by the office, let Elspeth clean off any traces that hex may have left. But ah can tell how tired you are. So head home and take the morning off. Should anyone call for you, ah will tell them you are indisposed, an' not tae be disturbed."

"Thanks, boss." I managed not to yawn down the phone at her, but all the aches and pain of the past day or so were now ganging up to make themselves heard. And the buzz I'd gotten from whatever Elspeth had used to counter the wolfsbane was definitely fading. All I wanted now was to get home, close the door and fall onto the nearest surface that even remotely looked comfortable.

After feeding Bear. I wasn't *that* exhausted to forget how much the furry behemoth had helped out today, and also to remember how much the sod liked to complain if he woke up hungry.

"Oh, Morgan, before you retire." Jessica's voice intruded as thoughts of deep pillows and comfy duvets dragged at my attention. "You should know. The three associates of Gary Weatherby. Ms MacElvy has done an initial examination and is confident she can remove all traces of the totems from them. They'll be under watch fer any signs o' withdrawal, but the witch nae fears for their safety."

"However." She went on, and I shook the dreams of sleep from my head, to focus. "Both Jacob and she went back tae find this hidden room in the university, but nae trace of it was tae be found. Someone got there first and closed it down. Ah've put watchers out for this professor, but he has nae been seen at his registered dwelling since you visited. It is likely he has gone tae ground."

"I'd guessed he would." I cursed under my breath, knowing it had been too much to hope we'd sweep him up too. "What about the poppies?"

"Miss MacElvy has some thoughts on their purpose, especially after your own encounter an' affliction. She has been able to glean some more details from the students, thought nae much more than worrying conjecture. For now, she has agreed tae see to their safe removal from the grounds." Jessica let her own frustration through with a sigh of her own. "Ah really want tae talk tae this man, Morgan. If what she thinks is his intent, then the man is harmful indeed an' needing tae be stopped."

"No argument there. The shit Gary pulled, the stuff he taught him? The kid tried to open the bloody Veil." I growled. "So we have nothing?"

"Morgan. Remember who you speak tae." She reprimanded me lightly. "We never have *nothing*. Now, go get some sleep."

The lined clicked off, and I settled back into the cab seat.

So the students would probably be fine, that was one good thing out of this mess. If anyone could wipe that shit from their souls or whatever it bonded to, Elspeth could. Hopefully she'd also jinx any memories too … leave them with vague thoughts of an old friend they didn't see anymore, and most likely a desire to take a break from their studies to go do something with their lives. Mortals accepted such random changes in their youth's behaviour with barely a flicker of worry, which made thing that much easier to clean up this sort of mess.

Shit, I'd forgotten to ask about Cerce and her gang. That was another loose end to tie up, no matter the witch's vocal protests that they were not the guilty party. She was up to her neck in the trade of wolfsbane, and the professor had given some to his *hexenwolfen* in case any of us came sniffing. She was due another visit, that was for sure.

The cab finally pulled into my parking bay, and I signed away the tab without even bothering to check the price. Unloading Bear, I had enough sense to note the lack of any large, suspicious vehicles parked out front of the building … it seemed Cerce had pulled the watchers from my home, like a good little witch. If she thought that would do her any favours, she was in for a big surprise.

All I wanted now was bed. As I stumbled along to the main entrance, uncaring that anyone might see me in my current state of barely-together shredded clothing, I only noticed the presence of someone as I pushed open the door. They must have been waiting off to one side, just out of view, and stepped out as I almost made it through the door after Bear.

"Look, I'm sorry but whomever you are, can you please just fu…" I growled, not caring if it was the Morrigan come to congratulate herself on leading me a merry chase to find Felix, bloody Herne come to call me out over my attitude or the fucking Lord and Lady of Ivory, looking for the next weapon of mass destruction they'd managed to mislay. They could all go hang …

Long black hair, naturally curling as it fell to frame her slim face with firm features. Her Spanish roots showing in those deep dark eyes and long lashes, the upturned lips and that small, perky nose pebbled with freckles. A small scar over the left eyebrow, and that smile which mocked the world from her viewpoint.

I stopped in shock, biting back my words as Sarah Maria Connor, Doctor of Paleozoology. Currently working at the Natural History Museum, last seen when we broke into the place to stop the Mistress from ripping a hole in the Mortal Realm with an old world war sea mine Where we'd hexed her to stop her realising we were there. My Sarah. My ex bloody girlfriend.

Standing on my doorstep, clutching a small wooden box to her slim chest.

She smiled tentatively at me, taking in my battered condition.

"Ah, hi Morgan. Is this a good time?" She gestured to the old battered box in her hands. "Some old lady stopped by whilst I was waiting for you, and left this. Said it's what was owed or something? Said I should give it to you."

I numbly took the box, still trying to get the fact that my ex-girlfriend was standing on my doorstep.

"So, look, if it's not a good time?" She broke the silence of my thoughts grinding through the exhaustion and strain of the past day, even as other parts of me frantically tried to grab the reigns and take control. "I can always come back … ?"

"Coffee." I managed, words finally lining up in my hazy brain. "You like coffee? You want to uh, go someplace and grab a coffee?"

Sarah flashed one of those million-watt smiles, and hooked her arm through mine.

"I'd love that." She leaned in and then out again, cocking her head. "And, Morgan … why do you smell like you've been rolling in the Thames?"

Any other day, just any other day. And she had to show up on this one.

Seriously, which immortal had decided my life needed to be this much of a joke?

So, towing a thoroughly disgruntled Bear back out into the fresh air, we headed out and off to find coffee.

Morgan's story, and that of the Pack, continues in Book 3 – The Furry and the Furious.

Available now.

About the Author

Born fourth son of the sprawling Cameron Clan, JP Cameron was introduced to the wonder of words and story-telling with the magical tale of The Hobbit, as one of the first books he remembers.

Taking The Lord of the Rings to primary school as his book for class set his feet firmly on a path, an endless road and a love of the fantastical, strange and magical.

Through school, work and into adult life (what little of that he knows), JP continues to expand his library and scope of writing, exploring other genres and inventing strange new worlds. But his love of fantasy remains at the core of his writing. Living with his wife and their hairy behemoth disguised as a Chow Chow in the green rolling hills of West Sussex, he is often found gazing happily at bookshelves groaning with volumes by Sir Terry Pratchett, Terry Goodkind, Terry Brooks and many, many more authors not called Terry.

Otherwise you may meet him up and down the UK coastline, celebrating a rich and happy history of piracy in fine company.

His published works to date include Tales of the Blade, and The Spire set, and now his debut into dark fantasy – The Lycan Files.

Find him at @bandycoot_74 for tweets and questions.

Printed in Great Britain
by Amazon

59961022R00159